HEIR OF EMBERS AND ASH

CLAIMING ELFHAME
BOOK TWO

J.M. WALLACE

Heir of Embers and Ash

Copyright © 2022 by J.M. Wallace

Cover Art by GetCovers
Interior Art by Etheric Designs

All rights reserved.

No portion of this book may be reproduced in any form without written permission from the publisher or author, except as permitted by U.S. copyright law.

ISBN 9781737880646

www.jmwallaceauthor.com

HEIR OF EMBERS AND ASH

CLAIMING ELFHAME
BOOK TWO

J.M. WALLACE

Contents

Dedication		VII
Mortal Realm		VIII
Mortal Realm Right		IX
Elfhame		X
Elfhame Right		XI
1.	Chapter One	1
2.	Chapter Two	16
3.	Chapter Three	31
4.	Chapter Four	42
5.	Chapter Five	64
6.	Chapter Six	82
7.	Chapter Seven	95
8.	Chapter Eight	109
9.	Chapter Nine	117
10.	Chapter Ten	134
11.	Chapter Eleven	149
12.	Chapter Twelve	159

13. Chapter Thirteen — 169

14. Chapter Fourteen — 187

15. Chapter Fifteen — 194

16. Chapter Sixteen — 203

17. Chapter Seventeen — 217

18. Chapter Eighteen — 234

19. Chapter Nineteen — 245

20. Chapter Twenty — 253

21. Chapter Twenty-One — 262

22. Chapter Twenty-Two — 271

23. Chapter Twenty-Three — 282

24. Chapter Twenty-Four — 289

Acknowledgments — 295

Also By — 297

About Author — 298

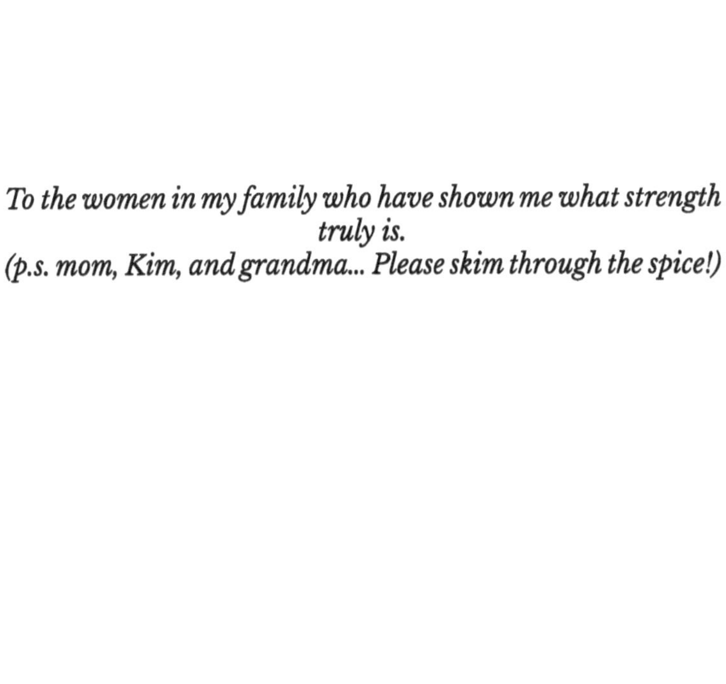

To the women in my family who have shown me what strength truly is.
(p.s. mom, Kim, and grandma... Please skim through the spice!)

MARENTH
N
W E
S
NEVENE
Western Sea
Rose Manor
Blackthorn Vei

AMARAN
Eastern Sea
Royal Palace
Mortal Realm

Autumn Court
Blackth
Western Sea
Unseelie Palace
Winter Court
Elfhame

orn Veil
Seelie Palace
SPRING COURT
SUMMER COURT
Eastern Sea
N
W
E
S

Chapter One

There were moments, when the moon was at its highest, that Kelera swore she could hear the stampede of hoofbeats amongst the stars. The three days that had passed since fleeing from the Unseelie territory in the Winter Court felt like a lifetime ago, and things were without a doubt, going to get much worse before they got better.

Running a hand through her mass of dark, wavy hair, she sighed and looked up at the night sky from where she was lying in the sand. It was late, and she knew she should try to get some rest, but she couldn't stop herself from searching for any sign of the horde of warriors that had thundered past them the other night—the night of her binding ceremony with Adrastus.

She nearly scoffed out loud at the absurdity of the last few weeks that had led to her being magically bound to the youngest prince of the Unseelie Court. Never in a million lifetimes would she have expected to be here, in this position.

Biting the inside of her cheek, she tried to distract herself from the tears that threatened to fall. She would not cry. Not now. She was done with all of that. She would do everything within her power to honor the vow she had made to never cower before anyone again.

Holding off the despair that often tried to creep in at the late hours of the night, she continued to stare, unmoving, at the sky. But instead of ancient Fae on horseback, only a blanket of dazzling Elfhame stars blinked back at her.

The Wild Hunt was still a mystery to her. If she hadn't seen them firsthand, then she would have believed them to be nothing more than a tall tale. Mere whispers in stories. But after seeing them ride in the direction of the Winter Court with her own eyes, she couldn't help but wonder now if they were the reason why the Night Riders who served the Unseelie Crown—Samael's crown—hadn't come for her and Adrastus yet.

The Night Riders. Kelera shuddered at the thought. Rolling to her side, she welcomed the sound of the waves crashing nearby, wishing they could wash away the terrifying images creeping into her mind. The Night Riders were a threat she feared nearly as much as Samael himself. The horrifying race of men who had been turned to wraiths by King Cyrus' magic was the last thing she wanted to face. Even the threat of bounty hunters did not strike fear in her soul like the Night Riders did.

But at this moment, there were no hoofbeats. There was no sound of the Wild Hunt or the skeletal Night Riders. The only sound was that of the waves crashing in the ocean nearby and Adrastus' steady breathing beside her. His eyes—irises filled with three shades of forest green—were closed, with his heavy lashes casting soft shadows on his face. His dark raven hair was covered with sand and curling at the nape of his neck. There truly could not be a man more beautiful than him in the whole world.

Kelera rolled to her other side with a blush. It was silly and irresponsible of her to be admiring the way Adrastus looked when their very lives were at stake. This was their third night on the run, and she was still trying to wrap her mind around her situation. Adrastus blamed it on the shock of what had happened to her in Samael's room of shadows, but she knew it ran deeper than that.

She had gone from a lady of the mortal court to a wanted criminal, being hunted like an animal for her alleged part in the death of King Cyrus of the Unseelie Court. That, of course, was Samael's handiwork. He craved her Seelie magic for himself and wanted his brother dead. With her power in his hands, and Adrastus out of the way—unable to challenge him for the Unseelie crown—then Samael would be free to wreak havoc in both Elfhame and the mortal realm.

That was not to say that she was completely innocent. A shiver crept up her spine as she closed her eyes and thought of the turning point that had gotten her here. The night that Samael had taken her to his torturous room. She could still feel the unbearable pain of ice cutting into her skin and the hopelessness in her chest at seeing Adrastus about to die at Samael's hands.

Her eyelids were growing heavy now, but her mind wouldn't still long enough to let her drift off peacefully. Sleep was a thing she suspected would never come easily to her again, and tonight was no exception. There had been many times in Kelera's life when she felt the weight of guilt like stones stacked upon her shoulders, but this was unbearable. She clenched her hands into fists and a tear rolled down her cheek. Regardless of Samael's false allegations about King Cyrus' death, she was guilty of murdering Prince Ammon. No one would care that it was an accident. Even *she* blamed herself for losing control of her magic in that horrible cavernous room.

Knowing she would find no peace tonight, she turned over once again on her side and watched Adrastus sleeping peacefully. He had done well at hiding his own anxieties as they traveled through the beaches of the Summer Court over the last couple of days. But there were times where she caught a glimpse of the twitch in his jaw or the gritting of his teeth and knew there was a storm brewing in his mind. She figured either he was too proud to drop his strong facade, or he was trying to keep a brave face for her so she wouldn't panic and make things worse yet again.

His own sort of mask, she thought with a sigh.

She wrapped her arms around her stomach and drew her knees up, trying to quell the rising nausea. In a matter of weeks, her life had been flipped upside down. Elfhame had turned her into a killer. Forced to hide, leaving her people in the mortal realm to live amongst an unnamed traitor. And as if that wasn't bad enough, she had gone through with a magical binding spell, connecting her magic to Adrastus' power. She was bound to a man who, by all accounts, should have been considered her enemy. But he was different from his father. It had taken her a while to see it, but he was a better man than the rest of them.

She took a deep breath, trying to relax the tension in her shoulders. Tomorrow, they would reach one of the fishing villages. Would she feel safer there? Or would the terror and guilt in her heart be a constant companion for the rest of her days? Exhaustion finally crept in, carrying her off to a restless sleep.

Kelera rolled off of her blanket and woke with a start as the soft, warm sand touched her cheek. Memories of dirt being kicked into her face in the fighting pits flashed in her mind, bringing back a familiar sinking sensation in the pit of her stomach.

"We need to move." The urgency in Adrastus' voice brought her back to the present.

"Why? What's happened?" She looked around but saw nothing out of the ordinary. They were alone in the sandy terrain. She could see Fae in the distance pushing boats into the water, but they were so far away that she couldn't make out the details of their faces. She envied them, going about their everyday life with such certainty and confidence. Were they even aware of the threat that hung over them, now that Samael controlled the Unseelie Court? Would they be prepared if he invaded their beautiful beaches, bringing with him chaos and destruction?

Adrastus packed their bags in a hurry, pausing every few seconds as if looking for any sign of threat. His voice was a low rumble as he said, "There's been word from Gadreel."

Kelera's heart did a flip at the mention of Adrastus' older brother. Gadreel had become her friend during her time in the Unseelie Court and had risked his life to help them escape. To her dismay, he had stayed behind to play their spy in the palace that was now controlled by Samael. As much as she trusted that Gadreel could take care of himself, she was still worried about him.

"H-how? What did he say?" Kelera scrambled to her feet and took her bag from Adrastus. She swung it over her shoulder with one hand and shook sand from her hair with the other.

"One of the palace ravens brought it." Adrastus clenched and unclenched his fists, making the veins in his muscular forearms stand out. Kelera watched him carefully, waiting for him to explain why he was so agitated. He blew out a frustrated huff as he continued, "The problem is, I don't know how long ago he sent the message. We've been traveling for days now, so there's no telling how long it took the raven to track us down. Things are escalating much faster than I was prepared for." He rolled his sleeves up to reveal the rest of his sun kissed arms. The Summer Court sun had been good to him and Kelera was having trouble taking her eyes off of him, until he continued, "The Wild Hunt and the Night Riders clashed. It seems the Wild Hunt prevailed, nearly wiping out the whole lot of them."

Hope bloomed in her chest. She had faced a Night Rider when she had helped her best friend, Princess Cierine, escape captivity in the Unseelie Court. It was strange to imagine that it had only been mere weeks since then. It didn't help that the terror in her heart was still as fresh as if it had happened yesterday. She shivered, even though the sun was offering plenty of warmth. "But that's amazing news, right?"

Adrastus spoke through clenched teeth with a growl. "Samael is making new ones."

"Samael? But how can he..." she trailed off when she saw the grimace on Adrastus' handsome, scarred face. A scar reaching from brow to jawline. One that nearly matched her own. Scars given to them both by Samael.

They hadn't mentioned Samael's name out loud since the day that Adrastus had rescued her from his cavernous torture chamber. She had wondered often if he was grieving for his father and his oldest brother—if he, too, had his own brand of guilt weighing on his heart for the part he had played. If he hadn't come to stop Samael from binding himself to her power, then he wouldn't be on the run. If he hadn't been framed for poisoning the king, then he himself would be on that throne.

Adrastus explained, "When Samael crowned himself king, he inherited the power that comes with it—my father's power. With it, he can create new Night Riders."

Disbelief and pure horror shook Kelera to the core. She took a shaky breath and swayed slightly. The legend that Mira—the mortal servant who had betrayed her, Cierine, and the other women when they tried to escape through the blackthorn veil—had spoken of, said that King Cyrus had used unfathomable power to destroy the very souls of men he'd believed had plotted against him. By doing so, he created the horrifying beasts that rode on horses with rotting flesh. They were unstoppable wraiths, doomed to serve the King of Unseelie for eternity. If Samael could make his own Night Riders, then there was no telling how many poor souls he would turn. He could be building an entire army of them for all she knew.

Kelera clenched her fists, and her magic flared slightly. It popped and fizzled under her skin, and she began to blow out a series of short breaths, attempting to regain control. She whimpered as a small fire bloomed in the sand in front of her. Adrastus' power tugged on hers, drawing it back and settling it down again. Then he stomped the flames out quickly.

She blushed, embarrassed by her lack of control. Adrastus furrowed his brow. But she didn't give him a chance to speak as she asked, "If Samael can create new Night Riders, then is it possible for someone to create more of the Wild Hunt?" She felt foolish asking. It showed just how ignorant she was to the ways of Elfhame and its ancient magic.

Adrastus answered without making her feel like the clueless halfling that she was as he said, "I wish it were possible. The men who make up the Wild Hunt are not cursed or created by magic that any living Fae wields. They ascend to the position in death. It is considered an honor to ride with them."

Kelera swallowed her disappointment. It would have given them the upper hand. If it was a mystery on how the Wild Hunt ascended, then it would surely be a mystery as to how many of them there were.

She returned to the matter at hand. It was best to focus on what they could control. "So, what does Gadreel want us to do?"

Adrastus hesitated and eyed her as if waiting for her magic to spin wildly out of control at any moment. Not that she blamed him. The shame of what she had done to Ammon washed over her again. But this time, mixed with the blistering sun of the Summer Court, the guilt was almost suffocating. Her legs burned from walking in the vast sandy terrain. There was no time to slow down, though. And she found reassurance in knowing that his magic was bound to hers, anchoring it when needed.

Adrastus pressed his lips together before answering, "He wants us to stay safe."

"Oh, is that all?" Kelera scoffed.

"No." Adrastus shook his head. "He says that an emissary to the Seelie Court will meet us near the Spring border. In a few days' time, there will be a festival. That is where he will be waiting for us."

Ah, yes, the Spring Court, she thought. The Seelie territory where Gadreel's lover, Oliver, would also be waiting for them. Where they would seek out a force strong enough to stand against Samael and his army. It also happened to be her birthplace. She grasped the locket that hung around her neck as a reminder of the mother who had given it to her before abandoning her. She shook away the curiosity that came with the prospect of finally seeing the territory that she hailed from, choosing instead to focus on arguing with Adrastus.

Her brow wrinkled as she considered their options. "I thought Oliver was our way in. Why can't we just go straight to the Seelie Palace? Meeting a stranger in the woods sounds like a waste of time to me."

A sly smile graced Adrastus' lips. "Is that what you would call our meeting? A waste of time?"

Heat prickled at Kelera's cheeks. She thought back to how Adrastus had defended her in the woods against Vazine and his wolf-like form. It had been the first time they had met one another face to face. Who could have imagined that one small moment would lead to all of this? He had helped her that night. And whether she had known it or not, he had helped her since. She stifled a smile and shrugged. "I suppose there are exceptions." Then more seriously, turning back to the matter at hand, she said, "But I don't like having to jump through all these hoops."

As if he had been ready for the argument, he didn't even blink as he replied, "We can't just stroll into the Seelie Palace and demand an audience with the Queen and her council."

Kelera raised her chin. "Why not?"

"I am an Unseelie Prince. And you are..."

"A halfling," she finished.

He gave her a sympathetic smile. "Yes. And whether it is the truth or not, we are both wanted for treason with the Unseelie Court. We wouldn't even make it past the gates of the Seelie Palace without being detained for questioning."

"But surely Oliver—"

"Oliver is my brother's lover." Adrastus pinched the bridge of his nose and Kelera wondered if it was the heat or the stress that was getting to him. "Many in his court look down at him because of his affiliations with the Unseelie. He would likely be considered biased. They will not listen to him alone."

"So, this emissary is our ticket in?" Kelera had to admit it made sense. The mortal court wasn't all that different. King Tristan never would have allowed rumored fugitives into the heart of his palace without someone to vouch for them.

"He is. Gadreel says that he is reliable, with nothing to tie him to Unseelie. But he is a fair man and, more than that, he is sympathetic to our cause." Adrastus placed a hand on her arm. "We are going in blind here. We don't know how much the Seelie truly know of Samael's plan. If he has been careful not to show his hand yet, then they may be reluctant to believe that he plans to take all of Elfhame. Convincing them to give us an army will be no easy task."

Kelera wiped the sweat from her brow and picked up her pace. Her magic still burned just beneath the surface, building with an intensity that matched her anxiety and guilt. She gasped as Adrastus' cool, soothing magic intertwined firmly with hers. It came in waves of fire and ice, washing over her like the tide she could see in the ocean ahead of them.

When she first agreed to the binding spell, it had been an act of desperation. Her magic had been wildly out of control. Because of the danger it posed, she couldn't return home for fear of hurting her father and those she cared about. And her instincts had told her she could trust him to save both his people and hers. Yet, here they were, wandering through the Summer Court, living like criminals on the run.

She stumbled through the sand beside Adrastus until he slowed and said, "We will stop to rest there." He pointed in the distance to a small village by the water. The houses were placed on stilts to protect their residents from the rising tides. His voice was rough from the heat and lack of water thanks to their dwindling supplies, as he said, "It's a fishing village. The Unseelie guard wouldn't dare venture this far into the Summer Court for risk of showing their hand too soon. We should be safe there for the time being. As long as we keep our heads down, no one will suspect a thing.

We'll stay for the night, then continue toward the Spring border in the morning."

Kelera squinted at him in the bright sun. His skin was glowing with a blooming tan, while hers was dry and freckling. It was taking a lot of effort to follow a plan she hadn't made herself, but the thought of having shelter and a bath in freshwater sounded divine. She'd never considered herself one to rely on simple comforts, but growing up in the mortal palace had apparently influenced her more than she cared to admit. She couldn't imagine how the solitary Fae who moved from place to place, never having a permanent home, managed.

And the thought of being within the safety of solid walls brought a sense of comfort to her. They were exposed here in the dunes. Every shifting of the sands set her on high alert—ready for one of Samael's minions to step out from the shadows to drag them back to face their punishment.

Adrastus came to a sudden stop and reached into his bag. "Here," he said, handing her a delicate dress made of nearly sheer fabric. "Put this on."

Kelera took the dress and gave him a questioning look with her brows raised. "What is this?"

He began to unbutton his linen shirt, tearing it off and shoving it into his bag. His body would have reminded her of a marble statue with lean, sculpted muscle if it weren't for the scars that ran along his chest, arms, and back. She'd known from the first moment she saw him that he was a man who had lived a violent life, but that didn't stop her heart from hurting for him.

He explained as he put on a fresh shirt made of a lighter fabric than the one he'd been wearing. "Gadreel wanted to make sure we'd blend in when we made it to the village." He smiled fondly as he talked about the one brother he *did* care for. "He's always thinking ahead. Slipped them into the packs before we fled."

Clutching the lightweight dress in her hands, she smiled too. Surely, the dress would be more comfortable in the sweltering summer heat. And she wanted nothing more than to shed the filthy clothes she was currently wearing.

Kelera raised a finger and spun it in a circle. Adrastus took the cue and turned away so she could change. She felt incredibly vulnerable, changing in broad daylight so close to the fishermen and the village. As fast as she could, she slipped out of her dirty travel clothes and into the dress. It was like nothing she'd ever worn before. Light and airy, but covering her modestly. She would have to thank Gadreel when she saw him again for giving her something tasteful.

She cleared her throat to let Adrastus know she was done changing, and they continued on their way. Though the heat wasn't as stifling now that she was wearing the style of the Summer Court, she couldn't help but sweat as dark thoughts crept into her mind with each step she took. The village in the distance looked quaint, but that didn't mean dangers weren't lurking around every corner there. Samael would stop at nothing to get to them. He did not like to lose. Her nerves were raw from the constant paranoia, and she knew deep down that she wouldn't truly feel safe until they reached the Spring Court, where their possible allies were waiting.

She clasped her hands together, trying to hide the way they trembled slightly, before speaking. "How long until we reach the Spring border?" Time was of the essence, and she still had her father and the other mortals to think about. The knowledge that Samael was building an army was more unsettling than she had words for.

If only she had a raven of her own to send word to them...

Adrastus interrupted her thoughts as he answered, "Two, maybe three days if we hug the coast."

Unsatisfied with the answer, Kelera said, "Every day we spend here is another day that my people are in danger. When I bound my power to yours, you promised to help them as well as the Fae of Elfhame. Who knows what else Samael is planning now that your father is dead...?" She stopped herself short, feeling sorry to have brought up his father. Adrastus was the bastard prince, an outcast in his family, but King Cyrus had still loved and respected him in his own twisted way. She wasn't sure how Adrastus truly felt about his death, and they had rather avoided the subject altogether.

Adrastus sighed and gave her the same speech he had been giving her since their first morning in the Summer Court. "Walking across the dunes leaves us exposed to both the elements and Samael's bounty hunters. Staying along the coast is the best course for now."

"Perhaps if we could find a way to send word to my father... a raven perhaps, then—"

Adrastus frowned. "Only a Fae can pass through the veil. When we reach the Spring Court, then we can try to find someone willing to cross the blackthorns with the message."

She didn't care to voice her mixed feelings about that, so she pursed her lips together and remained silent. For the better part of each day that they traveled, she'd been weighing her options. She could go with the messenger to warn her people. Which could lead to disaster if her power spun out of control without Adrastus nearby. Or she could allow a messenger to go without her while she stayed in Elfhame just long enough to help Adrastus in his quest to stop his brother and in the meantime, get control of her magic.

He offered a hand to Kelera as they made their way down a steep sandy dune. Still irritated by his answer and her predicament, she pulled away to scramble down the hill on her own. Just when she thought she would make it down effortlessly, her foot hit a loose patch of sand and she yelped as she slid the rest of the way down on her butt.

By the time she reached the bottom, she was covered in the soft white sand. Even her dark wavy hair was entangled with it. Adrastus howled with laughter. It was a surprising and infectious sound. She would have laughed too, but wasn't willing to give him the satisfaction. He hurried down the hill, sliding through the sand on his feet with grace. She pretended to sulk as he reached her and extended a hand to help her up. This time, she took it. He pulled her up and into his chest.

Breathlessly, he said, "You can trust me when I offer my help."

"We shall see." She knew he was speaking of the help he offered her to get down the dune, but her mind was still on the earlier offer to help her warn her people of Samael's plans to uproot the blackthorn veil that separated the two realms. Once he did that, then there would be nothing standing in his way—nothing to protect the mortals who were no match for the magic of the Fae.

She refrained from bringing the subject up again and followed him toward the village. The day was unbearably warm, especially after she had grown used to the bitter cold during her time at the Winter Court. She drew her hair back and tied it with a ribbon she had torn from the discarded dress she'd been wearing when they had made their escape from the Unseelie Palace.

Adrastus was smiling at her, and the heat of a blush crept across her face. "What is it?"

"Your ears... You haven't bothered to cover them as much since I first met you."

It was true. At some point, she had stopped trying to cover the pointed tips of her ears. She had gone most of her life trying to hide any attribute that gave her away as the daughter of a Fae woman, but here in Elfhame, leaving them uncovered gave her a small sense of freedom. Not wanting to dive into the topic with Adrastus and admit how much this world was growing on her, she simply said, "Well, you said we had to blend in."

He had also once said to her that she needed to stop trying to be what others wanted her to be... She glanced at him uneasily. He too had grown on her, but she certainly wasn't going to give him the gratification of saying it out loud.

He gave her a knowing look. "Of course."

Chapter Two

The houses in the modest fishing village were vibrant with bold and wonderful colors. It was almost like seeing color truly for the first time ever. In comparison, her home in the mortal realm was a dull and listless place. Kelera craned her neck to get a better view of the homes. They stood raised with wooden stilts off the ground to escape any unruly tides.

Then she stole a glance at Adrastus, watching as a cool sea breeze graced the air, ruffling his dark hair. His eyes seemed to glisten as he looked at the charming little town. He pointed ahead to a large inn. "We will take up a place there for the night. Oh, and Gadreel has given us these." He pulled parchment paper from his leather bag and handed them to her—they were identification papers with Oliver's signature flourished at the bottom.

She balked at him. "Husband and wife?"

"I think Gadreel thought it to be a sort of joke." He winked. "But the details are unimportant. All that matters is that these papers will allow me to lie about who we are, so long as I am simply stating what is on them."

She raised an eyebrow. "That's quite the loophole."

Adrastus gave her a mischievous smile, his eyes crinkling slightly at the corners. The tension in his jawline and shoulders dissipated, leaving him looking like the young man he truly was. It brought a surprising sense of relief to see him like that.

He ignored her statement about the loophole and said, "It also gives us a believable reason to be traveling together and staying in close quarters." Kelera looked at him in disapproval. It was scandalous enough that they'd been sleeping mere feet from one another the last few nights. What would her father say if he knew she was staying in the same room as a man who wasn't actually her husband?

Adrastus quickly elaborated, "We are safer together. Should we need to defend ourselves or flee, it is best that we be as close to each other as possible."

Kelera sighed. He had a point. Samael delighted in using his shadow magic and the idea of him or one of his minions slipping into her room in the middle of the night horrified her. Bending the mortal realm's code of conduct for an unmarried woman definitely beat the alternative to being vulnerable to attack, so she pressed the matter no further. And she had to admit she would need Adrastus' help to navigate yet another peculiar part of Elfhame. Being with him gave her a sense of security.

The prickling sensation of magic brushed the surface of her skin as if accompanying her thoughts. Since unleashing the power she had left dormant for so long, she had become accustomed to the warmth that surfaced with it. But it would take time to grow used to the chill from Adrastus' magic that accompanied it now. It was like a never-ending ebb and flow of fire and ice.

Her stomach growled as they approached the village. They'd been living off of the provisions Gadreel had packed for them. But the stale bread and dried meat had hardly been satisfying. She longed for a warm meal. "Do you think the inn will still be serving breakfast?"

Adrastus rubbed at the stubble on his face. "I doubt it. And it may be some time before they have lunch ready." He scanned the village around them and pointed to a building with sun bleached wood. "The tavern will be our best bet if we want to find a decent meal." He paused for a moment, then added, "And a strong drink."

Kelera followed him eagerly, already dreaming of the food that awaited them inside. They walked up the sturdy wooden stairs that led to an open door and the sharp scent of spices graced her nose. Her stomach rumbled again, and she practically leapt inside.

The tavern windows were wide open, allowing the sun to light the room. A refreshing breeze blew through them, giving Kelera a nice reprieve from the heat of the mid-morning. It was a stark contrast to the warm, cozy tavern Adrastus had taken her to in the Winter Court village.

Here, patrons were lounging lazily on comfortable chairs, cooling themselves with bright feathered fans. They were drinking shimmering gold liquid from tall flutes and smoking from long wooden pipes. Best of all, they were paying no mind to her and Adrastus.

Adrastus led her to a small table in the corner, positioned so they could see the entrance. *Strategic*, she thought to herself. If anyone came in looking for trouble, she and Adrastus would spot them first and be ready.

Adrastus pulled a chair out for her, then dragged his own close to hers, so they were both facing the door. Having a full vantage point to watch for anyone coming in who may appear out of place gave Kelera a semblance of control. Something she had been sorely lacking these last few weeks. She squeezed her hands together and placed them on her lap. Between her hunger and gnawing anxiety, she was having trouble relaxing.

Adrastus, however, was the epitome of ease. He sat back and called for a waiter with a gentle wave of his hand. A man with brilliant amber eyes brought them two flutes, and a decanter filled with the golden drink. She leaned into Adrastus once the man walked away. "What is this?" She gestured to the decanter with a small nod of her head.

Adrastus chuckled. "I can assure you it's safe. It is a drink for vitality—the sort of magic the Summer Court is well known for." He filled Kelera's glass first, then his own.

She sniffed at it, reluctant to drink anything that had been spelled by the Fae. It smelled like oranges with a mysterious bitter note to it. Despite her hesitation, after two days of rationing water, she was practically drooling at the prospect of something cool and tangy on her tongue.

Her palms were sweating as she said, "I suppose we can use all the strength and energy we can muster." Then she took a chance and sipped at it. It was refreshing with hints of fruit, but not too sweet. She took another drink and waited for something to happen. Adrastus was watching her curiously. She rolled her eyes. "What?"

"Nothing." He smirked at her as he drank.

The drink's magic lapped over her like a wave splashing against her ankles. She was suddenly very awake. Her body was buzzing with all of this energy she didn't know what to do with. She stared at Adrastus with wide eyes. "It works!"

He laughed haughtily. "Yes, that it does."

Kelera fidgeted with her newfound energy, tapping her foot rapidly under the table. Adrastus' gaze lingered on her, then he grabbed hold of her knee, making her stop. "You really should relax. There is no danger here. At least not at the moment."

"I don't understand how you can be so calm." She scanned the room, unconvinced by his reassurances that there was nothing to fear here. Samael could have sent any one of these Fae to capture them.

A man with dark curly hair and eyes the color of a sunset caught her eye. Giving her a dazzling white smile, he raised a glass to her, making her look away quickly. Adrastus shifted, looking over his shoulder at the man. Chuckling, he asked, "What's wrong, little thief? You act as if you've never had an admirer before."

Kelera looked back at the man and the heat of a blush crept along the bridge of her nose. Men in the mortal court weren't nearly as open with their affections as they were in Elfhame. The traditions of courtly manners had been imposed on her for so long that attention like this still caught her off guard. Even after witnessing Gadreel's pleasure party back in Unseelie.

Not wanting to seem rude, she smiled back at the man before turning to face Adrastus again. He was staring at her with sincere fascination, his green eyes luminous in the sunlight drifting through the open windows.

She laughed at herself for acting like a schoolgirl and tried to defend herself as she uttered, "Men in Elfhame are far more flirtatious than the men in Nevene." She took another sip of the summer drink in front of her. As she set it back on the table, she ran her finger along the rim of the cup. "Anyway, men in the mortal court never did show much interest in me."

Adrastus nearly choked on his drink. "You're kidding."

Kelera pursed her lips. Until Alexander asked for her hand in marriage, she'd had no other prospects. It was one of the reasons why she had been so keen to make the match work. It was the reason she had tried so hard to appear flawless in front of him—hiding the tips of her ears and watching what she said around him.

A couple at the table next to them waved to grab Kelera's attention. The woman was slender, with her arms draped over her companion's shoulders. She smiled softly as she said, "You two make a lovely couple."

Adrastus leaned in close to Kelera, wrapping his arm around her and pulling her into him. He smelled like the ocean. Like salt and sunshine. The couple beamed at them as Adrastus replied, "That is very kind of you."

"What brings you to our little village?" The man's accent was heavy, like the other Summer Court Fae they had encountered. It gave her a slight sense of comfort, knowing he wasn't an Unseelie sent there to entrap them.

Adrastus tensed as he started to speak, "We're here for... on..."

His tongue won't allow him to tell the lie, Kelera thought. "We're here on holiday," she lied instantly. "For our honeymoon, actually." To solidify the story, she leaned in and kissed Adrastus softly on the corner of his mouth. His body relaxed, and he gave her shoulder a light, grateful squeeze.

"How amazing!" The woman squealed. "So are we!"

Her husband called for the waiter. "A round of drinks for the entire room! We're celebrating." The tavern erupted in applause as the patrons cheered for the newlyweds.

Adrastus raised his cup to the couple. "Cheers! To everlasting love."

The people around them shouted drunkenly, "To everlasting love!"

She leaned against Adrastus, basking in the small moment of contentment. It would be fleeting, she knew, but it was worth taking in while she had the chance. She looked around at each of the faces in the room. They were bright and cheerful. Would she be like them one day? An image of Ammon's lifeless eyes flashed in her mind, destroying any semblance of hope. After what she had done, perhaps she didn't deserve to be like these people. Her fingers flitted to the locket around her neck, and she rubbed her thumb along the vine engravings, trying to calm herself—a nervous habit she had yet to break.

Adrastus nudged her in the shoulder. "What's wrong?"

"Nothing," she lied as she took a sip of the freshly poured drink nearby.

"You're doing that thing."

Furrowing her brow, she asked, "What thing?"

Adrastus nodded to her hand. "Whenever you're nervous or upset, you reach for that locket."

He was beginning to know her too well. Kelera lowered her hand, placing it gently in her lap. "I think the drink is getting to my head." She forced a laugh that sounded more nervous than humorous.

Adrastus continued to look at her as if he knew it was more than that. So, she tried again, "I was just," she paused, letting out a heavy sigh. There was no use lying to him when he could see right through her. "I was thinking about that day in your brother's room..." She drifted off, afraid of saying too much around all the strangers in the tavern.

Music began to play from the opposite side of the room. A woman strummed beautifully on a string instrument; eyes closed as if she were lost in her own song. Adrastus gave Kelera a lopsided smile and his eyes lit up as he said, "You just need to focus on the moment." He stood and offered his hand to her. "Care to use some of that energy in a dance?"

She hesitated. "I don't know if we should." She moved to rub at the locket around her neck again, but caught herself.

"It's one dance, little thief. Considering our perilous situation, it would be a shame not to cherish these precious moments." His lips parted slightly as he leaned in with his hand still extended.

Kelera bit her lip as her eyes darted to the dance floor and then back to the beautiful man standing before her. Her stomach fluttered when she looked into his eyes. He was right, in a way. They were running for their lives and even once they reached the Spring Court, there was no telling what danger they would still have to face. And sitting here sulking was not going to bring Ammon back. If she and Adrastus were to die tomorrow, then would she regret not taking a moment to enjoy one little dance?

Maybe it was the Summer Court drink that gave her the courage, or maybe it was simply that Elfhame had made her bolder over the last few weeks. Regardless of what drove her to it, she placed her hand in his and allowed him to lead her to a small clearing between the tables. The melody was soft and seductive, and he pulled her close to him. The intimacy of it sent a slight tingle sweeping up the back of her neck and across her face.

They swayed to the music, and Kelera struggled to find her footing. It was rather embarrassing. When she was a girl going through training as a lady of the court, she had spent hours perfecting the steps to popular dances. She'd known exactly what to do and when to do it.

Dancing here in Elfhame was strikingly different from dancing in Nevene. Back in the mortal court, dancing was like a game of chess. You were expected to move in a precise choreography based on the song that played. She'd been so eager to be the perfect courtier that she had appreciated how rule-based and rigid the dances were—it was easier to follow along that way. But here, in Adrastus' arms, dancing was like art. They allowed the music to guide them, moving their bodies without thinking of where their feet or hands needed to go. Soon she was utterly lost in it.

Her eyes kept drifting to Adrastus' face. There was a soft smile on his lips—the lips she had kissed not so long ago in his private rooms at the Unseelie Palace. Despite the blood and sweat that he had been covered in, she had wanted him. She'd wanted to know, even if for just a moment, what it would be like to be with him. It had been a kiss that had awakened something in her.

Her gaze dropped to his chest where his shirt revealed his tan, scarred skin and she tensed. Adrastus looked down at her and joked, "You need to loosen up." He drew her into him and she arched her back as he placed his hand on the small of it. His fingers traced little circles along the thin fabric of her dress. It then occurred to her that there was barely anything standing between his touch and her bare skin. She sucked in a small breath.

She nearly shuddered in pleasure as he said low, "Dancing should be sensual. It is something that should be done with feeling."

Kelera let out an uneasy laugh. "That doesn't come easily to me."

"Perhaps that is because no one has ever showed you how before."

She thought of Alexander, her betrothed, who was waiting for her in the mortal realm. He had been a reasonable match, but she had to admit they didn't know each other well. They hadn't had that chance. "In my world, that is something a *husband* shows his wife."

Adrastus grinned wickedly and leaned in to whisper in her ear, "Then it is a good thing that you and I are playing the part of husband and wife."

Shivers drifted through her. Breathlessly, she said, "Yet, you and I are not, in fact, husband and wife."

She started to draw away from him, but he stopped her, grabbing hold of one of her hands. He placed it on his chest and led her back into the dance. He tilted his head back and squeezed his eyes shut. When he looked down at her again, there was no smile. "I didn't mean to upset you." His hand drifted to her face and his fingers hovered carefully over the scar running from the corner of her eye to her jaw. "I only want you to be happy—to move past your fear and trust yourself... and me."

Kelera hung her head slightly. "I'm trying. It's just hard when all I've ever known is fear. Fear that if I show what I truly am, then I will be seen as a monster. That if I don't do things in a certain way, then I, and those closest to me, will be punished for it." Her fears weren't unwarranted. She had been bullied in Nevene by girls like Drisella, had been shunned by King Tristan's courtiers, and even when she had finally been brave enough to use her magic, she had killed someone. Maybe she really was the monster they all believed her to be.

Adrastus' voice was bitter as he asked, "In the mortal court, you mean?"

"Yes. I'm afraid of what will happen when I return home." Would the mortals welcome her back into their fold? Would Alexander still want her? For all she knew, she could be going home to be considered a ruined woman.

Adrastus smiled sadly down at her, "I know you believe you belong in Nevene with your father and with Alexander," he frowned as he said his name, "but if you want my honest opinion—I think Elfhame looks good on you."

"I'm not sure I would go that far," she scoffed. "I've made so many mistakes here."

His eyes bore into hers. "But you're learning from them. If given the chance, you could do great things. If you are honest with yourself, do you believe the mortals would give you that chance?"

No, they wouldn't. The thought came immediately, shocking her. But she knew it deep down. The mortals' fear of the Fae ran too deep. Magic would always appear as a threat to them. Her father had known it from the start. It was why he had been so adamant about her fitting in amongst the humans. It was why she'd had to hide her magic, and why she had to work so hard to excel at mundane things like dancing.

She sighed and looked away from Adrastus, but said nothing. What could she say? How could she make him understand why she was torn? Elfhame offered freedom, but the mortal realm offered stability. She knew her role there and had already put so much effort into perfecting the part. Could she really throw it all away now?

Adrastus tilted her chin up to look at him. "I think you could be happy here."

The way he looked at her—like she was the only person in the room—stirred something inside her. "With you, you mean?" Shocked that the words had slipped from her mouth, she stopped moving to the music and drew away from him slightly.

Adrastus appeared to be just as surprised. "Is that what it would take? For me to ask you to stay?"

"No. I mean..." She tugged at her hair to cover her pointed ear and blushed.

"Would it be so bad?" His gaze was questioning as he raised his eyebrow.

Her chest tightened as she considered it. Staying in Elfhame would mean leaving behind everything she had ever known and worked for. It would mean a whole new life. The part of her that craved freedom told her that staying in Elfhame with Adrastus would be an adventure. One that she could only have ever summoned in her dreams. It would be a life that could give her what she'd been missing. But the other part of her—the one that still believed if she could return to Nevene and save the mortals from Samael, then she would finally have earned her place amongst them—told her she had no choice but to go back.

She pressed her lips into a thin line and shook her head. "I can't."

Adrastus lowered his arms slowly and stopped moving to the music. "You're still fighting against who you are and what you want. If you can just bring yourself to move past that..." There was a bitter note mixed with disappointment in his words.

"We shouldn't even be thinking like this. We need to focus on saving our people. It's not about what we may or may not want." She wrapped her arms around herself, putting as much of a barricade between her and Adrastus as she could.

Adrastus let out a low, frustrated growl and pulled her back into him. Her arms dropped to her sides and her heart pounded in her chest. His voice was husky as he said, "You cannot deny that there is something here between us." He pressed his body against hers and she stifled a gasp. The fabric of her dress was thin, crafted for the heat of the Summer Court, and she felt incredibly vulnerable. A sudden flush of warmth spread below her naval and down between her legs. Her body was responding to his, but her head was spinning with warring thoughts. She cared for Adrastus. They had a bond like no other she'd experienced with a man. And she desired him. She couldn't deny that. But none of that changed their circumstances. His brother was a danger to them all. And ultimately, she would have to leave Elfhame to return to her people.

Adrastus' voice was low, but there was no frustration, only truth as he said, "I am aware of our situation. But it doesn't change how I feel about you. I know you're starting to feel it too, but you're scared, so you're holding back." His hand slid down to her hips and pressure built in her body, making her lean into his touch—craving more of it.

Despite her lust, she said, "It's not about us, Dras."

"If you always wait to take what you want for yourself, then you will find one day that you are too late." There was a hint of regret in his voice as he said, "There will always be another threat lurking in the darkness. Another plot. Another battle. That is the way of the world, little thief. But it is in these moments that we must appreciate what life is handing to us. You can fight for your people and still claim something for yourself in the process."

Her heart was beating rapidly as she said, "I don't know how to do both." She was still melting under his touch, wishing she could let go of her doubts and give them both what they wanted—what she had begun to want since their first kiss, when he had won her from Samael's control in the pits. When he had saved her in a clash of shadows and ice.

As quickly as he had placed his hands on her, he removed them. He wove his fingers through his hair, tugging at the soft waves as he said, "It appears your body is ready, but your heart is not. I suppose I will have to wait for it to catch up."

Kelera's throat was tight as she said, "Maybe we should go back to the table."

Adrastus tried to smile, but it faltered as he agreed. "Yeah, let's get some food." He held out an arm, allowing her to pass first.

She could still feel the ghost of his hands on her body as she walked back to their table, with him following close behind. It wasn't right to desire a man who was not her betrothed—to allow herself to wonder what it would be like to take Adrastus up on his offer and stay here in Elfhame with him. What was wrong with her? She had spent her life suppressing her desires. But after a few weeks with this man, she'd lost all control of her good senses.

They sat in silence for a few moments. She couldn't think of anything to say to him. And it appeared he was done with the subject of the two of them for the time being. She watched the Fae around them, noting a couple in the corner. They were whispering to one another and every so often, one of the women would lean in to kiss the other on her neck. Kelera envied them and how easily they were able to show their affection.

It felt like she and Adrastus quite literally had the whole world resting on their shoulders. If all of that was gone, if Samael were out of the picture and they were just a man and a woman enjoying each other's company in a tavern, then would she be able to open her heart to Adrastus fully? Would she trade kisses with him in the corner like the women she was watching now?

Her mind was still at odds with the possibilities when the waiter returned. She was glad to see him carrying a plate piled high with fruit and cheese. She grabbed a strange-looking fruit that was shaped almost like a heart. Adrastus abandoned his sulking and took it from her, cutting it in half to reveal a bright red center with small black seeds. He handed her one half and bit into the other.

Kelera dug in, savoring every ripe bite. She was starting to relax, content to eat and listen to the music, until four rough-looking men walked into the tavern. Their skin was lighter than the rest of the Summer Court Fae, and they wore bark-colored clothing similar to Oliver's. Gadreel's lover was an emissary of the Spring Court, so judging by the similarities these men had to Oliver, they likely hailed from the same Seelie territory. Did that make them friends or foe? Her eyes darted to Adrastus so she could gauge his reaction. Considering his experience in the various courts, she trusted he would be the first to spot danger.

He was still lounging casually in his chair and didn't even bother to look up at the men. They walked by the table. The tallest one, who was built like a knight, reminded her of her father's right-hand man, Dodger. Her ribs tightened with a pang of homesickness.

The man caught her eye and a small look of surprise flashed across his face. Kelera's heart skipped a beat. Did he recognize them? Samael would have sent their descriptions out to every bounty hunter willing to take on a prince of the Unseelie Court. And judging by the weapons these men wore on their belts, they would be just the type for that sort of thing.

Chapter Three

K elera's palms were so sweaty that she nearly dropped her drink as she raised it to her lips. She was having trouble taking her eyes off of the men who had walked into the tavern, worried that if she looked away for even a split-second, then they would get the jump on her and Adrastus.

Adrastus' hand squeezed her leg under the table, drawing her attention to him. He gave her a subtle shake of his head. He either didn't want her to engage them, or he didn't think they were a threat. Either way, Kelera busied herself with the plate of food in front of her.

The men chose an empty table closest to her and Adrastus, making themselves comfortable with an air of arrogance. The tallest one surveyed the room with a smug look on his face, like he knew his men were drawing attention and enjoyed every bit of it. Their waiter hurried over to them with a tray of drinks and she could see his hands trembling ever so slightly. Judging by the way they laughed as the waiter scurried away, the men must have noticed it, too.

The tallest one, with long, braided hair, leaned back in his chair and winked at Kelera. Her face burned as she glared back at him. She had no intention of drawing attention to herself, but she didn't like bullies. She'd put up with enough of them as a child and when she was under Samael's captivity. Adrastus squeezed her leg in warning, but she ignored him. Magic buzzed in her palms, eager to hit a mark.

The man raised an eyebrow and scratched at his bearded face. "Is there a problem, little lady?" His friends turned their scrutiny to her as well.

One of them had an eye patch made of cracked black leather. He leaned on the table and piped in. "Looks to me like she's in search of some real men to keep her company."

Her magic progressed from a slight buzz to intense heat. Adrastus grabbed her hands and his cool magic wound around them, dimming her power until it was a dull pulse. Coolly, he said, "The lady is just fine as she is, but your concern is touching." He stood and gestured for Kelera to do the same. They were drawing attention as the other patrons whispered and looked in their direction. Tension heightened, ridding the room of the comfortable atmosphere it'd had moments before.

She averted her gaze from the men as she rose from her chair. Adrastus tossed a few coins onto the table for the waiter and turned her toward the door, ready to leave. But the tallest man stopped them. "Wait, we didn't mean anything by it. We've been on the road so long it seems we've forgotten how to act around someone as civilized as yourselves." He smiled broadly and snapped at the waiter. "Drinks! For our friends here." Then he gestured to two empty seats. "Have a round with us."

Adrastus kept his composure as he replied, "A generous offer, but my…" He drifted off, looking helplessly at Kelera.

Taking the lead, she stuck her chin in the air and said, "My husband and I must be going."

"Your husband!" The tallest man, who appeared to be the leader of the group, slapped the man with the eye patch on the back of the head. "We've insulted the bloke's wife." He held his hands to his heart. "Now we really owe you a round of drinks. We insist."

Kelera wanted to kick herself for drawing attention to them in the first place. She should have minded her own business. She fidgeted with her locket as she waited to see what Adrastus would do. This time, she would follow his lead. The men, though rugged, didn't seem to be an immediate threat. But it could be an act to get them to drop their guard.

Adrastus shifted on his feet. After a moment, he smiled back at the men. "It would be idiotic to turn down refreshments on such a warm summer's day." As he led Kelera to the table, he leaned in and whispered to her, "It might be wise to see what they know. If they're here for us, then it's best that we confront them in a controlled environment, rather than be ambushed on the road."

A wise choice. But one that she wouldn't have made. The thought of a confrontation when her magic was on the constant verge of chaos worried her, especially with so many innocent bystanders in the tavern. There was no telling who would be harmed if she lost control again. But she trusted Adrastus' judgment enough to follow his lead, so she took a seat between him and the leader of the group. The waiter brought a wooden jug of ale for them to share and practically ran from the room. Whoever these men were, they were notorious in the Summer Court. She could feel eyes on her and noticed that everyone in the room was watching them warily. It didn't ease her nerves.

She kept her hands neatly on her lap, trying to keep her magic steady. If she allowed herself to focus on her fear, then her power could get out of hand. It didn't help that the man with the eye patch was looking at her like she was a piece of meat he would like to devour. When she made eye contact with him, he picked a knife up off the table and began to pick at his teeth with it. She looked down at her hands, willing her magic to stay dormant. Her fingers twitched from the strain.

The other two men, each donning braided beards and hair pulled back tight, paid no mind as they spoke in hushed tones to one another. The leader grabbed Kelera's attention when he asked, "So, what are two Spring Courters doing here? Running from the trouble?"

She wasn't sure what made him think they were from the Spring Court, but it was the second question that struck a real chord with her, causing her stomach to do a small flip. He knew they were on the run. She balled her hands into fists and tried to steady herself. Adrastus, on the other hand, appeared unphased. He was much better under pressure than she was. A skill he'd acquired in the Unseelie Court as he tried to undermine his family's cruelty toward the Lesser Fae. If only Kelera had that same talent.

He answered casually, "Just passing through."

The man with the knife narrowed his eye as he studied them. Kelera elaborated for Adrastus, "We are newlyweds and came here to celebrate." The more consistent details they gave, the better they could throw any suspicion.

"Strange time to do it, all things considered."

Well, that backfired, Kelera thought. Was this man trying to bait them? Trying to make them slip up and give themselves away? She bit the inside of her cheek as she waited for Adrastus to talk. He shrugged his shoulders and took a drink.

When she realized he wasn't going to say anything, she gave into her curiosity and spoke up. "What do you mean, all things considered?" If the men were here for them, she'd rather get it all out in the open and be done with the guessing games. And asking questions sure beat giving the wrong answer to the strangers.

The man with the eye-patch sucked at his teeth then said, "Considering the Queen ain't gonna make it through the month. Shit, I'd be surprised if she makes it through the week."

Kelera felt numb. The Seelie Queen was still fighting the poison that Samael had somehow slipped to her. It was a wonder how she had survived this long. The poison Samael had given to King Cyrus had worked quickly. Perhaps it was the Queen's Seelie magic that was allowing her to hold on as long as she had. It hadn't taken long for Kelera to learn that the Seelie Court was renowned in Elfhame for their healers. Then again, if the healers didn't know what was causing the Queen's illness, then maybe they wouldn't know how to help.

She feigned light interest, tapping her fingers on her cup as she asked, "Do they know what ails her?"

The braided man shrugged his broad shoulders. "The council's keepin' that one close to the vest. Guess we don't rank high enough to be privy to such things. But it came on fast, and she's not more than a few centuries old. I'd be inclined to think foul play."

Kelera shifted uncomfortably in the wooden chair. It was hard to tell what sort of rumors might be circulating around Elfhame about the Queen's illness. But the more worrisome question was whether Samael would wait until the Queen was out of play before advancing on Seelie territory. If the answer was yes, then the longer she held on, the more time that bought them.

Kelera studied the men's sullen faces at the mention of their Queen in peril. She couldn't be certain, but perhaps these men weren't there for her and Adrastus after all.

Adrastus finally spoke again. "We didn't realize things had gotten so bad. I admit we've been traveling for quite some time now. You know how word spreads on the road. You're never quite sure how much accuracy is in it."

The tall one spoke. "Aye, we know how it is."

Adrastus grabbed the jug and filled the tall man's cup before topping off his own. "So, what brings you lot here?"

He raised his glass in thanks to Adrastus and said, "Strong drinks and beautiful women, my friend." He took a deep gulp from his cup and wiped at his beard with the back of his sleeve. "If trouble's brewin' then we need one last reprieve."

Kelera couldn't help but wonder what these men did for a living. They reminded her of the group of mercenaries that Duke Cunningham had put together when Princess Cierine had been taken by Samael. They didn't look like farmers or courtiers. There was an edginess to them that worried her. If they weren't there to track her and Adrastus down, it didn't mean they wouldn't make a grab for them if they realized there was money in it for them.

The tall one choked on his drink. "We forgot our manners! My name's Ragnor." He nodded to the man with the eye patch. "That there's Jinx. And the two whispering to one another are Tepin and Chaz."

Adrastus raised his cup to each of them. He spoke slowly, annunciating each word as if it were a struggle to get them out. "I'm Talis and this is Sera." Kelera suspected that the smile on his face was from pride at finally being able to aid in their lie.

The fake names that Gadreel had put on their papers sounded strange being said out loud. She forced an agreeable smile, then held her breath, hoping that the men would believe their story. They showed no sign of recognition, which calmed her enough to steady her hands. She reached for her drink carefully and took a small sip, not wanting to get drunk, but too afraid that if she didn't appear to be drinking, then it would only draw more unwanted attention from the men. The ale was sour on her tongue and she wrinkled her nose slightly. She was never one to drink heavily, even at the extravagant balls in Nevene. There was nothing appealing about losing control of one's inhibitions. Better to be in control at all times.

Two women who had nothing but sheer robes draped over them sauntered by. One of them winked at Tepin and he pushed his seat back so quickly it nearly clattered to the ground. Chaz followed suit and the two of them followed the women into a shadowy corner of the tavern. Kelera stifled a smile at their eagerness. These men might not be the stoic types that they made themselves out to be. Rather, they were like so many other men she'd come across. Men who were in search of simple pleasures in order to escape the constant struggle that life had dealt them. They actually reminded her a bit of her father's knights. The thought of them gave her a hollow feeling in her chest. Would she have the chance to sit amongst those men again? Would she ever get to sit and listen to their boastful stories over the long dinner tables in the barracks again? She ignored the tightness in her throat and returned her attention to the table.

Jinx set the knife down and sighed as he watched his friends disappear into the dark corner of the tavern. Kelera spotted the women's shadows as they took their places on the men's laps. When she turned back, Jinx propped his arm on the table and rested his chin on his fist. "Lucky dogs." He looked so pitiful, she nearly spat her drink out. The change in his demeanor was so at odds with the brutish look of him that it was almost comical.

Ragnor patted him on the back. "Don't drag our new friends' spirits down. Buck up, man."

Jinx's eye shifted between Adrastus and Kelera and his mouth drooped in a frown. "You don't realize how lucky the two of you are. Findin' someone who'll stand by you through it all." He eyed the scars on her and Adrastus' faces, and she fought the urge to raise a hand to cover that side of her face.

Jinx drooped a bit further and said sadly, "Someone who will love you even if you're missin' an eye..." He gingerly touched the leather eye patch on his face.

Kelera bit her lip to keep from laughing. Feeling bad for finding humor in his pitiful state, she grabbed the jug and poured ale into his empty cup. The corner of his mouth perked up in a sad but grateful smile, and he raised the cup to her before drinking.

Adrastus chimed in. "Cheer up. There's someone out there for everyone."

Jinx perked up with a hopeful gleam in his eye. "You think so?" He looked at Kelera as if waiting for her to confirm it.

She cleared her throat and nodded optimistically. "Oh, yes, I'm confident there is a lucky someone out there who," she paused, searching for the right words, "holds the same interests as you." So maybe it wasn't the most romantic thing to say, but what did she know about love? She'd accepted an engagement out of expectation and duty. Alexander was a stranger to her, but marriage to him meant a chance at solidifying her place in society.

She glanced at Adrastus out of the corner of her eye. He was another story. She couldn't pinpoint what her growing feelings for him meant, but surely it couldn't be love. She trusted him and cared for him, and she clearly longed for him, but were those signs of falling in love?

And she certainly never had an example set for her at home. Her father claimed that he had been in love with her mother, but they had only known each other for one reckless night. Kelera always thought that her father had built up a fantasy in his mind to ease his pain. Either way, he had never remarried, insisting that his life was full enough with her and his knights in it.

Adrastus took hold of her hand on the table. He gave it a small squeeze and said, "I think you just have to believe it for yourself." Butterflies fluttered in her stomach.

Ragnor lifted his cup. "Cheers to that."

They all clinked their cups together. Kelera felt bad for judging Jinx so harshly. Judging the Fae based on their appearances was a bad habit she wanted to break. The mortals in Nevene went to such care to fit into the mold that society had created for them. But as different as the Fae in Elfhame were from the mortals in both appearances and power, they too had dreams and wanted to find happiness. *Deserved* to find happiness.

Ragnor began rattling on to Adrastus with tales of their travels. After a while, Kelera started to relax. By midafternoon, Ragnor and his men were drunk from the many jugs of wine they'd had sent to the table. Even Adrastus was having a good time, laughing with the men and exchanging funny stories about their time in the Spring Court. Of course, he had to twist the truth a bit, something that only Kelera noticed as he gripped his cup tighter each time he did it.

She'd noticed that the more Ragnor and his men drank, the less Adrastus drank from his cup. Then it dawned on her. He was getting them drunk. It impressed her how easily he played the part of a Spring Courter on holiday with his wife. Trying her best to play her part as well, she laughed and joked with the group when the opportunity arose.

To her relief, Adrastus controlled the conversation with ease, redirecting questions back to the men and encouraging them to share more stories. It was something she appreciated as she had never been to the Spring Court. It would have been difficult to pretend that she had if they had forced her to participate with tales of her own.

Jinx was telling them about a woman whose bed he'd fallen into, just to find that her randy husband had come home early from his trip. She'd been in the other room when the husband stumbled in and climbed into bed. Jinx barked with laughter as he said, "Should've seen the bloke's face when he rolled over to find little old me instead of his vixen of a wife!"

Kelera fell against Adrastus with laughter. A few of the other patrons sitting at the tables nearest to them laughed as well. The atmosphere in the tavern had shifted back to the way it had been before Ragnor's band had walked in. They no longer eyed the men warily, and it helped ease her paranoia.

At least until Ragnor cleared his throat and said, "Tell me, friends, what news have you heard from the Unseelie territory since being on the road?"

Kelera's body went rigid. "We, um—"

Adrastus swooped in with the save as he said, "We haven't heard much. Just that the king is dead and his son has taken the throne." That was the truth. They hadn't been in town long enough to hear any rumors and had been fortunate enough not to run into any travelers in the dunes.

Ragnor narrowed his eyes. "Aye. We've heard all chaos has broken loose. Seems the Prince of Shadows fancies himself the most powerful Fae ruler since the First King."

Adrastus eyed Ragnor over his cup as he drank. "What else have you heard?"

"That the Bastard Prince killed his own Pa. And that some halfling prisoner killed Prince Ammon. Tis' the craziest thing I believe I've ever heard." He laughed and took a sip of his drink.

Kelera tried to steady her rapidly beating heart. Trying to steer any possible suspicion away from her and Adrastus, she gasped, then asked, "Have they been caught?"

Ragnor shook his head. "Word is they're on the run with a bounty hanging over their heads." He shrugged. "But that's Unseelie business." He paused and gave Kelera a reassuring smile. "Rest assured, though, Milady, if any of that trouble spills over our borders, our men will be ready. But I'm sure it won't come to that and it'll all work itself out. You've nothing to fret about."

She forced a smile and took a deep breath. "I'm sure you're right."

Chapter Four

Ragnor stretched out in his chair lazily. As he did, his long legs reached under the table and he kicked Kelera with his boot. His laugh was deep and genuine before he said apologetically, "Sometimes I forget my own size."

Kelera gave a lighthearted shrug. "It's quite alright."

She'd recently lost track of how much Ragnor and Jinx had drunk. But judging by how flushed their faces were and how loud their voices carried across the room in a slur of words as they continued to tell their stories, they must have been feeling it pretty good.

Jinx spotted a lithe woman alone at the bar and sat up straight in his chair. He was practically drooling as he watched her. Kelera had once wanted her body to look like the woman's and had often compared herself to Cierine's petite frame. She peeked at Adrastus to see if he, too, was ogling the woman. Instead, she was surprised to find that he was staring at her. If Kelera had been standing, her knees likely would have gone weak. Surprised at the attention, she straightened in her seat and fought the blush that threatened to creep along her face.Ragnor drew her attention away from Adrastus' unfaltering gaze as he teased Jinx. "You don't stand a chance."

Kelera was inclined to agree, though she didn't say so out loud. The woman had a deep golden complexion and long silken hair. She was utterly flawless. Whereas poor Jinx was... well, he was less blessed by the fates in that area.

She had to admit the men were growing on her, though, and she was feeling more confident in their presence. A small warning voice in the back of her mind said, *It could all be a trick*. They were Fae, after all, and she had learned by now that the Fae had a talent for trickery.

Ragnor and Jinx stood and mumbled something about finding some companionship. The tavern was becoming crowded as the dinner crowd began coming in.

Adrastus leaned in and whispered to her, "This is an excellent opportunity to slip away."

There was tension in her shoulders all of a sudden. This would be the true test of whether or not these men were in the Summer Court for fun or for more nefarious business. Would they try to stop her and Adrastus from leaving? Would they follow them to the inn where they would rest their heads for the night? If they were bounty hunters, then they would have to make their move soon, wouldn't they?

She and Adrastus bid the men farewell and thanked them for the drinks. To Kelera's relief, the two brutes barely cast a glance in her direction. They waved to them over their shoulders, having already moved onto two other women smiling at them by the bar.

Kelera breathed a sigh of relief as she and Adrastus walked out the door and headed toward the inn. The breeze felt wonderful on her skin, cooling as evening approached. Though, tension still lingered in her shoulders and her neck, and she suspected it wouldn't go anywhere until they were safe across the Spring Court's borders. She still wasn't sure what to make of Ragnor and his men and as much as she had begun to relax in their company, she knew she needed to keep her guard up.

She and Adrastus reached the inn and climbed the sturdy wooden stairs. The heat inside the lobby was not nearly as stifling as she expected. Its wide-open windows, similar to the tavern's, allowed the summer breeze to flow freely past the white chiffon curtains. Adrastus approached the wooden desk at the front in search of the innkeeper. While they waited, guests of the inn wandered in and out. They paid Kelera no mind, but she couldn't take her eyes off of them.

Like some of the patrons back at the tavern, their skin varied in golden tans like the one Adrastus was getting, to brilliant, striking shades of brown. But it was their stunning eyes that had her captivated. The three rings in their irises, common in the Fae-folk, ranged from golden brown like the sand on the beaches to fiercely dark umber.

One small group standing off to the side began whispering to one another in excited, hushed tones. That is, until a man, taller than the rest, blurted out, "I heard he intends to drop the veil!"

Immediately, Kelera's interest peaked, and she craned her neck to listen in on their conversation.

A man standing across from him scoffed as he argued, "He wouldn't dare. The blackthorns have been there as long as any of us can remember."

Kelera's heart leapt into her throat when she realized they were talking about Samael. Apparently, word *was* spreading after all.

"*Some*," the tall man corrected him. "I was around when they were planted. Before that, we were free to explore any part of the world that we wished."

A woman with a smokey voice objected, "Exploring wasn't the only thing that was happening. Or do you forget why they were placed there in the first place?" She crossed her arms stubbornly. "Let us hope that his council talks sense into him."

Another woman stuck her nose in the air. "Queen Mabine will never allow it, anyway. The border reaches over Seelie land. He can't just go tearing into our territory."

If you only knew what he planned to do to your beautiful land, Kelera thought. She desperately wanted to warn them that far worse was coming, but she couldn't draw that sort of attention to her and Adrastus.

One of the women, the one with the smokey voice, caught her staring and Kelera smiled politely. Hopefully, she didn't think that she was eavesdropping... even if that was exactly what she'd been doing. Kelera fidgeted with her hands nervously as the woman approached her and said in her sultry voice, "Good day to you, friend. What brings you to the Summer Court?"

"My husband and I are here to celebrate our union." The lie was sliding off her tongue easily now. As if calling Adrastus her husband was the most natural thing in the world.

Adrastus laughed and added, "And to find a bit of a reprieve from our overbearing families." He gave her a wink, and the woman smiled in understanding.

Kelera tried not to scoff at the twist of his words. If only an overbearing family were the biggest of their worries. *Try insane and murderous,* she thought bitterly.

Adrastus solidified their story of being two Fae in new marital bliss as he took Kelera's hand. She assumed it was for the Fae woman's benefit, to make her believe their cover story, until he rubbed his thumb along her knuckles. Butterflies fluttered in her stomach at the intimacy of the touch until her mind took a turn. Again, she thought of Alexander. Her fiancé. If she could still call him that. He likely thought she was dead or, worse, trapped in Elfhame as a slave for eternity.

Kelera had gone into Elfhame to save Cierine, only to be caught at the border and sentenced to serve the royal family. If she hadn't gone through the blackthorn veil, or if she had been successful in bringing Alexander and the rest of the rescue party with her, then she might never had gotten captured in the Unseelie Court. If she had just stayed out of it all, then she might have been on her real honeymoon with Alexander at this moment.

The longing she'd felt for her return home—her return to him—in her early days trapped in the Unseelie Court had started to fade. Her life in Nevene was like a distant dream, overshadowed by her new reality here in the home of the Fae. So much had happened. She had only just begun to learn what she was capable of. And she had the sneaking suspicion that she would learn much more in the days to come.

Regardless of what challenges they had yet to face, there was no doubt that she was already forever changed. Knowledge of what her power could do—both the good and the bad—and her bond to Adrastus, would make it much more difficult to suppress her magic as she once had. What would that mean for her when she finally returned home to Nevene? Would she be forced to hide her true self once again, or would they be more accepting after her part in returning the princess?

Her conversation with Adrastus on the dancefloor left her with a lot to think about. Any time she had taken action based on her heart instead of her mind, had only resulted in strife—making her stand out in the mortal court, kissing a man who was not her betrothed...

"Isn't that right, darling?" Adrastus gave her hand a small squeeze.

She hadn't been listening and had no idea where the conversation had led. Trying to avoid seeming rude, she agreed, "Yes, dear." Then she smiled at the woman standing in front of them.

The woman bowed her head to them. "Well, I wish you all the luck of the fates. Enjoy your stay." She turned to rejoin her friends, leaving Kelera and Adrastus by the desk.

Adrastus turned Kelera away, never letting go of her hand. She looked at him with a furrowed brow. "I was lost in my thoughts. What was she saying?"

He leaned in so he could whisper to her, "She asked if we were eager to start a family. I told her, *incredibly*."

Kelera's eyes went wide. "That's an awfully bold thing to ask a stranger."

Adrastus chuckled. "You're the one who agreed."

"Unwittingly." She fidgeted with her locket and ignored the flush of heat that accompanied the thought of what inevitably led to having children. Another thought dawned on her. He couldn't lie. She furrowed her brow. "You said incredibly?"

His face was somber as his mouth tugged into a frown. He shrugged it off quickly and said, "I want a family of my own someday. She didn't necessarily specify who with." He paused awkwardly, then added, "We're just playing the part of two Fae who are madly in love."

Kelera suppressed an amused smile. "Of course."

Under his breath, he spoke with a serious tone. "We need to play our part well. The bounty on our heads will no doubt guarantee a king's fortune. We may have gotten lucky in the tavern with Ragnor, but any one of these Fae could be willing to claim it if given the chance."

Kelera glanced around at the inn's patrons. Suddenly, their beauty was lost on her, replaced with suspicion.

A short man waddled through the kitchen doors and up to the back of the desk. "Welcome! Welcome!" His bronze skin was glistening with sweat and he wiped at his brow with a kerchief.

Adrastus greeted him. "It is a pleasure to be here. This lovely woman and I were hoping for a room."

"Of course." The man beamed at them with a widespread smile. "I have *just* the room. Overlooking the sea. Oh, and at night, the stars will dote upon the two of you." He fumbled below the desk for a key. "Ah, here it is." He paused, then added, "Name's Ganch, by the way."

Goosebumps prickled along her neck, and she had the eerie sensation of someone watching her. She turned to see a man standing beside the window. He met her eye and whistled a sad song as he shifted to look out at the sea. She wasn't sure if it was paranoia or something more, but she could see by the way the other Fae in the room gravitated away from him that he was out of place here.

She was about to voice her concern to Adrastus when Ganch waddled around the desk, signaling for them to follow. The man by the window sauntered out the door and Kelera tried her best to shake off the unsettling feeling he left her with. She ascended the stairs between Adrastus and Ganch until they came to a room. He unlocked the door for them and threw it open wide, then handed the key to Adrastus and left them with a suggestive wink.

Adrastus stepped aside to let Kelera into the room first. She wandered in, taking in the fresh, bright, tropical floral bouquets that were placed around the room. There were wide double doors that opened up to a terrace overlooking the sea. The view was as breathtaking as the old innkeeper had promised. She could see over the horizon and spotted brightly colored dolphins playing with one another in the water. She had seen dolphins before in Nevene when she and her father had visited the coast, but these were not the same grey-blue creatures she had seen then.

She marveled at the shimmering, smooth, golden skin as the playful animals leapt in and out of the water. With every passing discovery she made here in Elfhame, she was more and more enchanted. She couldn't imagine what it would feel like to leave it all behind—to go back to the more mundane life that the mortal court had to offer.

She took a deep, pained breath. Allowing these thoughts in felt like a betrayal to her father who had risked everything for her. Her duty should be to him and him alone. Surely, she would find a way to be content with life in Nevene again.

There was a thud on the ground as Adrastus unloaded their bags. She left the terrace, wondering what else he had planned while they were waiting in the Summer Court. Her stomach did a small flip when she took in the narrow single bed. "Adrastus! What is this?"

"That?" There was sarcasm in his voice as he said, "That, Kelera, is a bed."

"*One* bed."

"Well, I couldn't very well ask for two. We are supposed to be newlyweds." He joked, "I know I am not familiar with the way things work in the mortal realm, but here in Elfhame, husbands and wives *share* a bed."

Kelera scoffed, "I know that. But you and I are not husband and wife. You cannot honestly expect me to share a bed with you." It was scandalous. Until she came to Elfhame, she had never even kissed a man... not until Adrastus. Her eyes lingered on him as he removed his shirt. Unwelcomed warmth moved down the center of her, but it wasn't the buzz of their magic. This was something more carnal. This was desire. She looked away quickly and busied herself with smelling the flowers on the table near her.

Adrastus sighed. "We have been traveling alone for days now. Sleeping just mere feet apart from one another. I do not see the problem with laying just a little closer..."

Kelera groaned. Of course, he wouldn't understand. She ran her fingers over the velvety petals of a bright pink flower as she said, "I am betrothed to another. My virtue is important."

"Would your fiancé not take your word for it?" He flopped onto the bed and placed his hands behind his head.

"I-I don't know."

He raised a playful eyebrow. "You do not know?"

"We don't know each other very well." Saying it out loud made her feel naïve and silly, like a schoolgirl who had not experienced the world yet.

"I see. So, this *fiancé* of yours... it is an arranged marriage?" There was genuine curiosity in his voice.

Kelera sat on the edge of the bed and fiddled with her locket. She didn't want to talk to Adrastus about her personal life. They were bound to each other for one purpose—to save their people. That did not mean she owed him any explanation for her life choices. Still, she found herself answering, "It is an arrangement that both he and I want."

"How very boring."

"I'll have you know Alexander is a gallant man of high standing and it is a good match." She turned to Adrastus so he could see the annoyance on her face, but his eyes were closed.

His comment still bothered her. Would marrying Alexander be dull? Especially now that she'd experienced so much in Elfhame? He certainly hadn't gotten under her skin the same way that Adrastus did. But what did Adrastus know of mortal matches and happiness? Curious, she called out to him, unsure of whether he was already sleeping and not really caring if she woke him. "Dras?"

"Hm?" He didn't open his eyes.

"Have you spent any time in the mortal realm?" The blackthorns had been planted ages ago, long before Adrastus had been born. But Fae had still been known to slip through. Samael, after all, had done it many times.

"I've been once." Just when Kelera thought he wouldn't elaborate on it any further, he said, "I was tracking a Fae man who had been stealing children from the southern villages."

"Oh," was all she could think to say. Before Samael's kidnappings had started, she'd only ever heard vague stories about children being stolen away in the night. It had always felt like a tall tale to her. She had been so far removed from the people of Nevene, safe in the confines of the palace, that she supposed she'd let it blind her to the troubles that the commoners near the border had faced. The very people who would be directly in the path of any nefarious Fae who ventured into the mortal realm if Samael was successful.

She was so lost in thought that Adrastus' voice made her jump as he said, "I can't say I cared for it. Your mortals were frightened and helpless. Thinking that iron and horseshoes would protect them. Their homes were in shambles from years of neglect. I couldn't help but wonder what sort of king allowed their people to live like that. Or what sort of men would leave their people so defenseless?"

The hint of disgust as he spoke of Nevene and the mortal rulers grated on her. Her first instinct was to defend King Tristan. She'd been raised in his court. Had seen him crowned. But Adrastus wasn't wrong. The people had relied on superstitions for so long that they had no idea how to truly protect themselves. And King

Tristan had become too complacent, thinking that the blackthorns made them untouchable.

She held her tongue. Adrastus had every right to look upon that sort of leadership with contempt. He had seen the same troubles in his own kingdom when his father ruled. His people had been subjected to the pits—forced to fight for entertainment. And Adrastus had done everything he could to help the people in the villages at the risk of his father finding out. If he had known what his youngest son had been up to, then there would have been a price. One she was glad Adrastus hadn't been forced to pay.

After a few minutes, his breathing became steady and even. A sign of sleep that she recognized from their nights on the run together. Leaving him to rest, she went out to the terrace, and sat in one of the small wooden chairs beside a short breakfast table.

As she watched the dolphins in the distance, she couldn't help but wonder if she was making mistake after mistake. Since coming to Elfhame, she had fumbled her way through their court and through their customs. She had offended the Unseelie King, misjudged the people, and played a part in the murder of a prince. With so much on the line, she couldn't afford to misstep any longer.

She sat like that, contemplating the mess she was in and listening to the sounds of the ocean mixed with Adrastus' snores until the sun began to set. The sky was painted with brilliant hues of orange and red. It was at that point that she decided one thing was for sure. She would need to be patient—with herself and with Adrastus. What other choice did she have?

She breathed in the salty sea air, trying to find some semblance of peace. The threat of danger still lingered in the back of her mind, making it feel as if she had something constantly weighing on her chest. So, she did the only thing she could think to do and focused on the moment—of how she was safe on the terrace with Adrastus nearby—and was finally able to catch her breath.

She stayed there until the sun set and a crisp night breeze blew through her hair. She could no longer see the dolphins, but she could hear them as they flipped and splashed in the distance. She envied their freedom. The expectations of others did not shackle them. They were free to be what the stars had always intended them to be. Would she ever experience that? Or was she fated to be tethered to a life where she would be forced to keep part of herself hidden?

She bit her lip as she stood to go inside. Going back to the mortal court in Nevene would be an adjustment. But it was something that she didn't have to face now. Right now, at this moment, she needed sleep.

Adrastus was still in a deep slumber. He looked peaceful, with his chest rising and falling gently. Kelera stepped up to the bed and paused. Yes, things had certainly changed for her since coming to Elfhame. Never in her life would she have thought she'd be sharing a bed with a man who wasn't her betrothed. An incredibly handsome man whom she'd kissed...

She climbed into the bed, careful not to wake him. She didn't undress, hoping to maintain some ounce of decorum. Slipping under the covers, she let out a slow, steady breath and settled onto the soft mattress.

Adrastus rolled toward her slightly, resting his leg against hers. It sent another unwelcome shiver down her spine, and she fought the impulse to move closer to him. Instead, she studied his face in the moonlight. His lashes were dark and heavy, casting small shadows on his tanned cheeks. His raven hair was a ruffled mess with a strand settled over his scarred eye. The glamor he used to hide the rest of the scars his brothers had inflicted on him held strong. She'd seen the scars with her own eyes the night that he dropped the glamor in an attempt to frighten her.

But she'd felt no fear, only heartbreak. His family, all except for Gadreel, had ridiculed him for what he was—a bastard born of Seelie and Unseelie blood. It had hardened him. Forced him to hide the parts of him that his family deemed weak. She supposed they were a lot alike in that aspect. They had both been taught to feel shame for their Seelie blood and the power that came with it.

Without thinking, she reached her hand out and moved the hair from his face. It was soft beneath her fingertips and her breath hitched in her throat as she felt his power course through her in a sudden rush of ice and fire. She withdrew her hand and stared up at the ceiling. What was she doing? Why was she so drawn to him? It couldn't be the magical bond between them. She'd been grappling with these feelings before he'd ever suggested the ceremony.

She closed her eyes tight, willing sleep to come. Hoping that it would give her a reprieve of her tangled mess of thoughts and feelings. After a while, the sounds of the waves crashing against the beach sang her to sleep like a lullaby.

As she slept, she dreamed of home. Cierine's childhood home, Rose Manor, stood in the distance. Kelera ran her hands through the poppies as she walked through the field. They were in full bloom and the fragrance was so overwhelming, she wondered for a moment if it was a dream at all.

Before she could take a step further, a hooded figure appeared only feet from her and she gasped. The figure turned, revealing hair as white as the fallen snow and a familiar, pointed face. Ammon. But it couldn't be. He was dead. Dead because of her. She stumbled back a few steps, trying to put distance between her and what she could only describe as a nightmare. "You can't be here."

His lifeless eyes bore into her as if they could see into her very soul. Blood trickled from his mouth and his voice was raspy as he called to her, "A debt owed to Unseelie cannot go unpaid."

And you, little thief, are the price. The memory of Adrastus' words to her at the blackthorn border echoed in her mind. Her heart raced and her magic bloomed to life in a rush of sparking heat just beneath the surface of her skin. Ammon began to walk toward her and the overwhelming feeling of her magic grew with each step he took. She shook her head and pleaded, "Please, Ammon. I'm sorry. I'm so sorry. It was an accident."

He continued to advance through the field, crushing the poppies beneath his decaying boots. Kelera tried to catch her breath, but couldn't shake the suffocating fear. He was here to collect a debt for the life she had robbed him of. She shut her eyes tight. *This is a dream. Only a dream. He cannot hurt me.* It wasn't enough to convince her. She felt her magic burning through her. It scorched her arms and her legs as she tried to contain it.

The guilt for what she'd done to Ammon was going to destroy her from the inside out. She wasn't strong enough to contain the chaos inside of her. She needed Adrastus. Without him to ground her magic, she would lose control again. What would happen if chaos unleashed in her dream? It was something she didn't dare want to find out.

Ammon opened his mouth to speak, but instead of words, a swarm of moths flew from it. His jaw came unhinged as they poured out, heading straight for her in a dark cloud of wings.

As the first of the small, black moths flew into her, she screamed. They stung as they hit her skin at lightning speed. But that was impossible. How could she feel pain if she was dreaming? The burning urge to release her magic grew as the moths continued to pelt her face and arms. She couldn't hold on much longer.

"Ammon, please! I'm sorry, I'm so sorry!" It was the stars' honest truth. "I didn't mean to hurt you. My magic was out of control. You must understand!"

Ammon shrieked as the moths burst from him in an endless stream. Her magic was going to erupt. She was going to hurt him all over again. Just when she thought she couldn't hold on to it any longer, someone gripped her hand. Adrastus linked his fingers through hers and, in a chilly rush, his magic wove itself into her own. The power that had been raging inside of her dimmed slightly. She could still feel its strength, but now it was accompanied by the steady drum of his power. It was as if her magic had been missing a puzzle piece and was now complete with Adrastus' magic winding around it. She felt grounded.

Adrastus shouted above Ammon's shrieks, "We have to let it out, Kelera! The longer you hold it in, the worse it will be when it's released."

Kelera nodded. She needed to trust him. She took a deep breath in and when she released it, their magic exploded through the field, turning the moths to ash. It stormed toward Ammon, but he didn't look afraid. Instead, he tipped his head to the sky and proclaimed, "The world will succumb to frost and be reborn in fire." He grinned as the magic burned through him. Fire consumed him, turning his twisted face—and the moths that flowed from him—to ash. It ravaged his pale skin and the smell of burning flesh filled the air. Soon nothing but dust was left in the fire magic's wake.

Kelera was horrified, but the fire was no longer building inside of her. Her muscles were weak and shaky at the sudden release of tension. Their magic ebbed, leaving only a small buzz in her veins. She looked around at the chaos she had caused. The entire field of beautiful orangish-red poppies was burned to a crisp. Their magic hadn't left one flower untouched. Warm tears streamed down her cheeks. She wiped at them angrily. This was why she couldn't return home. Not yet. If she did, she could destroy everything.

Adrastus was out of breath beside her, and she spun to face him. "Dras, how are you here?"

His eyes snapped from the scorched earth to her face. "You need to wake up now, Kelera." His voice was filled with fascination, mixed with something that sounded like fear.

Her vision blackened around the edges until it completely consumed her. When she regained her sight, she was staring up at the moonlit ceiling. She pressed her hands to her stomach, relieved to be back in the room, but it was short lived. When she sat up, her breath caught in her throat. The quilt on the bed was singed and smoking. Pillows were strewn around the bed as if someone had used them to put out the fire.

"Oh stars, what did I do?" Her body shuddered, and she began to sob. Even in her sleep, the real world wasn't safe. What was happening to her?

Adrastus' eyes were dark with shadows clouding the whites and he opened and closed his fists as if trying to regain his composure. Kelera swallowed back her tears. The dream had impacted his magic as much as it had hers. Another sob escaped her, accompanying the guilt she was suddenly overwhelmed with.

Adrastus' eyes cleared and his gaze snapped to her. He closed the distance between them and his strong arms wrapped around her, scooping her into the safety of his embrace. Kelera buried her face in his chest as he ran his fingers through her wild, wavy hair. His voice was soothing as he said, "Your magic just got a little out of control. It must have been from the fear you were feeling in your dream."

She couldn't wrap her mind around the fact that her magic had taken on a life of its own as she slept. If her fear was leaking out into the real world as she dreamed, then no one was safe. "I could feel pain. And my magic..."

He hugged her tightly. "I know."

"How were you there?"

Adrastus' voice was low. "Seelie dream magic. Our bond strengthened my presence there."

He'd entered her dreams before, giving her visions in warning before she came to Elfhame. But he had never been corporeal in her mind before. She wasn't sure whether to be grateful or horrified.

She sniffled and tried to dry her eyes. "Did you hear what Ammon said?"

The silence was excruciating until Adrastus said, "Yes."

"What did it mean?"

He lowered his eyes and didn't answer.

She repeated the words Ammon had spoken in her dream, "The world will succumb to frost and be reborn in fire. It's not the first time I've heard it. But what does it mean?" The only sound that followed those words were the waves crashing with the tide. She sat up to face Adrastus. "Please, all I ask is that you don't keep things from me."

He rested his hand on her leg, steadying her, and sighed. "It is an Elder prophecy. Passed down through generations. It is a prophecy of war."

She thought back to the night of their binding ceremony when the Wild Hunt had paraded through the sky. Adrastus had told her it was a sign of things to come, but she had assumed he'd been referring to their own journey.

Her voice quaked as she asked, "What does it say?" She dreaded the answer, but she needed to know what they were facing. If Adrastus was worried, then it must be something worse than any nightmare she might have.

His jaw twitched, and he said, "The Elders are the most ancient of our people. They are the beginning and the end. They have long presided over the fate of the realm. Only the King of Unseelie and the Queen of Seelie are permitted to enter their court deep beneath the hollow hills."

Kelera waited patiently for him to go on, but he grunted in irritation and rose from the bed. Her leg felt cold in the absence of his hand on it. He crossed the room to a small table laden with a decanter of wine. His voice was nearly a growl as he said, "We need a drink if we're going to talk about this."

Kelera agreed. The idea of an ancient group of Fae watching over the realm made her nervous. Their magic would have to be incredibly powerful to have kept them alive since the creation of Elfhame. Adrastus returned to the bed with two full glasses and the bottle. She accepted the wine from him and drank deeply as he sat down beside her. It was light and sweet. She took another long sip and waited.

Adrastus drank his in one gulp and poured himself a refill. "Long ago, the Elders called my father under the hill. It was long before I was born, so what I've heard has been bits and pieces passed through the court. There's no telling how much of it is accurate. According to legend, there will be a great war between night and day. Unseelie and Seelie will rise in a clash of power." He took another drink and wiped his face with the back of his sleeve. "'The world will succumb to frost' translates to the Unseelie rising to take control of Elfhame in its entirety."

Just like Samael wanted. He was the frost that threatened the world. Her mouth was suddenly very dry. She cleared her throat and encouraged him. "And…"

His voice was grave as he said, "And be reborn in fire. It means that the only hope for Elfhame is an heir to the Seelie throne that doesn't exist."

Hope bloomed in her chest. Samael and Kane—the brother who had taken Samael's side—were afraid of

Adrastus. They knew his power was stronger than theirs. Samael knew he didn't stand a chance at taking Elfhame if Adrastus was there to stand against him.

She tilted her head as the prospect struck her. "What if it's you? What if you're the lost heir? I know you must have heard the gossip in the Unseelie Court."

Adrastus' face twisted into something that resembled anger. "I am not the lost heir. The heir doesn't exist. It's a rumor. Born from court gossip and the idiotic hope that a savior will suddenly appear to make the world a better place."

Kelera couldn't accept that. "But Ammon said—"

"It was a dream, Kelera!" He jumped from the bed.

"*My* dream!" She leapt from the bed too. "I know nothing of Elders and their prophesies. This was a *vision*, Dras. And I had it for a reason." She needed to believe that this was the truth. That there was still a small sliver of hope to grasp onto. A way for them to save both Elfhame and the mortal realm. She grabbed Adrastus' hands and held tight so he couldn't pull away. "If there is even the smallest possibility that it's true, then you need to be ready to accept it."

He shook his head stubbornly. "Kelera, after the things I have done in the name of Unseelie—the people I have hurt, the lives I have destroyed—I am not a man worthy of that crown. I am nothing more than the bastard son of a king and whatever poor wretched soul he lured into his bed."

The memory of what Adrastus had done to the rogue Fae in the Winter Court made her hands tremble. She had seen what he was capable of when he had shattered that man's mind, but she also knew the shame he had felt afterwards when he had run into the palace to escape her and what she had witnessed. He might have done terrible things to appease his family, but that didn't mean he was the same as them. That didn't mean he wouldn't be a good king.

His brow was furrowed with worry and his voice softened as he said, "I do not want you to get your hopes up based on a fairytale. Our best hope is to go to the emissary in the Spring Court so we can gather a force to stand against my brothers."

She couldn't force him to believe in the prophecy. And lost heir or not, he needed to get to the Spring Court. With the help of the emissary, the council would listen to him and help him defeat Samael. She nodded and loosened her hold on his hands. In an effort to placate him, she said, "You're right. Whether the prophecy is true doesn't matter right now. We can do nothing for Elfhame and my people until we have allies to fight beside us."

Adrastus' face softened, and he released one of her hands. Still holding onto the other, he led her to the bed. They climbed in, tucking themselves safely beneath the blankets. Propriety no longer crossed Kelera's mind as he inched closer to her. She didn't want to be alone after the terror in her dream. He'd been right when he had said they were safer together.

They were a breath away from one another as they lay face to face. She stared into his eyes, counting the rings in his irises made up of beautiful shades of forest green. It was hard to believe that someone with such beauty had the same dark Unseelie blood running through his veins as Samael.

She thought next of Gadreel, the brother who had quickly become her friend at court, and Ammon who had never actually raised a hand to her even if he *had* chosen the wrong side. She had no doubt his death would haunt her for the rest of her life. Sleep would not come easy tonight with the guilt and the nightmare so fresh in her mind. Seeing him in the dream had torn open the wound in her mind that had been marked there when she'd dealt that killing blow.

Adrastus reached up and brushed her dark hair from her face. She leaned into his touch and whispered, "I'm afraid I'll see Ammon again if I close my eyes."

"You're safe here, little thief."

Kelera scoffed. "Safe for the moment."

"This moment is the only one that matters." The conviction in his words was almost enough to bring her peace of mind.

He wrapped his arms around her and her body gave in to the comfort, releasing all of her tension. His fingers brushed against her arms sending a pleasant shiver along them. When he pulled her closer, she didn't resist. Instead, she melted into him and sighed as he began to hum a quiet tune.

A yawn escaped her as she asked, "What is that?"

"It's an old Seelie lullaby. One that all Seelie mothers used to lull their babes to sleep."

Her eyes were growing heavy as he continued to hum softly. "There's something familiar about it."

Adrastus' hold on her tightened and his magic blazed to life in her veins, intertwining with her own. It flowed around them, blanketing them in its power. Kelera buried her head on his pillow and closed her eyes. She allowed his magic to envelope her head, burrowing its way deep into her mind. It was like a small candle lighting up the dark.

Too exhausted to fight her feelings, she embraced them instead. In this moment she belonged with him. The world around them could wait. Here in this room, she was safe. Adrastus had come to her rescue many times, proving that he wouldn't abandon her. A day may come when he wouldn't be around to protect her, but tonight she would sleep comfortably knowing that he was there.

She drifted off to the sound of his lullaby. As he hummed, visions of home danced in her mind, intertwined with memories of her childhood. She felt safe and loved as she danced with her father and Cierine in a field of fireflies beneath the night sky. That night, in Adrastus' arms, she slept better than she had in her entire life.

Chapter Five

The sand was soft between Kelera's toes. She drew her dress up to her knees and stepped up to the ocean's edge, letting the waves splash at her ankles. The salty air was refreshing on her skin and she closed her eyes to bask in it. If only the cool water and fresh breeze could wash away her worries.

The moment she had woken up in Adrastus' arms, all of the previous night's problems came flooding back. She'd slipped from the bed and walked down to the beach. She needed space and time to think. The Elder prophecy was still fresh in her mind, but she was trying to focus on their next step. They had to keep moving. Adrastus was sure that Samael would send scouts to track them through the Summer Court, and if they wanted to stay ahead of them, then they couldn't remain in one place for too long.

Part of her would be sad to leave the beautiful, white sandy beaches of the Summer Court behind. But she knew there would be no long-lasting peace for them there. Especially not if Samael had his way and got his hands on both courts that fell under Seelie rule. It would only be a matter of time before he tried to make the entirety of Elfhame in his image. What would that mean for the Fae here?

She shielded her eyes from the sun as she looked out onto the water, where several wooden boats bobbed up and down with the waves. They were impressive in size, holding a number of the solid-built Fae men at once. The boats swayed and rocked with the sea as the men stood steady, casting their nets into the water with expertise.

Meanwhile, women sat on the sands with children running carefree around them, collecting seashells. Kelera found a smooth rock to sit on. It jutted out slightly over the crystal clear water, allowing her a full view of the colorful fish swimming just below the surface. Their scales shimmered and flashed as they wove around each other.

She leaned down onto her stomach so she could get a better look and dangled her arms over the sides of the rock. Her fingers trailed along the water, sending ripples in their wake. Her sudden appearance made the fish shy away from her a bit, and she slowed her movements. She didn't want them to run away from her.

A wistful sigh escaped her. She didn't want *anyone* to run away from her. But is that what would inevitably happen when she returned home to Nevene? Would the courtiers scurry from her path like the fish when they learned of her newfound power? She had to make sure that didn't happen. She needed to use her time in Elfhame to get a grasp on it without relying solely on Adrastus. Even in her own dream the night before, she had relied on his magic to keep her grounded.

She turned her attention back to the families playing on the beach. A man swung his daughter around and they laughed as they tumbled into the sand. She watched them thoughtfully and soon found herself missing her own father. Sir Aldric had done all he could to give her a happy childhood, but he was a knight through and through. His duty was to his men and the protection of the realm. She had grown up seeing how heavily that responsibility could weigh on a person. It left little room for quiet moments like this where all that existed was family.

She wondered what sort of family life Alexander would offer her. He was often traveling with his father, and though he was no warrior, he certainly had his fair share of responsibility. His family oversaw a large portion of Nevene, tending to the villages and taxes in them.

The man crouched and signaled for his daughter to watch as he spun the sand with his magic. It followed his fingers, transforming into a castle. The detail was remarkable as the sands obeyed his every command. The little girl clapped wildly and threw her arms around her father's neck.

The way the man's eyes sparkled at his daughter's delight reminded her of Adrastus. She had seen that expression on his face when he thought no one was watching. What sort of father would *he* be? He'd surprised her when he had said that he longed for a family someday. He, like her own father, felt the pressures of duty to his people. Yet he still made a point of enjoying the rare moments of happiness. He enjoyed dancing and visiting his friends in the village. Balance was something he had mastered, and something told her it would make him a good father... and husband.

Loud laughter caught her attention, and she glanced down the beach to see the men from the tavern. Ragnor and his men were planted firmly in the sand with wooden fishing rods dangling lazily from their hands. They were passing a flask around and seemed to be in good cheer.

They must have found some companionship after all, she thought to herself as she eyed them cautiously. There was a tightness in her gut as she watched them. They had been pleasant enough with her and Adrastus in the tavern, but they were still strangers. And she couldn't afford to let her guard down when her life was hanging in the balance.

She gazed down uneasily at the water, running her fingers through it to create tiny ripples. Broad scales flashed before her eyes and she withdrew her hand with a gasp. "What in the world?"

She squinted to get a better look at the shadowy depths of the water. It was far too large for a fish—closer to the size of a person. She held her breath, waiting for it to swim by again. Curiosity got the better of her as she leaned down as close to the surface as she could get without falling in. At first, she saw nothing but her own reflection, that is, until a stranger's face rose to the surface to look back at her.

She screamed and scrambled back as a frighteningly stunning creature rose out of the water. The woman stopped with her head and shoulders above the water and stared at Kelera curiously. Then tilted her head side to side as if it was Kelera who was the oddity.

Kelera had never seen anything like her. Not even in the storybooks in the mortal court. Her skin was pale and glittering, with small scales coating it. Her eyes were dark pools with no whites and her hair was long and tangled with seaweed, making it hard to tell where the seaweed stopped and the hair began.

The creature flashed cramped rows of razor-sharp teeth and a soothing melody escaped her lips. Kelera leaned forward, forgetting the danger, and wondering why she had been taken aback by the woman's presence.

Cool magic tugged on her. It was like the tide trying to pull her out to sea. Kelera was so mesmerized she didn't hear someone approach.

Firm hands pulled her away from the creature and she was startled to see Adrastus. His teeth showed as he snarled at it, "Back. Now." His eyes began to cloud once again with the shadows that were as much a part of him as his own soul.

The creature whined at the sight and floated a few paces back. Kelera snapped out of the trance, blinking furiously. "What is that thing?"

Adrastus pulled Kelera up so they were standing together on the rock. "It's a siren." He ran a hand through his hair. "I forget how sheltered from this world you are." He smiled smugly at her.

Kelera raised her chin in defiance. Even if he was right, she wasn't willing to admit it—not with that look on his face. "I am not sheltered."

He frowned at her. "Regardless, you just almost got yourself drowned."

"Oh." Kelera felt a little nauseous. She had been so engrossed by the siren and her song that she hadn't realized she'd been in danger.

He sat on the rock and eyed the siren warily. She was bobbing in the water and staring at them with a strange intensity. "She probably sensed weakness," he explained.

His words stung. He had sung her to sleep last night, and today he was insulting her. It rubbed Kelera the wrong way. "I'm not weak." Her words were firm, but her resolve wasn't. She was, after all, dependent on him for the time being.

He gaped at her. "I didn't mean... I just meant that she could likely sense you weren't using magic to protect yourself."

Kelera softened slightly. "Oh, I see." She sat beside him and watched the siren carefully. Her tail splashed out of the water. It was a brilliant color of orange and red, like the sunset. "So how do I do it? Protect myself with my magic, I mean."

"It's fairly simple when you have control. Think of it as a blanket. You have to reach for your magic and wrap it around yourself. It will help keep creatures like this from getting into your head. Don't mistake it for making you invincible, though. She could just as easily tear your throat out with her teeth, but she couldn't force you to come to her willingly."

Kelera ignored the horrible imagery and asked, "Can you teach me?" They would have to get moving soon if they were going to stay ahead of the scouts, but surely they had a little time to spare. And she would feel a lot safer knowing a few basic defenses in case the worst were to happen.

Adrastus raised his eyebrows in surprise. "Of course." He leapt to his feet and offered a hand to help her up.

She laughed at his eagerness. When they'd been in the Unseelie Palace, he had been tense and prone to shutting her out. He'd admitted to being reluctant to let others see how much he cared for the people of Elfhame for fear his father would discover what he was up to. Hiding the aid he'd given to sick villagers and working in secret with Gadreel to keep Samael from gaining too much power.

But here, under the clear skies of Seelie, he was lighter. The tension in his shoulders and in the way he spoke to her was gone. This was the version of him that she had only caught short glimpses of in Unseelie. This was the man she'd seen in the moments where she allowed him to get close to her—to kiss her. Part of her wished that she could make him feel like this all the time. She feared that he would once again put on his mask of indifference and irritation when they reached the Spring Court and had to get back to the urgent matters at hand.

Adrastus walked around her and leaned in close. His breath was hot on her ear as he spoke. "Deep breaths." Kelera obeyed, breathing the salty air deep into her lungs. Adrastus' voice was intense as he said, "Good. Now embrace the magic inside of you. Like the flutter of a butterfly's wing. It dances just under the surface." Kelera welcomed the steady flow of magic as it coursed through her. It was soft and subtle, so different from the wild chaos she had known before.

She whispered, afraid to lose her concentration. "Now what?"

"Now imagine you're taking hold of it with your hands and wrapping it around you like a scarf to keep out the winter chill." He whistled for the siren and the curious creature began to sing her song. It drifted along the water's surface and tugged on Kelera—beckoning her into the siren's arms.

Her breath hitched in her throat as she began to panic. "I can't." She wished she had been taught how to control her power when she was younger. If she'd had the time, then she was confident she could have perfected the art of using magic.

"You can." Adrastus trailed his fingers along her arms, sending shivers down her spine. "Focus on my touch. Don't worry about the world around us. All that exists is us and our power." Kelera imagined her magic flowing up with Adrastus' touch.

His voice was low and soothing as he whispered, "Magic isn't something to be perfected." She looked up at him, surprised once again that he knew her so well. He nodded toward the siren and she returned her attention to it.

Still running his hands along her skin, he elaborated, "Your power is not science, but rather a feeling. And feelings are often unpredictable and imperfect. Now *feel* the blanket of magic as if you are really holding it in your hands. Allow yourself to lead it where it needs to go."

In her mind, she pictured a blanket of stars, like the ones she loved to look at in the Elfhame sky at night. There was a flicker of peacefulness which she allowed to bloom in her mind. She visualized the blanket wrapping itself safely around her ears and her mind, keeping the siren's song out.

She was no longer entranced by the tug of the siren's call. All she could feel was the warm embrace of her magic and Adrastus' powerful hands on her arms. She gasped, "I did it."

There was pride in Adrastus' voice as he said, "I knew you could."

Kelera sat on the smooth rock with her feet dipped into the water. Adrastus was sitting close with his arm touching hers. Their magic continued to pulse together, and it felt right. Like his shadow and ice magic was soothing her chaos rather than trying to snuff it out.

Adrastus was sitting quietly beside her, letting her bask in her accomplishment. She'd been so proud of herself and she wanted to practice using her power to defend against the siren just a little longer.

By now the creature had lost interest and instead chased the small colorful fish around the rock. Kelera took a bite of the cinnamon coated bread Adrastus had brought for her. She savored every last crumb, knowing that it would be a while before she had another meal this decadent.

Adrastus yawned and stretched out on the rock, laying on his back while she ate. Kelera leaned down on her arm so she could watch him and smiled. "You're not a terrible teacher, you know. You made more progress with me in a matter of minutes than Gadreel did in days." She nearly scoffed at the memory of the endless hours she and Gadreel had spent in the dusty library at the Unseelie Palace, trying to unlock her magic.

Adrastus shook his head slightly. "Today was all you. Back home, you were frightened. Afraid that Samael would take your magic for his own uses. And you were scared to accept your Fae blood." He squinted up at her. "You're different here. I see you letting your guard down more, even if you're reluctant to do so. Your confidence is growing." He smiled as he closed his eyes so he could continue basking in the sun.

Kelera laid back beside him. He wasn't entirely wrong. Though she was still afraid of what would happen if Samael caught up to them, she felt safer with Adrastus by her side. It gave her a different sort of confidence.

Curious, she asked, "Would the veil you just taught me work to protect me from other Fae?"

Adrastus nodded.

"Like Samael?" The way Cierine had cowered on the floor in the Unseelie Palace when Samael had conjured her fears from the shadows flashed through her mind. Nightmares and terror were an Unseelie specialty.

"If you can strengthen your ability to do it, then yes."

Kelera twisted her hair around her finger. "And does it shield against dream magic as well?" Dream magic was a Seelie gift. She didn't mind when Adrastus used his abilities on her, but the thought of someone else rummaging through her mind as she slept or conjuring visions when she was awake unnerved her.

"That too," Adrastus said cautiously.

"I just meant, if some strange Fae decided to pay me a visit..."

He chuckled, "I know what you meant."

"Oh, good." She closed her eyes, enjoying the heat of the sun on her face.

"I wouldn't blame you, though, you know." When Kelera didn't respond, he continued, "If you did want to have a way to protect yourself from my magic. When I'm using it, I lose myself in the power. At least Samael can control his shadows. I've burrowed into minds and shattered them like panes of glass without trying. It started when I was young." He laughed bitterly. "You should have seen my father's face the first time I did it. He was so proud."

Kelera leaned in to get a fuller view of him. Adrastus had tried to frighten her when they first met. Had tried to convince her that he was like his father to keep her at a distance for fear of his plans being ruined. But things were different now. They were connected in a way that was more permanent than marriage. Their bond kept his magic at bay as much as it did hers.

There was a slight tinge of guilt for bringing the subject up, and she placed a comforting hand on his arm. "You are better than them, Dras. I know that. And you should know that I do not fear you."

He sat up. His eyes shined as he looked at her with what appeared to be relief. Reaching out a hand, he brushed her hair behind her ear. She wondered for a moment if he might lean in and kiss her. But instead, he lowered his hand and said, "We should be going. If we leave now, we can make it to the Spring border by nightfall. Our new friend will be waiting for us." The way he said 'friend' was unnerving. They, in fact, didn't know the emissary. There was a chance that he would deny them the help they needed.

"Are you worried he'll change his mind about helping us?"

Adrastus offered his arm to her, and she looped hers through it. He sighed. "We'll have to make a good impression on him. Oliver has vouched for us, but it will be up to you and me to solidify our standing and convince him to believe us."

Kelera glanced over her shoulder to take one more peek at the siren. The enchanting creature smiled at her slyly, then dove into the water, disappearing from Kelera's view. Part of her was sorry to see the siren go. She wondered what other magnificent creatures awaited her on their journey. She only hoped she would be ready to face them and any other obstacles.

"Then I suppose I must put my charm to good use," she teased, and snuck a glance at Adrastus. A hint of a smile was splayed across his face, along with a small dimple in his cheek. He really was stunning to look at. Not just in the way that all Fae had an ethereal quality to them. He wasn't perfect. There were scars that ran deeper than his skin. But the fact that he still found the ability to smile like that showed her how resilient he was.

They walked arm in arm along the beach. To any of the families looking at them, they would appear like any other couple enjoying the warm summer morning. Kelera tightened her grip on him without thinking. What would it be like if they really were just a man and woman who had come to the Summer Court to celebrate their new marriage? Her heart hammered in her chest and her cheeks warmed with a blush.

She sighed. It was a nice thought. But it was a fairy tale. And their situation was exactly the opposite of that. They were fugitives. And they needed to stop basking in the sunshine and remember that if they wanted to stay alive.

She looked up at Adrastus as a question dawned on her, "Can I ask you something?"

"Anything," Adrastus said without hesitation.

"If Samael finds us," she paused at Adrastus' frown, then continued, "*if* he finds us, what do you think he'll do when he realizes he can't bind my magic to him?"

Adrastus' frown deepened. "It's hard to say. He's always been so unpredictable. The lines he is willing to cross shocks even me."

"Do you think he'll be able to take the Seelie territory without my magic?" He had been so adamant about using her Seelie power to give him an advantage. She desperately hoped that without it, his plans were severely damaged.

Adrastus tensed. He stopped and turned to face her. "Kelera, I honestly don't know. I wish I did, but being out here means being cut off from information. Until we reach the Spring border, I won't be able to say for sure, and I don't want you getting your hopes up."

Kelera placed her hand on his chest and his heart pounded beneath her fingers. "I know, Dras. I am preparing myself for the worst."

"I think that's best. Especially if he is, in fact, turning new Night Riders." He placed her arm around his and they began walking again.

They turned north, ready to follow the coast up to the Spring Court border. Everyone seemed to believe that her mother hailed from the land of eternal spring in Elfhame. With so much happening over the last few weeks, Kelera hadn't considered what it would mean for her to see the land where she came from. Would she feel a deeper connection to the magic there?

She opened her mouth to ask Adrastus, but the man she had seen in the common room at the inn the previous day caught her eye. She recognized him instantly with his slicked-back hair and a permanent sneer on his face. He avoided Kelera's gaze as he strutted up to a cluster of boats.

She stopped in her tracks, still clinging to Adrastus' arm. He studied at her with his brow knitted in a questioning gaze. "What's wrong?"

Kelera tilted her head slightly in the direction of the man. He was lingering near the fishermen, who were readying their boats to sail. The Summer Court Fae didn't pay much attention to him as they continued about their business, but she couldn't help noticing how out of place he looked. He was prepared for a lengthy travel with a heavy bag strapped to his back. And he was fully dressed, unlike the fishermen who waded barefooted in the water with their pants rolled up.

She eyed him like a hawk as he leaned against one of the boats and scanned the beach. Then she noted the dagger on his belt. It was hard to tell if Adrastus had noticed it too, as he had gone completely silent. But she knew better than to count out his ability to observe his environment.

She nudged him in the side. "I saw him at the inn. Something about him feels off."

Adrastus nodded, "I agree."

"So, what should we do?" All the confidence she had been filled with earlier faded away. A siren confined to the water was one thing. An experienced bounty hunter on land was another. If that was even what he was.

She peered over her shoulder at the families sitting idly by on the beach. The little girl from earlier was splashing in the tide without a care in the world. What if she was caught in the crossfire? What if Kelera couldn't control her magic against this stranger and someone innocent paid the price for it?

A strange tug, like a string pulling at her wrist, startled her. The tingle of her magic flared to life in response and she swept it over her like she had done to block out the siren's call. She looked at the stranger to see his dagger was already drawn.

Adrastus' magic roared in response, sending a jolt of power through Kelera. He was calling on the full strength of their combined magic. She didn't resist as he drew it from her, settling it in a twist of shadows and light at their feet.

The man bounded for them, running faster than Kelera thought would be possible on the soft sandy beach. Adrastus pulled their magic up, making a veil between them and the man. It twinkled in the sunlight, and she could still see the man through the thin layer of shadows that flowed around them.

Behind them, parents began shouting at their children, and Kelera turned to see them fleeing. Everyone except for Ragnor and his men. Their brows were furrowed in confusion, but they didn't hesitate to draw their weapons. It was as if it was a reflex for them.

Adrastus positioned himself between Kelera and the stranger. He was so focused on the frontal attack that he didn't see the danger that she saw approaching from behind. Ragnor's band reached them just as the strange man did.

Kelera turned to face Ragnor and his men while Adrastus faced the man. She tried to warn Adrastus, but the man had his full attention as he chuckled in amusement. "So it's true. The bastard and the bitch thought they could find sanctuary in the Summer Court." He clucked at his teeth and added, "The stories were wrong about you, your Highness. I thought you'd have been smart enough to keep a lower profile. Instead, I find you out here teaching your halfling whore how to play with her magic."

Ragnor snarled from behind them, *"Your Highness?"*

Kelera pooled her magic into the tips of her fingers, ready to direct it at Ragnor and his men if they stepped out of line. She caught a glimpse of some of the Fae from the beach lingering behind them, waiting to see how things played out.

Her rapid breathing matched the pulsing magic in her veins. She shouldn't have asked Adrastus to stay a bit longer. They should have taken their breakfast on the road and gotten away from all the innocent bystanders. They shouldn't have allowed themselves to be surrounded by all of these men who were, by all accounts, strangers to them.

She looked around, sizing up the men who outnumbered her and Adrastus. Ragnor and Jinx were standing behind them while Tepin and Chaz flanked their sides. These men were standing between them and their freedom.

She snuck a glimpse at the slick haired stranger standing in front of Adrastus. The man raised an eyebrow and shouted over Adrastus' shoulder, directing his question at Ragnor. "There's a cut in it for you if you help me take them in."

Kelera was holding her magic over her mind, hoping it wouldn't falter if she had to defend herself in a physical fight. Ragnor and Jinx exchanged a look, then nodded at the stranger. Kelera felt a stab of betrayal. She hadn't expected them to defend her and Adrastus, but she couldn't shake the disappointment that came with how easily they'd agreed to turn on them.

The stranger's dagger flashed as he advanced on Adrastus. But Dras was too quick. He wrapped his shadows around the man's wrist, knocking the dagger from his hand. The man shouted for Ragnor and Jinx to help him, but Kelera turned on them. "Do not do this."

Ragnor winked at her. Confused, she looked at Jinx, who was already calling on his own magic. Small vines broke through the beach, sending sand flying in their wake as they grew. Kelera took a deep breath in, ready to unleash her magic if she needed to. The innocent Fae who still lingered nearby, and the fishermen who had simply come down to the beach to begin their workday, scrambled away. A few who were closest to the village fled. Some of the fisherman began to shout at them, but didn't dare step any closer.

Adrastus had hold of the stranger now, wrapping shadows around his throat and sending the man to his knees. Adrastus was strong, but he, too, struggled to control his magic. If he was outnumbered, there was no telling if he could take them all on without any innocents getting hit in the crossfire.

Fear overwhelmed Kelera, making her power burn in her veins. She couldn't use her magic against these men. Not if it meant risking innocent lives. Her panic surged as she felt herself losing control. She pleaded with Jinx, "Please, I'm begging you, don't do this."

Jinx tilted his head to the side and smiled at her. "I wouldn't dream of it, Milady." The roots he'd called up from the depths of the land shot up through the heavy sand.

Kelera scrambled to take hold of her magic, but it slipped from her grasp. Small fires sprouted from thin air around her feet, and she stomped them out before they could catch on her clothes. As she struggled to put out the fires she had caused, she left Adrastus exposed. Her stomach twisted into knots as she saw Jinx's vines head for him.

She shouted, "Dras!" But he was so consumed with the power he was wielding that he didn't hear her. Adrastus was going to die because she was too weak. She cried out as the vines shot past him and straight into the stranger's chest. It tore through his skin. She gasped as Jinx balled his hand into a fist and pulled. With the quick movement of his hand, the roots followed with the man's heart wrapped tightly within. Blood dripped from the dark bark and the stranger's eyes rolled to the back of his head as he fell to the ground with a thud. Jinx had killed the bounty hunter. They had taken her side—had saved them.

Adrastus turned toward Ragnor and Jinx with his magic still flowing around him. His eyes were clouded with shadows again and he looked ready to destroy everything in his path. His magic raged like a storm and Kelera's knees weakened with the sensation.

She called out to him, "Dras, look at me!" The power was consuming him. Kelera threw herself in front of him, digging her fingers into his shoulders as hard as she could. "Dras!"

She focused on her power, imagining a veil that she could place over his magic. Wrapping her power around his, she felt it buckle and give way to her strength. His eyes cleared, revealing the beautiful rings of green, and Kelera breathed a heavy sigh of relief.

With a furrowed brow and eyes full of concern, he whispered her name. "Kelera." And placed both of his hands on the side of her face. "Did I hurt you?"

He scanned her for injury and she tried to calm his nerves as she said, "No, I'm okay. We're okay. Thanks to them." She gestured to Ragnor and his men.

Ragnor bowed to Adrastus and said, "Your Majesty."

Adrastus shook his head. "I am not the King."

Ragnor winked at them. "Aye, not yet."

Kelera stared at the men in disbelief as he and Jinx knelt before Adrastus. When Ragnor stood, he continued, "As you said, word travels on the road. We had a hard time believing that the Unseelie King's crown had been claimed by the Prince of Shadows. That he was hunting down his own brother for the death of the king. Prince Samael's conquests are notorious in the Spring Court. Didn't make sense that you'd poison your own father out of spite or that a mere halfling girl would be able to take down a prince of royal blood and magic. And we certainly never imagined that Samael would be strong enough to take the throne over you, Prince Adrastus."

Kelera grabbed onto Adrastus' sleeve to steady herself. She raised her chin as she asked, "What interest do you have in who rules the Unseelie Court?" She tried to ignore the whispers coming from the fishermen, who had inched closer for a better look at the carnage. Their cover here was blown. It was no longer safe for them in the Summer Court.

Jinx released his hold on the roots and they retreated back into the ground. He dusted his hands off as he said, "Prince Samael is a greedy son of a bitch. It's not lost on the Spring Court that his ambitions reach beyond the Unseelie borders."

Ragnor chimed in, "We seem to have a common enemy. And for that, we will help where we can."

Adrastus eyed them warily. "Who are you really?"

Ragnor chuckled as the rest of their band stepped closer. Then Tepin and Chaz took their place behind Ragnor as he said, "We are Guardians of the Wildwood."

Adrastus looked impressed as he regarded the men with a newfound respect. "You're in line to join the Wild Hunt."

Ragnor tipped his head and put his calloused hand to his heart. "Only if we're worthy." He looked around the beach. "For now, we really should get moving if we're going to stay ahead of these traitorous bastards."

Chapter Six

Kelera's legs burned from trudging along the sandy beach for the last few hours. The bounty hunter attack had shaken her to her core. She'd been living for days with the constant echo of a threat in the back of her mind, but all the anticipation couldn't have prepared her for an actual ambush.

Having just been faced with their first bounty hunter, the danger felt more imminent. A fresh sense of fear was setting in now. Was this going to be the new normal—constantly ready for monsters to appear, even in the broad daylight. Kelera wanted to kick herself for getting so comfortable during their stay in the Summer Court. What had she and Adrastus been thinking by drinking and dancing, and wasting time watching sirens in the water?

They'd given Samael too much of an opportunity to catch up. If one bounty hunter had found them, then surely there would be more on their tail. And who knew what power the other hunters would hold?

Nausea rolled in her stomach. The tension was shared amongst the group. No one spoke for a long time and the pace they were traveling at was excruciating. Kelera's legs would have given out from the unsteady trek through the sands, if it hadn't been for the terror embedded in every nerve of her body. It was the only thing pushing her forward.

They hugged the coastline for the better part of the day, hoping to throw any bounty hunters off by taking the less direct route to the Spring border. Kelera kept a watchful eye on their new allies. She wanted to trust them, but after getting jumped on the beach, she couldn't fully relax.

Tepin and Chaz stumbled drunkenly behind her. It seemed they had made quite the dent in that flask of theirs while they'd been fishing. Meanwhile, Ragnor and Adrastus talked up ahead.

Ragnor laughed at something Adrastus said and patted him on the back. After that, Adrastus slowed, stepping into place beside Kelera. He was silent for a moment before saying, "You're upset."

Kelera rolled her eyes. "And you're not?"

"But you're upset with me." He raised an eyebrow.

She relented. "I'm more upset with myself for getting so comfortable. I shouldn't have allowed us to linger on the beach."

"Kelera, that bounty hunter would have caught up to us either way. He knew exactly who we were and where to find us. Consider what would have happened if it had been just the two of us on the road."

Kelera fumbled at her locket. Again, he had a point. It was becoming quite the habit of his.

To drive his point home, he said, "If we hadn't been on that beach, then the Guardians wouldn't have been there to help."

"We got lucky, Dras. They could have just as easily sided with the hunter. Then where would we be?"

Adrastus grabbed hold of her hand, drawing it away from the locket, and ran his thumb along her knuckles. Her frustration dissolved with each stroke. She walked beside him like that for a while, content to be in his presence. He was trying his best, just as she was. That's really all they could do until they reached the Seelie Palace.

Jinx joined them, walking quietly on the other side of her, his eye alert and his gaze was shooting to any and every sound. He shook his head. "We're too exposed out here. I don't like it."

Kelera looked around at the sandy dunes. There wasn't a soul in sight. She couldn't even spot boats on the horizon anymore. It made her feel better knowing there were no strangers happening upon them. She shrugged. "At least no one can sneak up on us here."

Jinx sneered at her and sucked at his teeth. "Don't be so sure of that, Milady."

As if conjured by his words, the sands in front of them began to shift. The ground quaked and Adrastus side-stepped around until his back was pressed against Kelera, shielding her from whatever was happening on the beach.

Ragnor swore under his breath. "Damn you, Jinx."

Jinx growled, "Oh, come on now, this one wasn't my fault." He unsheathed the dagger at his side and the others followed suit, drawing multiple weapons that Kelera hadn't even seen them carrying. She'd noticed they were armed, but had no idea they had been hiding so many blades on their person.

The sand lifted off the ground, whipping around them like a storm. Kelera shielded her face with her hands and shouted over the winds, "What's happening?"

The sands settled as quickly as they had risen, and in the midst of the beach stood an incredibly beautiful woman. Her skin was coated in soft silvery sand, but Kelera could see stunning eyes beneath, as blue as the sea beside them. The woman flashed a dazzling white smile at them as she said, "I hoped you would pass through my domain. Very foolish of you all."

Adrastus inched back, causing Kelera to back away from the woman as well. He spoke over his shoulder as he warned her, "She's a sand-wielder... a Summer Court witch. We need to get out of here."

Ragnor agreed, "The sooner, the better."

The sand-wielder frowned. Her voice was grainy, like sand being rubbed on a hard surface as she said, "Not so fast, boys. I have it on excellent authority that those two are wanted by the High King."

Adrastus snorted. "Is that what he's calling himself now? His arrogance knows no bounds."

Kelera clenched her hands into tight fists. They had to be referring to Samael. If he was proclaiming himself as the High King, then that could only mean that he was no longer keeping his plans a secret. He was announcing to the entire realm that he meant to take it all for himself.

The sand-wielder hissed. It was an unnatural sound coming from such a beautiful creature. "It is your own arrogance that will be your downfall." She lifted her hands and with them, another sandstorm began to circle around them. It cut between Adrastus and Kelera, pushing them apart.

Kelera gritted her teeth. She was tired of being pushed around. Her magic rose to the surface as if eagerly awaiting her to grab hold of it. It yearned for release, and in this moment, she was happy to oblige. Her only hope was that Ragnor and his friends would be quick enough to get out of her way if things got out of control.

Adrastus was no longer visible as the sand-wielder fixated her power on him. She was burying him in the storm. Perhaps it was because she thought Kelera was less of a problem. Little did she know that Kelera's unhinged magic was the bigger threat at the moment. Her muscles tensed with her mounting power. She raised her hands, mimicking the movements of the witch.

Thinking back to her lessons with Gadreel, she focused on the elements around her, knowing that her magic would be strongest if she drew on the power of the Seelie Court. Spotting the ocean out of the corner of her eye, she tried to imagine it washing over her. *Feel it*, she reminded herself.

There was no sign of Adrastus as he was trapped under the witch's sand spell. Ragnor and his men fruitlessly attacked the sand-wielder, but she deflected their blades as her body's sandy form shifted with each strike. Fear began to cloud Kelera's focus and her magic buckled for a moment. What if she wasn't strong enough to control it?

The sand-wielder snarled at her. "You think to use your meager halfling magic against *me*?"

Something crept underneath the sand, and Kelera gasped as a massive, dry, scaly tail emerged. The sand-wielder's tail snapped on the ground like a whip. Sweat dripped down Kelera's back, reminding her of the whip that had torn through her skin at the King's revel in the Winter Court.

Light bounced off of the large needle sharp stinger at the end of the witch's tail, blinding Kelera for a moment. Just long enough for a strike. She squeezed her eyes shut and threw her hands up in a defensive reflex, waiting for the pain to come. But it didn't. When Kelera opened her eyes again, Chaz was standing between her and the witch. He opened his hands out to the sun, drawing the rays in with his magic. As he did, it bounded from his hands and onto the witch. She shrieked in agony as it burned through her tail, crystalizing it. Still, through it all, she kept her hold on Adrastus.

Every instinct in Kelera's body screamed for her to run far away from the monster. But in her core, she knew she wouldn't. *I'm stronger than this.* Kelera balled her hands into fists. She wouldn't leave Adrastus behind. There was no time for second guessing and doubting herself. They'd come too far together to be defeated by this creature. If they were going to die on this journey, this was not the way it was going to happen.

Enough, Kelera thought with determination. *I will not cower.* She sucked in a breath, and a rush like icy water from a coursing river coursed through her body as her bond with Adrastus bloomed to life. His magic steadied hers until she was able to take hold of the tide. Envisioning the water in her grasp, she tugged at it with her outstretched hands.

She held her head high and concentrated on calming her mind as she focused only on the waves and where she wished them to go.

To her shock and awe, the sea answered her call. A mountainous wave rose over the beach. Kelera imagined it whirling together, much like the sand-wielder's sandstorm was doing over Adrastus. Then she met the witch's eye, and with a sly half-smile, Kelera ravaged her with it. The water overtook the witch.

The pride swelling in Kelera's chest was quickly replaced with rising panic as more water rushed in like a tidal wave. If she lost her grip on it, then it wouldn't just drown the sand-wielder—it would take Adrastus too. She bit her lip, slowing the water down with each steadying breath she took. As if responding to the fear of losing Adrastus, her magic veered into the sand-wielder only, leaving Adrastus free of the water.

The witch's screams were drowned out as the waves continued to crash into her. It didn't stop until it washed her away. When it dissipated, there was nothing left of the Summer Court witch but a heap of wet, muddy sand.

Adrastus coughed and choked as he spat sand out of his mouth and wiped it from his eyes. He was completely covered in it, but Kelera leapt into his arms, anyway. The sand was rough on her cheek as she rested her head against his shoulder. She gave a nervous laugh. "I did it."

Jinx's voice behind them was awestruck. "By the stars. You just controlled the sea."

"Yes, she did." Adrastus took hold of her chin gently and their eyes met. His grin said everything that he must have been thinking. He was proud of her. He leaned in, his lips parting slightly.

Kelera followed suit, leaning in for a kiss, but Ragnor's voice cut through the moment. "We need to keep moving. There could be more nearby."

Kelera pressed her lips into a tight line. She and Adrastus stood, dusting the sand from their clothes. Then he grabbed her hand, and they ran.

Once they were farther down the beach, they slowed their pace. Far off in the distance, a brilliant green tree line stood tall and dense. The sunlight shone on the trees, bringing to life an array of greens, much like Adrastus' eyes. Something in her heart warmed at the sight. She came to a stop and whispered, "Is that?"

Ragnor finished, "The Spring Court, Milady."

Kelera had never been so eager to walk into a forest before. But there was something unmistakably familiar about the magic that was emanating from the tree line up ahead that drove her to pick up her pace. The closer they came to it, the more her magic pulsed in her veins. It was as if the very magic that the Spring Court held was one and the same as the magic she'd been born with.

She reached for the locket hanging around her neck. Its intricate vine and thorn carvings were familiar under her fingers. What surprised her, though, was the longing in her heart. It was a longing she hadn't known in nearly a decade, since she was a young girl and had often thought of her mother.

Chaz's sudden groan stopped everyone in their tracks. They were all exhausted from the confrontation with the sand-wielder, and she couldn't blame him for needing to take a breather. But when she turned to look at him, her heart dropped. His face was a pallor of sickly green. Had the sand-wielder made contact with that horrible stinger of hers? As if acknowledging her question, Chaz's eyes rolled, revealing only whites in them and he dropped like a wounded deer.

Ragnor cursed loudly as he raced to him. Kelera and Adrastus dropped their packs and rushed to their side. There was no sound coming from Chaz now as he lay in a crumpled heap. Ragnor turned him on his back with a grunt and removed his weapons with quick, fluid movements.

Nothing could have prepared Kelera for what was waiting for them under Chaz's jacket. The witch's stinger had, indeed, made contact with him. There was a small puncture wound that would have appeared harmless had it not been for the skin rotting around it. It was an angry wound, bruised and black, but more concerning was the green and yellow pus coming from it.

Tepin sounded like he might be sick as he said, "Rag, you gotta do something, man."

Hope dawned on Ragnor's face, lighting up his eyes. He turned to Adrastus and said, "You have healing magic, right? We've heard the rumors. Your power rivals the healers at the Seelie Court."

Kelera nodded eagerly as Ragnor spoke. Healing magic was difficult to master, but she knew first hand that Adrastus was capable of wielding it. He'd healed the wounds on her back after she'd been whipped at the revel and then again after Samael had sliced into her face.

Adrastus, however, didn't look nearly as confident as she felt. His jaw twitched, and he nodded gingerly. "I can try... but I can't guarantee anything. The venom is already working its way to his heart."

He pointed to a thin black line that was progressing slowly from the wound to Chaz's chest. Kelera hadn't noticed it before, but she saw it now and it was clear that this man's life was in grave danger.

Jinx begged, "Just try?" His voice cracked. "You have to try." The helplessness in his words broke Kelera's heart. She hadn't had the opportunity to get to know Chaz well, but these men were brothers in arms, if not in blood.

Without another word, Adrastus held his hands out over the wound. Kelera could feel his magic before anyone else could see it. It was warm and powerful, like the sands under the summer sun. Ragnor and the others gasped as a glow bloomed beneath his hands. It engulfed Chaz's wound until Kelera could no longer see the black, dying skin around it.

Adrastus furrowed his brow as he concentrated. After a moment, he growled in frustration. Instinctively, Kelera put her hand on his shoulder and whispered, "You can do this. Draw on my magic if you need to."

He smiled gratefully at her and closed his eyes. His magic wrapped around hers. There was a tug as he pulled it from her and made it flow into Chaz. The glowing light of Adrastus' power bloomed brighter with hers to accompany it, and Chaz stirred. He didn't open his eyes, but he was waking back up. It was working.

Suddenly, a sensation of ice wove itself around the magic Adrastus was drawing from her. It stung, like someone had plunged her beneath icy water. She gasped, "Dras, what's wrong?"

"Fighting the venom is taking too much power. My..." He strained as he continued, "Unseelie magic is trying to interfere."

She could tell by the tremble in his hands that he was afraid. The threat of his Unseelie and Seelie power intertwining was something he feared. She could feel it too, now, allowing her to sense the volatile nature of it for herself. It was suffocating, like the shadows of his Unseelie power were trying to smother out the warmth and healing efforts of the Seelie magic. But instead of snuffing it out, the shadows were melding into something else—a new kind of power.

Kelera shivered. Guilt mounted with each ragged breath Chaz took. She froze, brokenhearted for the life she knew deep down they wouldn't be able to save. This wound was because of her. Because he'd stepped in to help her. If she hadn't needed protecting—if she'd been stronger—this wouldn't have happened.

Adrastus growled under the pressure of his magic. She might have needed saving back on the beach, but right here, right now...

A thought dawned on her. If she could pull more of her magic to the surface, then it would tip the scales. His Unseelie power would be overpowered. But if she did that, she would be putting everyone at risk... even Adrastus. Chaz cried out in agony and Kelera looked down to see that the venom was spreading faster, as if fleeing from Adrastus' magic.

She had to act now. She shut her eyes tight and focused on the warm breeze of the Summer Court. She concentrated on the sun shining on her face and embraced it, letting it fill her entire being. If the Summer Court had powers of healing and vitality, then she would draw on that. It fueled her magic, and she led it to the path of Adrastus' power.

A man's life was depending on this. She couldn't take back the pain she had caused or the life she had taken in Samael's room of shadows, but she could start her amends here and now by helping Chaz. She let out a steady breath as her magic met Adrastus' and flowed into the wounded man.

This was going to work. She just needed to push a little harder. She clung to the hope that she could finally use her magic to help save a life rather than destroy it. That is, until she heard Jinx sob, "It's too late. He's gone."

Kelera opened her eyes. Chaz's chest no longer rose and fell with life's breath. The marks from the sand-wielder's venom had pooled around his chest. It had poisoned his heart. Her breath hitched in her throat at the sight of him, and her magic snapped back into her. She cried out in pain and Adrastus reached for her. But her mind was already filled with turmoil. She hadn't been strong enough, or fast enough. If she wouldn't have doubted herself, then she could have helped sooner. Someone was dead again, because she failed.

When Adrastus' hands met her skin, he hissed and pulled back quickly. Kelera blinked at him through tear-filled eyes. Now she was hurting him, too. Was anyone ever going to be safe around her?

His voice was gentle and soothing as he said, "Kelera, this was not our fault. This is the witch's domain, and she was incredibly powerful." He reached for her again, slowly this time.

Kelera pulled away from him, afraid that she would burn him or that her magic would explode like it had before. "Don't, okay? Just don't." She scrambled from the sand and walked a few feet away while Ragnor and his band of men said goodbye to their friend. She couldn't bear to watch as they wrapped him in a blanket from his pack and started gathering driftwood from the beach.

They were solemn as they worked together to build a small pyre for their fallen comrade. The man who had agreed to help her and Adrastus and had lost his life because of it. She spotted Adrastus out of the corner of her eye as he approached her. He gave her space, standing a few feet away. She sighed. "Who else is going to pay the price for standing against Samael with us?"

Adrastus' voice was low and rough as he said, "These men knew the risk when they made the decision to help us in that tavern."

Kelera turned to him in disbelief. "And what of those caught in the middle? The Fae and mortals who haven't chosen any of this. Cierine, Alexander," her voice broke as she added, "my father."

Adrastus closed the space between them and took hold of her shoulders. He was firm as he said, "We will do everything we can to protect them. Once we get to the Spring Court—"

"We'll what? Build an army to fight your brother and his monstrous force?" She wanted to pull away, but she feared his touch was the only thing keeping her standing. Her legs were shaking, and she felt dizzy as smoke filled her nostrils. She glanced past Adrastus to the fire that Ragnor and his men had started. The fire that would carry their friend into the afterlife.

Adrastus turned to look, too. They watched as Ragnor and the others circled around the fire. Ragnor bellowed out the last rites, "Rest now, brother, for your next journey will begin soon. May you ride atop the stars. May you be granted a steed amongst the warriors of the afterlife, destined to claim your place beside Woden and his sword. May you find glory in the afterlife as you did in this one."

Jinx and Tepin pounded their fists against their chests and shouted in unison, "Glory to the Wild Hunt!"

Kelera watched in silent fascination. The men clearly mourned the loss of their friend, but they were not saying goodbye forever. The gleam of pride in their eyes told her that they truly believed they would see Chaz again. She envied their strength and confidence. It must have been nice to have that sort of faith in something.

When they finished, they turned to her and Adrastus. With a nod of his head, Ragnor led the way up the hill and toward the fiercely green tree line. They weren't going to hold the death of their friend against her. And for that, she was grateful, even if she still blamed herself deep down.

Adrastus held out his hand. "Ready?"

Kelera nodded as she linked her fingers with his. She had no idea what to expect when she crossed over that border, but having Adrastus and these brave men by her side gave her enough strength to take the first step.

Chapter Seven

The sun had gone down by the time they reached the Spring border and Kelera's spirits were about as dark as the night sky. The ache in her heart hadn't subsided. She couldn't change what had happened to Chaz, so she did her best to focus on the moment. The air was cooler here, and she wasn't sure if it was from the setting sun or the change in season they were coming to. It was still strange to hear how each court of Elfhame was in an endless cycle of the same season.

Back home in the mortal realm, she had always loved spring the most. After a long winter, there was nothing more enchanting than hearing the sounds of birds singing again or seeing flowers blooming in the palace gardens. There was something freeing about being able to go outside in the fresh air after being cooped up in the warm confines of the palace.

She stood before a beautiful tree line, now, with evergreens that towered high above. She let go of Adrastus' hand and took a step closer to them. Her power stirred within her like a cat purring at its owner's touch. The Fae she had met during her time in Elfhame had speculated that her mother was from the Spring Court. Between her appearance and her magic, they were sure of it. But she hadn't known enough of this world to be convinced... until now.

As she stepped over the border, she felt it. The magic of the very ground on which she stood enveloped her like a warm embrace. It danced over her skin and tears filled her eyes. This time, the tears weren't from loss or pain. There was no mistaking the heat radiating through her chest for anything other than joy. She clutched her locket tightly and looked around in awe.

The Spring Court was as alive as her magic was. There was no other way to describe it. The sounds of birds and other wildlife were music to her ears, and she swore she could hear the breath of the trees surrounding her. Like the sparkling ocean of the Summer Court, the forest here in the Spring Court was vibrant with color like she had never seen in the mortal realm. It was as if the stars themselves had blessed the land, gifting their twinkling light on everything that grew here.

She turned slowly, wanting to soak up every bit of it. She didn't want to miss one detail of this, hoping she could sear it into her memory. The thought of forgetting it when she returned to the mortal realm pained her.

Adrastus' chuckle broke through her captivation. She turned to find him, Ragnor, and the others leaning lazily against various trees. They watched her with amusement, and she blushed. Ragnor, Jinx, and Tepin, after all, resided in the Spring Court.

Ragnor smiled broadly at her. "Welcome to the Wildwood, Milady."

"It's more beautiful than I ever could have imagined." Her voice was filled with awe.

"It is blessed with endless spring bounty. I may be biased, but it is the most glorious place in all of Elfhame." Ragnor gave Adrastus a sharp look, as if challenging him to say otherwise.

Adrastus shrugged his shoulders. "It certainly has its charms. As does every other court in Elfhame." He returned the pointed look, and both men laughed good-heartedly.

Jinx led them through an overgrown brush toward a clearing. Snickers came from the trees and Kelera had no trouble identifying the mischievous winged creatures as pixies. Smaller Fae creatures were notorious for creeping across the veil into mortal territory. Once upon a time, Kelera had doted upon these types of Fae—leaving gifts for them in the garden or chasing them through the tall grass. That is until her father warned her of the dangers they posed to her and her security in the mortal court.

Seeing them now, though, brought her no sense of dread or embarrassment. Stumbling across pixies was as natural here as seeing a butterfly back in Nevene. Adrastus nudged her in the side and pointed to a branch. Two beautiful women with a green shade to their skin and long, flowing hair tangled with orange and purple flowers stared down at them. There were no whites in their eyes, only the color of tree bark.

Kelera sucked in a breath at the shock of their appearance. "Are they... safe? To be around, I mean?"

Adrastus chuckled. "They're safe as long as you give them their space. And as long as you don't offend the forest."

Kelera raised a brow, never taking her eyes from the women who were doing a splendid job of balancing on the thin tree branch. "Offend the forest?"

Adrastus explained, "They're dryads—nature spirits. They tend to the forest and won't hesitate to strike down anyone who dares to bring harm to it."

"Wow," was all Kelera could say. She looked back at the dryads one last time as Adrastus led her away and swore one of them winked at her.

As Kelera climbed through the brush that led to the clearing, one of the branches snagged on her dress, tearing it along the side. She was definitely not dressed for a trek through the woods and made a mental note to change when they reached their destination.

She whispered to Adrastus, "How far to the Seelie Palace?"

"A day or two's walk. The emissary will be waiting for us once the moon reaches its peak. We'll make camp tonight and continue on in the morning." He frowned at the tear in her dress. Taking a step closer, he lowered his voice as he asked, "Are you okay?"

"I'm fine. I'm more worried about them..." She nodded toward the men who had become their unlikely allies. They were gathered around a small fire they had built and passing a flask to one another.

Adrastus smiled sadly. "They'll be alright. Guardians of the Wildwood don't mourn like the rest of us."

"Because they believe their friend will join the Wild Hunt." Kelera had picked up that much. "But how can they be so sure?"

Adrastus ushered her to the fire as he said, "They have faith."

"But you have doubts."

He frowned. "I have never witnessed it for myself, nor have I met anyone who has. But who am I to deny them their beliefs?" They reached the fire, and Adrastus continued, "They dedicate their lives to achieving glory in the name of Elfhame. Their sole mission in life is standing up for injustice and protecting the people of these very woods. If they are found worthy, then they believe they will find a place for themselves amongst the Hunt."

Jinx raised the flask. "Aye. Glory in the Hunt. Chaz was a fierce warrior and died for a worthy cause." He bowed his head to Adrastus before taking a drink. Kelera's face burned with a blush, knowing he'd overheard their conversation.

She sat on her bedroll, which the men had graciously laid out for her. Adrastus took a seat beside her, scooting close enough that their legs were brushed up against one another. Tepin pulled dried meat from his pack and passed it to Kelera. She hadn't realized how hungry she'd been and savored the smokey flavor as she bit into it. It settled heavily in her stomach, but she continued to eat, nonetheless.

Contentment soon fell over their little band. Between sips of the flask being passed around, the men were sharing stories about Chaz with fond smiles on their faces. Still, she could see in their eyes that they were mourning. She sympathized with them, though she had never lost anyone close to her before. She'd mourned the absence of her mother, but it wasn't the same when you were grieving for something you never truly had to begin with.

Adrastus was contemplative beside her and she took the opportunity to ask, "What happens to other fallen Fae? The ones who don't join the Wild Hunt?" In Nevene, the mortals talked of a beautiful paradise where souls would join their loved ones in death. But she hadn't heard anyone talk of such a place here in Elfhame. The mortals had never mentioned it either or included it in the books they kept on the Fae. To them, the Fae were dark creatures who didn't deserve to find peace in the afterlife. It had often made her wonder what would happen to her own soul in the end.

Adrastus scratched at the growing scruff on his chin. It had been a while since he'd last shaved, and Kelera liked the way he looked with it. He answered, "They simply return."

"Return where?"

"Their magic returns to Elfhame, joining the collective power of the land. It is what you feel now." She gave him a puzzled look, and he chuckled. "I know you feel it in your magic. Your power is connected to the ancestral magic of the Spring Court. Same would go for a Fae who was born in Autumn or Winter."

It was true. The moment she stepped into the Spring Court, her magic had seemed fuller somehow. Like a storm that was finally settling.

"What of their souls?" It was strange to say out loud. It made her uncomfortable to think about death. Who was to say souls even existed? Maybe their bodies simply returned to the earth along with their power.

"Souls reside deep beneath the ash trees," he paused, with a tilt of his head as if searching for the words. "It is an underworld of sorts. *Under the hill, beneath the ash trees, the Elders await you with the keys.*" He gave her a lopsided smile. "It's a nursery rhyme parents tell their children. The keys to a place with no pain and no tears..." He ran his thumb along Kelera's cheek where a tear had fallen. After all that had happened today, it was both comforting and heartbreaking to think of a place like that. She wanted desperately to believe that if Samael succeeded and took their lives that it wouldn't truly be the end for them.

She asked no more questions, happy to sit quietly with Adrastus by her side.

The Elfhame stars covered the sky like tiny fireflies twinkling through the canopy of the forest. Adrastus had insisted that they get some rest before the moon reached its peak. It was then that they would meet the emissary from the Seelie Palace.

Kelera wouldn't have minded the wait, had it not been for the nervous knots in her stomach. There was still so much uncertainty about how this meeting would go, and she desperately wanted to get it over with. But there wasn't anything she could do about it.

In the meantime, she was forced to sit with her thoughts. She laid back, staring up, and basking in the soft glow. The glittering night sky was another thing she was going to miss about this strange realm. The list of things she would miss seemed to be growing by the minute. She couldn't remember a time where she had seen such beauty in Nevene and the prospect of going back to the mundane landscape brought an ache to her heart.

At least she would be reunited with her father and with Cierine. And Alexander? She didn't know anymore where they would stand when all of this was over. Keeping track of how much time had passed since she had crossed the blackthorn border was becoming difficult. Would he have moved on? Did he consider her lost to their world for all of eternity? She wouldn't blame him. More than that, what would he think of the magic that had awoken inside of her? Or the scar on her face?

Her stomach quivered as these questions filtered through her mind. It was obvious from the start that they were strangers to one another. And never before did she think that it was a hurdle she couldn't jump. But would that be enough for her now? Having to face yet another obstacle? No doubt it would force her to revert back to her old ways—doing everything within her power to please others so they would like and accept her. It was so unlike what she had with Adrastus...

Ragnor's hardy laugh broke through her thoughts. His body shook as he laughed and said, "When I first found Chaz, he was a scrawny little son of a bitch. Villagers were complaining about a thief stealing their livestock in the midst of the night. So, Jinx and I decided to put a stop to it, expecting to find a pack of fearsome bogie responsible for it." He leaned forward and became very serious, drawing Kelera into the story as he said, "So, we set a trap. We laid in wait, ready to destroy the thieves when they came for the sheep we had fenced up at the edge of the woods. Imagine our surprise when a skinny little kid hopped the string that we'd set to catch him and set the beasts free!"

Jinx chimed in. "Turns out he wasn't stealing them to make a profit or to devour them to appease his unsatiable hunger like we'd expected. He just didn't like seein' them caged up!"

Kelera sat up, resting on her elbows, and laughed now too. "That was very sweet of him."

Jinx nodded. "That's who Chaz was; always looking out for those who couldn't look out for themselves."

Ragnor sighed. "That was the night we asked him to join us." His eyes met Kelera's. "You see, Guardians of the Wildwood are tasked with the protection of all of Elfhame's creatures. Magical and mundane, big and small. And that's why we are willing to risk our lives to aid you in your quest."

Jinx added, "Samael has never shown any regard for life. Not even in his own territory." He eyed Adrastus. "We know of the pits."

Adrastus shifted uncomfortably beside her. She wondered how he truly felt about what his brothers had been doing. She knew he cared for the villagers in the Unseelie territories, but he'd been forced to tread carefully—afraid if he showed his hand too soon and allowed his family to discover that he was working to keep power from Samael's hands, that they would destroy him. Had they done that, then there would be no one in Unseelie to stand between Samael and the power he hungered for.

Ragnor spoke carefully. "We know they were throwing their own people into those pits as punishment. We also heard that you've taken to the arena yourself."

Adrastus raised his chin slightly. "I have. Though I have only ever matched with the warriors of our court—men who entered willingly."

Ragnor looked skeptical with a lifted brow, but said, "I can respect that."

There was a tense energy around the campfire now, having delved into the more serious subject. Kelera bit the inside of her cheek as she thought of Samael. What would happen when they faced him again? It was only a matter of time. If Adrastus raised an army in the Seelie Court to confront Samael and his forces, then it would surely mean war. Would she still be here when it happened? She wanted desperately to avoid it. Her place was beside the mortals. Would they also be dragged into the confrontation?

Ragnor kicked at the dirt before speaking as if he didn't want to ask the question. "Lady Kelera, back at the beach, and again on the coast, your magic seemed... rather erratic."

Kelera gulped, embarrassed to have to explain herself. "Yes, I am only half Fae."

Ragnor cleared his throat. "We'd heard it was a halfling girl who had fled with his Highness here. We also heard that Samael is after you because he wishes to bind himself to you."

"Yes," Kelera answered carefully. She wasn't sure if she should tell them that she was already bound to Adrastus, making it impossible for Samael to bind with her.

Ragnor guessed anyway, "You are bound to him." He tilted his head toward Adrastus. "I've noticed the power that emanates from the two of you in a fight. It can be easy to spot bound magic if it's powerful. And the two of you..." He whistled and wiggled his eyebrows.

"Yes," was all Kelera said.

Ragnor clicked his tongue against his teeth and then chuckled as he said to Adrastus, "That royal jackass brother of yours will be mighty pissed when he finds out."

Imagining the look on Samael's face when he realized his bastard brother had achieved what he so desperately had tried to, gave Kelera a bit of glee. Smugly, she said, "Yes, he will be."

The men all laughed now, each taking turns to show off their impression of Samael when he inevitably found out. Once the laughter died down, Ragnor grew a bit more solemn. "Can I give you a bit of advice? Though I'm no expert on the matter."

Kelera took a drink from the flask and tried not to wince as the liquid burned her tongue and throat. "At this point, I'll take all the advice I can get."

Adrastus laughed beside her and rolled his eyes. "You never say that to me when I offer."

Kelera nudged him in the side. "That's because you're a know-it-all."

Ragnor smiled softly. He leaned forward, resting his elbows on his knees. "You have power. True power. Power that many would envy. I can sense it emanating from you like pollen in the wind."

Kelera shivered. How many other Fae could sense it? King Cyrus and Samael certainly had, to her dismay. Surely it would be better if her power was undetected and contained so no one would want to destroy her or take it from her. That is what got her into this whole mess in the first place.

But there was no envy or hunger in Ragnor's eyes as he spoke of it. Instead, his brow was furrowed with worry. Worry for her. He continued, "Do not let it control you. That amount of power can be seductive and all consuming. And if you allow yourself to fear it, then you've relinquished your control of it."

Kelera bit her lip, thinking of Ammon. "I will remember that." Satisfied, Ragnor sat back.

This time it was Tepin who spoke. His voice was gruff, like he'd spent his life shouting. "What would your mortals think of you being bound to a Prince of the Night?"

Her jaw dropped as she searched for an answer that wouldn't offend all of them. "I can't really say. But I can tell you that my father has always been loving and supportive."

Jinx hollered. "Must be to take one of our own to bed!"

Ragnor elbowed him in the side and Jinx blushed apologetically. The men changed the subject, talking about other powerful Fae they had come across over the years. Adrastus joined in, swapping stories and drinking from the flask. But Kelera was still pondering the previous conversation. What would her people think of her now? When she first came to Elfhame, she had been afraid to use her magic. She'd spent so many years afraid that if anyone in Nevene knew of her it, then they would exile her and her father. Afraid that using it would bring trouble to the palace and the people who resided there.

Then, once in Elfhame, when she had learned to access it, she had killed Ammon. Nothing scared her more now than the thought of her magic overpowering her and hurting innocent people. How was she supposed to move past that fear? It was easy for everyone to tell her not to be afraid, but they had no idea what it was like for her. Mortal blood ran through her veins as well as Fae and, because of that, her power was volatile. It wasn't her fault she couldn't control it, was it?

Jinx roared with a yawn and laid back on his bundle. Tepin followed suit and Kelera worried they would all fall asleep before they had a chance to meet with their contact from the palace. Adrastus moved his bedroll closer to hers until the two were touching.

She raised her eyebrow at him. "And just what do you think you're doing?"

He shrugged nonchalantly. "I'll feel better if I'm near you."

"So I can protect you?" she teased.

He rolled his eyes. "So, if any more of Samael's bounty hunters pay us a visit, I don't have to worry about getting to you in time."

She laid back down on the soft roll and looked up at the sky. Adrastus lingered in his position of sitting upright until she said, "Fine. Get comfortable." She added quickly, "But not too comfortable."

He laughed as he settled into his bedroll. "As you wish."

What she didn't say out loud was that she didn't wish it. She thought of the night before when he had hummed to her and held her until she drifted off to sleep after the nightmare. And of the way his hands felt on her hips when they danced in the tavern. Her mind told her not to let him get too close, but her heart was beginning to tell her that it was too late for that. She couldn't deny that she felt safe with him. He'd been trying to protect her since Samael had first found her. And even if she hadn't known it, he'd been trying to help her in his own misguided ways.

Still, she would leave this place as soon as she had the chance. She was promised to Alexander and owed loyalty to the mortals. Though they had not accepted her wholly, they had not turned her away like her own Fae mother had.

Movement above the trees caught her eye, drawing her mind away from her worries. At first, she thought they were shooting stars, they were moving so quickly.

But then she heard the faint sound of hoofbeats. She glanced at Adrastus, who was also watching the sky.

She whispered to him, afraid to disturb the others. "Is that..."

"The Wild Hunt."

"Where do you think they're going?"

"It's hard to say. No one knows where they reside, and it has been centuries since they've been spotted." There was worry in his voice as he said, "They appear at times of great strife. A sign of war."

"But surely, if they attacked the Night Riders, then we can count on them to stand with us." The word 'us' slipped from her mouth naturally, and it startled her. This was not her war. Not until it reached the mortal border.

But it was too late to take it back. Adrastus looked at her in surprise. "I don't know. The prophecy foretells that they will stand with the lost heir."

Kelera sighed. "Dras, I know you don't want to entertain the possibility but—"

"Don't, Kelera. Please leave it alone." He looked across the fire to where the others were laying. "Do not fill these people with hope that we cannot deliver on."

She rolled close to him, careful to speak so only he would hear. She was nearly nose to nose with him as she said, "I've *felt* your power. I know your magic is unmatched. And you were born here in the Seelie Court. You might not believe it, but do not tell me to close my mind to the possibility that there may be some mystical forces at play here that could save your life."

"It is not my life that I fear for." He leaned forward until his forehead was pressed against hers. Her heart warmed at the gesture, and she allowed herself to stay that way until music echoed through the trees. She pulled away and propped herself up on her elbows. "What is that?"

Jinx let out a loud whoop from across the fire, making Kelera jump in alarm. Before she could register what was happening, Jinx and the others were up and pulling their boots on. He shouted, "No rest for the wicked, boys!" He added, "And lady."

Adrastus sat up and put his boots on as well, with a resigned look on his face.

Kelera followed suit. "I don't understand. What's happening?"

Jinx jogged over to her and swooped low so they were face to face. "Tis' a celebration, Lady Kelera. One to top all others." He held out a hand and helped her to her feet.

"But we have to meet the emissary..." Kelera's confusion was genuine. They were waiting for an incredibly important meeting. The last thing they should be doing is following music through the forest in the middle of the night. Especially with the threat of bounty hunters around every turn of their journey.

Adrastus shook his head. "I told you there would be a revel."

"You mentioned a festival, but you didn't say we would be attending." She wasn't sure how she felt about having such an important meeting in the midst of a major celebration. Would the emissary think it insensitive of them?

Realizing all eyes were on her, she sighed in defeat. It was clear the Guardians were excited about the revel. And if the man was waiting there for them, then what choice did they have but to go?

The music was growing louder, like a beacon, signaling for its revelers to follow.

"Very well," she said. "What is the celebration for?"

Adrastus held his arm out gallantly. "It's Beltane, little thief, and when the music calls, we must answer."

Chapter Eight

K elera had heard of Beltane. They celebrated it in Nevene as well. It was a festival to honor the peak of spring and the coming of summer. It was also the day of her birth. She frowned. She hadn't even realized her birthday had come. That meant she was twenty now. She thought of home. It was summer there when she had left the mortal realm. Did that mean she had been celebrating her birthday at the wrong time her entire life? She chuckled at the ridiculous thought.

Her arm was linked around Adrastus' as they walked down a narrow pathway, and she whispered, "I don't understand. Is a party really the best place to hold such an important meeting? And what if we're recognized by someone?"

"This is where he's expecting to meet us. And don't worry, I'll take care of the other thing." He smirked at her and her curiosity peaked even more.

Though she didn't consider a revel in the Wildwood the most appropriate place to meet with a man of the Queen's court, she followed behind Ragnor's men quietly. The Fae seemed to find fun wherever they could, and maybe this was just how things were done here—including official business. Besides, she couldn't ignore the intrigue of seeing a springtime revel for the first time.

She winced at the memory of the last revel she'd attended. Where Samael had beaten an innocent boy and cracked a whip across her back. *Samael is not here,* she reminded herself. But still, her eyes couldn't help but wander to the shadows.

They ducked below some low-hanging branches and came out into a small clearing surrounded by a thicket of trees full of flowers. They were so fragrant that the scent filled the entire clearing like a cloud of the expensive perfume Kelera had seen ladies of the Nevene court fight over at the market.

She followed Adrastus around the perimeter of the tree line, keeping to the shadows. The Fae were all too busy with their fun to notice them. Adrastus nodded to a jumbled pile of masks laying nearby. Jinx reached down and started to pass some back to them. Adrastus put one on that resembled a raven with a beak over the nose. It matched his hair and made him look very mysterious. He handed her one that had dazzling white feathers on it and a beak that nearly matched his, only this beak was a soft orange. Black paint lined the edge of the beak and the circles cut out for her eyes. It was a swan. And it was beautiful.

"Beats the last mask I wore," she joked, but it fell flat. Something dark flickered in Adrastus' eyes and she regretted bringing up the horrible mask Samael had forced her to wear in the Unseelie Palace. The one that had taken away her individuality in an effort to remind her that she was below him. A mask that had marked her as his property. Trying to make up for the remark, she added, "It's lovely, Dras."

A smile graced his beautiful face and brought one to her own. She placed the mask over her face and was relieved to find that it wasn't as stifling as Samael's. She reminded herself that this was simply a way to make her blend in with the other Fae who would not turn their noses up at her. They were all here to celebrate together. This mask would protect her. At least, that's what she hoped. Who knew where Samael's bounty hunters were lurking or if they had been able to track her and Adrastus over the border? It would simply be a matter of time...

"Let's get you out of that dress." Adrastus was looking at her with an arrogant smirk on his face.

"Excuse me?" She looked around for Ragnor and the others, but they had already joined the revel, blending in with the other residents of the Spring Court.

Adrastus held up a beautiful white dress that was laced with delicate swan feathers. "You'll stick out with the torn summer dress."

"Where did you even get that?" Kelera glanced around at the revelers, afraid that whoever the dress belonged to would be furious that someone had swiped it.

"Travelers often join these sorts of revels. So there is always spare party attire strewn about. I promise you, no one will miss it."

"If you say so." She took the dress and looked around for some place to change. There was no way she was going to strip in front of all these strangers. She thought back to the time when she felt the urge to dance naked beneath the light of the moon when she was in the mortal court and blushed. It seemed like a lifetime ago. Now that she was here with the opportunity to behave however she pleased, it was intimidating.

Noting the half-dressed Fae dancing around the bonfire, she guessed it wouldn't be frowned upon here at the Beltane revel to do so. She glanced back at the trees and asked Adrastus, "Would you mind?"

He gave her a lopsided grin. "Helping you out of that dress?"

Her face flushed. *"Keeping a lookout."*

He gave her an extravagant bow. "It would be my pleasure."

Shaking her head, she ducked under the branches and slipped behind a large tree. She untied the summer dress and let it slip from her body. She wrinkled her nose at her undergarments. They had to be filthy after the day they'd had. It would be nice to get out of them, but she had no others to change into. To her dismay, Adrastus had grabbed only the dress. *Men*, Kelera thought to herself. She looked around self-consciously and slipped them off too, praying that the dress wouldn't be too revealing.

She should have known better here in Elfhame. The Fae exuded a confidence that mortals did not. Modesty wasn't revered here in the same way as it was in Nevene. She pulled the new dress over her head and gasped. It was stunning and fit her like a glove. It was low cut. A little revealing for her taste, but the light cotton beneath the feathers kept her warm enough in the cool spring air, without being stifling. And thankfully, the multitude of feathers covered up the fact that she wasn't wearing anything underneath.

She peeked around the tree to discover that Adrastus had his back to her. She snuck up behind him and tapped him on the shoulder. His eyes widened when he turned to face her. A "wow" escaped his lips, and Kelera felt like butterflies were fluttering in her stomach.

She was glad for the mask hiding the blush she knew was blooming on the bridge of her nose. "Well, what are we waiting for?" She slipped past him and into the crowd.

Fae danced with wild abandonment around the clearing. There was a band of creatures playing music off to the side. They were a mismatched looking bunch. One with horns on the top of his head and sun kissed skin. Another with rough skin that at first glance looked like tree bark. But they were all sporting the same carefree smiles. The flute player was the most interesting of the bunch. He was shorter than the rest, with the legs and bottom of a goat but the torso and face of a man. His ears were floppy and bounced as he danced around their makeshift stage.

If she had happened upon a revel like this weeks ago when she'd first come to Elfhame, she would have been appalled. The storybooks in the mortal realm spoke of revels where the Fae would lure virgin women in to dance until their feet broke. But there were no mortals here other than her. There was no malice in any of the partygoers' eyes. Instead, there was acceptance and joy.

She searched the crowd, looking for anyone wearing palace garb. It was possible that they wouldn't dress the way emissaries in Nevene dressed—in gently pressed pants and a jacket bearing the royal crest. She wrinkled her brow and asked Adrastus, "How will we know the Queen's emissary when we see him?"

Adrastus shrugged, but there was no hiding the twitch in his jaw. Kelera watched him closely as he took a drink offered to him by Jinx and said, "Let us hope that *he'll* find us."

Kelera gave him an annoyed look. Was he trying to calm her nerves by pretending he wasn't worried? If so, it was backfiring. It would be preferable for him to admit he's worried as well so they could address the situation head on.

She sighed. "We can't just wander around aimlessly. If Fae have traveled from all over the Spring Court, then he might not be able to tell us apart from the rest."

"We'll just have to wait and see." His words were strained as he scanned the crowd. "If he doesn't turn up by the time the moon begins to descend, then we will take action." He offered some of his drink to her, but she shook her head. Handing the cup to a random man nearby, he turned to Kelera and asked, "Shall we dance while we wait?"

She shook her head, more vehemently this time. "Now is really not the time."

Adrastus opened his mouth as if ready to argue, when someone in the crowd blew a horn. A man with a long tail like a lion jumped up on an abandoned tree stump and announced, "Here ye, here ye!" The crowd went quiet as the Fae turned to listen to him. He continued his proclamation, his tail twitching behind him. "We restless souls have gathered here to celebrate new life and awakening. May your souls stir with newfound energy and may you leave here tonight in good health and even better spirits!"

The crowd erupted with a cheer, and Kelera couldn't help but smile. The Beltane celebration back in the mortal realm was much more mundane than this. King Tristan delighted in hosting a grand ball where the same old hors d'oeuvres were passed around on silver plates and ladies of the court fought over which eligible bachelor they would get to waltz with.

This was so much... more. The Fae were ready to celebrate with purpose. They were honoring the true holiday and not using it as just another excuse to show off wealth and status. She tilted her head as the crowd quieted down to a hush again.

The man's eyes twinkled in the starlight as he continued, "Tonight, we celebrate our land by crowning someone here who is worthy of honoring the Goddess of the Earth."

Kelera's eyes widened in awe as the man extended his hands, allowing a soft golden light to extend from his palms. It wove through the crowd, circling each woman that it passed. Kelera leaned into Adrastus and whispered, "What's happening?"

Adrastus sounded as enchanted as she was with the display of magic as he said, "Whomever his magic touches will be crowned for the night. It is an honor bestowed upon the kindest soul amongst the revelers." The light continued to wind around the partygoers, leaving behind women with frowning faces—disappointed at not being deemed worthy of the title. It crept closer to them and Adrastus added, "I've never seen it for myself. This is my first Beltane revel."

That explained why he was just as intrigued as she was by the whole ritual. Her skin warmed as the light made its way to her. She held her breath as it twinkled around her arms and hands, running up around her chest and beneath her hair. It tickled her skin, sending goosebumps along her arms.

It continued to sparkle around her, weaving its way up to the top of her head, and murmurs swept through the crowd. She was frozen in place, unsure of what to do as the light settled on the crown of her head.

The man clapped his hands together, and the sound echoed through the clearing. "Our Goddess of life and light!"

The Fae in the crowd went absolutely wild in response. They cheered and clapped, closing in around her so that they could get close enough to reach out to her. Adrastus' presence was constant, the scent of him behind her. Her body stiffened as Fae after Fae lined up to touch her hands or her feet. Others brought offerings: gifts of wine, fruit, and feathers.

The man whose magic had crowned her stepped forward at last. He bowed at the waist and grinned at her as he rose. "Milady, your name?"

"K-Sera," she caught herself before revealing her real name, still unsure of whom to trust. In theory, they were safer in the Spring Court, but that didn't mean there was no danger of strangers passing through with knowledge of the bounty. Strangers who would jump at the chance for Samael's favor and reward.

"Lady Sera, well, for tonight, you are our Goddess." His grin turned mischievous, and he winked at her before continuing, "And as such, tradition calls for you to honor one in the crowd to be your chosen."

"Chosen what?" She glanced back at Adrastus, whose eyes had gone wide beneath his mask. Her stomach sank. What did these Fae have in store for her?

"Your chosen mate, of course." He gestured wide to the crowd with sparks flashing from his fingertips in purple and blue. "As we celebrate life and love, you must choose one lucky man or woman to honor with your favor."

Kelera twisted around to look at Adrastus again. "Does he mean?" She mouthed the word, "Sex?"

Adrastus bit his lip, and his eyes watered as he tried not to laugh. "It is symbolic, is it not?" He rose his voice so the man with the tail could hear him.

The man's eyes brightened with what Kelera swore was magical light and not the shine of the moon and stars. "If you so wish it to be. Tonight, *you* make the rules, Milady."

Kelera breathed a sigh of relief. Adrastus' magic pulsed in her veins with an icy chill, reminding her that there was only one real choice here. She couldn't risk being separated from him, after all, right? She gestured to Adrastus and declared, "I choose him."

Chapter Nine

K elera was grateful for the warmth from the blazing fire. A cool wind ruffled the white feathers on her dress as Adrastus stepped forward as her chosen mate. There were a few disappointed mumbles in the crowd, but most cheered again. They parted to leave space near the bonfire where others had been dancing before.

The man gestured to the clearing. "If it pleases you, you may first honor one another with a dance."

Adrastus held his hand out to Kelera. As she accepted it, he smiled sweetly and said, "See, I knew you would end up dancing with me."

She shook her head but couldn't stop a slight smile from spreading across her lips. "How do you do that?"

Music began to play softly, and the crowd gathered to watch them. Adrastus placed one hand on her hip and gripped her hand firmly with the other. "Do what?"

"Allow yourself to just... *be*." She swallowed heavily, trying to ignore the way his eyes darkened as he looked down at her. He certainly had a way of making her heart flutter.

"Growing up in the shadow of my father and brothers made me realize that if I don't let myself bask in the minor glimpses of light, then I would become the very thing I fear. Darkness breeds darkness. And I have done everything within my power to fight that."

Kelera was thoughtful as he spun her around the fire to the beat of the music. "That is precisely what would make you a decent leader."

Adrastus chuckled, but his shoulder tensed under her hand. "Not the lost heir thing again."

Kelera shook her head quickly. "No, not this time." She gripped his shoulder lightly. "If," she paused and correct herself, "*when* Samael is defeated, the Unseelie Court will need a king. Who better to lead them into the light than you?"

He leaned in close, his breath smelling of sweet, honeyed wine. "I am afraid that too much of my father's blood runs in my veins. What if I can't control it on my own? Bound to you, the volatile nature of my magic is tempered, but on my own... I fear I would fail my people."

The raw truth of what he was admitting to her struck a chord. Fear of embracing who and what she was had been a recurring theme in her life. It was something the two of them shared.

She took a deep breath before speaking. "I was afraid that if I admitted to myself that my Fae blood was something I liked or could be proud of, then I would be betraying my father and his people. But hiding that part of myself only made me weak. Being Fae is half of who I am, just as being half Seelie and Unseelie is who you are. How can either of us be confident and strong if we're too busy being ashamed of that?"

Adrastus gave a grunt of approval as if he'd been waiting a long time for her to admit about herself what he already knew. There was a hint of triumph in his voice as he said, "Perhaps the fresh spring air has done you some good."

Kelera swatted at him playfully and laughed. "You know, you seem happy here, too. All things considered."

He laughed as he repeated her words. "Yeah, all things considered. It's different here. I don't feel the pressure that I do back home. No one is watching and waiting for me to mess things up. No one is whispering about my power and what that will mean for the court. There is no need for violence and anger. I can just be me. I can be..." He trailed off as if trying to find the right word.

"Free," Kelera finished. She felt it too. "I wish we could stay here forever."

Adrastus' gaze snapped to her and his lips parted slightly as he studied her face. "In Elfhame?" He was looking at her with an intensity that surprised her.

"I just meant... here in the Wildwood." She scrambled for a defense. Had she meant Elfhame? She hadn't really been thinking when she spoke. She'd been caught up in the moment.

"But would you?" He asked.

"Would I what?" Kelera bit her lip, nervous about where this was going.

"Would you stay in Elfhame? I know you didn't want to entertain the idea in the tavern, but I think if you just give it some real thought, you might see that there truly is a place for you here."

Not this again, she thought. She pulled back slightly and busied herself with straightening the soft, airy folds of her dress. A few couples had joined them on the dance floor now, swaying with their bodies pressed close to one another.

Kelera returned her gaze back to Adrastus. The thought of staying in Elfhame hadn't really crossed her mind much—at least she didn't want to admit it had. And she wasn't sure why he seemed nervous to hear her answer.

Finally, she said, "I couldn't leave my father behind."

"But if things were better here? If this realm was safer for someone like your father?"

"Is that what you want? For Elfhame to be safe for the mortals?" Her eyes bore into his. She'd never asked what his plans for Elfhame would be if they were to defeat Samael. She knew he would make a better ruler than his horrible brother, but he was still a son of the Unseelie crown. What if he was right about the darkness inside of him? Would he and the mortals be able to repair the damage done to the treaty between them?

He gritted his teeth. She knew he would have to tell her the truth. Was he struggling to find a way to twist his words? Finally, he answered, "They are not our responsibility. I believe some of the Fae would welcome them if there was a treaty in place to protect both them and us as well. But the safety of mortals in Elfhame would fall to your mortal king. If King Tristan cannot move past the mortal blood my brother has spilled in his room of shadows, then I fear we may never be able to rebuild the relationship between our two realms."

Kelera felt like disappointment would swallow her whole. King Tristan was ruled by fear. Trust would not come easily for him. Especially not now. But she understood what Adrastus was saying. Trust was a two-way path, and both realms would need to be willing to extend a hand in friendship if they were going to live peacefully. What would happen if the mortal realm and Elfhame couldn't reconcile their differences? If they couldn't forgive past transgressions?

"Dras, you know I have to go home." She was surprised at the regret she felt as she said the words. It wasn't that she thought she belonged in Elfhame with the Fae, but rather that she wasn't sure *where* she belonged.

Not fully mortal, and not truly Fae. She was like a feather floating on a breeze, being bounced from place to place—destined to never belong in any one spot. Destined to never feel at home.

Adrastus shrugged his shoulders. "I know."

They slowed to a stop and Adrastus led her away from the bonfire and dancing Fae. He laced his fingers between hers and she welcomed the way his hand fit together with hers like a puzzle piece.

What if he really did want her to stay in Elfhame when this was all over? There was nothing to indicate that he wasn't genuine when he'd said those things to her. Even though she knew she couldn't, a tiny part of her warmed at the idea of him wanting her to.

As Fae passed by them, a few would reach their hand out to touch her gently on the shoulder or hair. She couldn't help but wince at the honor they were showing her. If only they knew she was a halfling sent there to beg their kingdom to go to war. They likely wouldn't be so eager to bestow their good graces on her then.

Adrastus nudged her in the shoulder and pointed to the tree line. "Look."

Jinx was standing with a voluptuous woman who had a thin veil of fabric wrapped around her. It hugged at her curves, covering only her breasts and below her hips. She ran a finger over Jinx's eye patch and he looked utterly besotted.

Kelera laughed. "Do you think he's finally found love?"

Adrastus draped his arm around her shoulders. "At least for the night, he has."

Kelera stayed still, enjoying the feel of Adrastus' muscular arm around her. It felt natural, as if they were two friends at a party together, just enjoying the moment. She supposed that's what this actually was. She did enjoy seeing the way the Fae flitted around the clearing.

"Care to dance?" A man who looked to be in his thirties appeared at her side, holding out a tanned hand. Soft lines formed at the corners of his brown eyes as he smiled at her.

She shook her head. "I appreciate the offer, but I should really stay with my friend here." She inched closer to Adrastus.

The man looked Adrastus up and down. "I'm sure he won't mind, will you, chap?"

Adrastus eyed the man, then said, "The lady makes her own decisions." He paused, then added, "But I make no objections."

The man puffed out his chest with satisfaction. But Kelera didn't take his hand. She stood on her tippy toes to whisper into Adrastus' ear. "What are you doing?"

Adrastus brushed her hair away from her ear to whisper back, "Ragnor and the Guardians are all within range. And this will give us a moment to seek out the emissary. I'll be right here, don't worry. Besides, we don't want to make anyone suspicious, do we?" He pulled back and gave her a wink.

Easy for him to say. He wasn't the one being summoned to dance with a stranger. In an effort to go along with it, she reached out and took the man's hand. "One dance can't hurt."

The man gave her hand a gentle squeeze. "That's the spirit!"

They joined the revelers around the fire and the man led her in step to the music. As they moved around the clearing, Kelera kept an eye on Adrastus, reluctant to lose sight of him. There were a lot of Fae here, and she didn't want to get lost in the crowd.

The man didn't speak as they danced, and Kelera was content to enjoy the moment in silence. She didn't want to risk saying anything that could reveal why she was really in the woods.

As the second song came to an end, he bowed to her. "That was lovely. You are quite the dancer."

"A compliment I am happy to accept." She gave him a slight curtsey and smiled genuinely at him.

The man tipped his head to Adrastus, who was speaking with a small cluster of Fae. He was watching Kelera as he spoke to them, and she smiled at him. The man leaned in and said, "It seems your companion is occupied. Shall we grab a drink?"

Kelera weighed her options. Adrastus was clearly still looking out for her and the drink table was only a few feet away. He would be nearby, so she didn't see the harm in it. "That sounds great."

The table was filled with decanters of wine and plates piled high with food. After eating nothing but dried meat in the last few hours, the food here looked too delicious to pass up. She grabbed a small cloth from the table and loaded it with thick crusted bread and spread berry jam on them. The man offered her a short horn of wine.

"My name is Bothwell, by the way."

Kelera swallowed the food she had shoved into her mouth—not her most lady-like moment—and said, "I'm Sera."

"Well, *Sera*," he emphasized the false name, making her breath catch in her throat. She stilled until he continued, "are you finding the revel to your liking?"

"I am." It was the truth. Being on the run with Adrastus was teaching her to bask in small moments of pleasure. At this rate, she never knew if it might be her last.

Bothwell took a long drink of his wine. "I come here every year. I wasn't sure I'd make it this year though with the Queen in the state that she's in."

Kelera wasn't sure how to respond. She took a large sip of the wine to buy herself time. The man surely assumed she was a member of the Spring Court. Should she appear saddened by his words? Or hopeful? Instead, she opted to say, "It is important for us to celebrate life even in times of hardship."

"Spoken very elegantly, Sera. That is, after all, the true spirit of Beltane—the celebration of life."

Her head buzzed from the wine. It was rather potent. Absentmindedly, she said, "It's my birthday." She wasn't sure why she shared the information, but it was nice to tell someone.

Something flickered in Bothwell's eyes, and she couldn't pinpoint exactly what it was. He set his drink down on the table. "Is that so?"

"Yes. Twenty years ago on this day." She stopped herself before she could say, *Twenty years ago, on this day, my mother brought me into this world. Only to abandon me months later.* What would things have been like if she hadn't? How different would things have turned out if she had been raised alongside the Fae in the Spring Court? She never would have fallen into Samael's clutches, that was for sure. She would have known how to control her power... But she also would never have known her father. The man who had raised her with love, warmth, and affection.

Adrastus excused himself from the group and started walking in her direction. *And I never would have met him*, she thought to herself. Would her path have crossed with Adrastus' if she had grown up in Elfhame? Or would she have been just another Fae in the crowd to him?

She took another sip of the wine, enjoying the way it warmed her throat and chest. Was she sharing too much with the stranger? She hiccupped. *Uh oh, this is why I don't drink.*

Bothwell leaned against the table and tilted his head. "Your parents, they still reside in the Spring Court?"

Kelera stilled. "My father is... abroad. And my mother..." The word was like ash on her tongue. "She has been absent for quite some time."

"I'm very sad to hear that."

Bothwell's eyes narrowed as he watched her. She'd said too much and needed to watch her words more carefully. Suddenly, her mouth went dry, so she took another drink.

She only relaxed slightly when Bothwell changed the subject. "Your companion seems rather... uneasy." He gestured to Adrastus, who was approaching them now. "Afraid I might steal you away?"

Kelera giggled at Adrastus' furrowed brow. "Oh, that's just Dras being Dras." Her eyes widened at the admission of his real name. *Shit*. A laugh escaped her, and she covered her mouth with her hands. This wine was potent.

Bothwell flashed a smile at her. "I see." He bowed his head. "It is a pleasure to meet you, *Lady Kelera*."

She opened her mouth to deny it, but there was no point. The jig was up. Adrastus was going to be so cross with her. Instead of anticipation, another laugh bubbled from her throat.

Adrastus had reached them now, placing himself between her and Bothwell. Kelera hiccupped again between giggles. "I believe I may have slipped up."

Bothwell pipped up quickly, "Oh no, my dear, you have nothing to fear from me." He extended a hand to Adrastus. "Allow me to formally introduce myself. I am Bothwell Greenguard, high master of the Queen's council. Oliver says the two of you have a rather bold request of me."

Adrastus hesitated, then took his hand. "We are honored that you have agreed to meet with us."

"Ah, I simply wanted to see you both with my own eyes before risking my reputation."

Kelera took another sip of wine and wiggled her eyebrows at him. "Like what you see?"

Adrastus' brows knitted together as he stared at her with shock. "Wha—"

Bothwell chuckled. "What I see are two Fae who honor the Spring Court and their traditions. It would be my pleasure to discuss things further. Perhaps you can tell me of your strife on the way to the palace tomorrow."

Adrastus argued, "Time is of the essence."

Bothwell held a hand up. "The trouble will still be there when we wake. Tonight is not a night for problem solving, it is a night for rejoice. I will be waiting for you here when the sun sets its eyes upon us."

Kelera tried to listen to Adrastus' response, but the forest was spinning around them as if it were dancing to the Beltane music. Was this part of the Spring Court's magic? She looked down at the wine in her hand. Perhaps it would be best to stop drinking. She reached out to set the wine down on the table, but she misjudged the distance and it clattered to the ground. The wine had definitely gotten to her.

Embarrassed, she bent down to pick it up, but tumbled down next to it. By the stars, she never would have allowed herself to get this drunk in the mortal court. The ridiculousness of it all sent her into a fit of laughter.

Adrastus leapt to her side and glared accusingly at Bothwell. "What did you give her?"

Bothwell looked genuinely confused as he replied, "Just some wine."

Adrastus picked up the horn that she had dropped and sniffed at the drops that were still left inside. He cursed under his breath, "Dammit. Elfwine."

Bothwell sounded baffled as he said, "I didn't mean any harm. I thought..."

Kelera didn't hear the end of his sentence because Adrastus had already scooped her up into his arms and was carrying her away from the table. She peeked over his shoulder and waved merrily at Bothwell. He waved back hesitantly before being joined by the other revelers. They raised their cups to toast to their goddess as she was carted away by her chosen mate. She beamed back at them and blew them a kiss.

Adrastus was still carrying her, and she leaned back in his arms to look up at the stars. They seemed to shine brighter in the sky, and she swore they were dancing just for her. She draped her head back to look at the party, which was becoming increasingly far away. Suddenly, an upside-down Jinx stepped into view. He had foregone his mask and his face was flushed.

Kelera giggled. "Why are you so sweaty?"

His one eye widened with surprise. "Is she *drunk*?"

Adrastus growled. "On Elfwine."

"Oh." Jinx's face fell into a frown and Kelera giggled again because, from her upside-down angle, it looked like a smile.

Adrastus repositioned her in his arms, bouncing her around and making her feel ill. "The emissary has made contact, but refuses to hear more from us until the celebration is over."

Jinx sounded joyous as he said, "A man after my own heart."

Adrastus snorted. "I'm taking her back to the camp. Let the others know. We'll see you back there."

"Don't wait up." Jinx raised his flask, then bounded back to the revel.

Why did they get to have all the fun? Kelera pouted as Adrastus carried her through the forest. "Why do they get to stay? I didn't want to leave yet."

"You're drunk. You need to sleep." His voice was clipped. He was displeased with her. Such a pity.

Kelera closed her eyes. Maybe he was right. When they reached the camp, he laid her down on her bedroll, and she rolled to her side. He took his place beside her, removed her mask, and brushed her hair from her face. His touch felt exquisite, like she could feel it in her soul. *Stars, I should not have drunk all that wine.*

She sighed, "It's my birthday, you know."

He ran a hand through her hair. "Happy birthday, little thief."

She relished in the way he said the nickname he had given her when she had stolen Cierine away from captivity and taken her and the other mortal servants to the border—the servants who had died because of her failure. "I could have been happy here, you know. The servants, Ammon, and Chaz, would still be alive. If she had wanted me, then things would have been different."

Adrastus' voice was low and husky as he said, "You don't know that your mother didn't want you. We don't know why she left you with your father."

"I could have been free here." She sighed as sleep claimed her.

It was still dark when she awoke. Adrastus was sitting at her feet, tending to the fire. She watched him for a moment—his tall, solid build, and the way his shoulders slumped as if something were weighing on him.

"Dras." Her voice cracked as she called out softly to him. Her head was pounding from the wine, which had thankfully worn off by now. It was a relief that her mind was no longer fuzzy and that her thoughts were clear once more. *Note to self,* she thought, *do not accept drinks from a stranger at a revel.*

Adrastus turned to her and pasted a smile on his face. She could tell it was forced when it didn't meet his eyes. "Feeling better?"

"Not so much. My head feels like it's filled with rocks."

"Here, this will help." He handed her a flask. When she scrunched her nose at it, not wanting anymore alcohol, he said, "It's water from the spring."

Gratefully, she took it and drank deeply. The cool water soothed her throat and the throbbing in her head started to fade away. Then she asked, "How long have I been asleep?"

"A few hours."

That explained why she wasn't feeling the effects of the wine anymore. Sheepishly she said, "I'm so embarrassed... I've never actually been drunk before." She groaned as memories returned. "Oh stars, I hate to think what the emissary must think of me."

"Don't fret. He seemed quite taken with you, actually. Besides, Elfwine does that to the best of us. And for a half mortal, I'm surprised it didn't have a stronger effect on you."

"What do you mean?"

"Elfwine has been around for a long time. Long before the treaty with the mortal court, it was used to drug mortals who happened upon our revels. It would cause them to forget themselves. They would dance into a sort of dreamland, then find themselves waking days or even years later to find that they never left the revel."

Kelera's stomach did a flip. Perhaps the history books in Nevene hadn't gotten it all wrong. "Oh," was all she could say.

"Kelera," Adrastus turned to face her with a serious look on his face, "when you said you would have been free had you been born and raised here in Elfhame..." He ran his hand through his dark raven hair as if waiting for the right words to come. "You could still have that, you know. The freedom."

Carefully, Kelera said, "If I stayed, you mean."

"Would it be so horrible?" There was hope in his voice and Kelera felt a piece of her heart break.

She mustered up the courage to say the words out loud. "The truth is, it wouldn't be horrible at all. All looming threats aside, if Samael was defeated and Elfhame and the mortal realm were both safe again, then I could be incredibly happy here. I wouldn't have to hide who and what I am. I wouldn't have to pretend anymore." She thought about Gadreel, Gilby, Tobias, and even Ragnor and his band. "And I have friends here. More friends than I ever had back in Nevene."

Adrastus took hold of her hands. "Then stay."

Her breath caught in her throat. Wasn't that what she wanted him to say before? That he wanted her to stay. But nothing had changed. It still wasn't safe and as much as she dreamed of a world where there was no threat to the people she cared about, it wasn't the reality.

"Dras." She put her hand on his face, running her thumb along the scar that matched her own.

His eyes bore into hers. "Stay, Kelera. I will make it safe. I promise you. I will fix all of this. Your father, Cierine, they will all be okay. I can help you find your mother if that is what you truly want. I can give you whatever it is that you've been searching for all your life. You just have to give me the chance."

She clung to the words he was saying. What he was offering was everything she'd ever dreamed of. To her, he was offering the world. He was offering a home. She leaned in until her lips met his. His mouth opened softly, and she slid her tongue against his. He tasted sweet, like the wine they had been drinking earlier.

His hands came to her waist, lowering her down onto the bedroll. His breath was coming faster now as he positioned himself over her. "I mean what I say, little thief. There is a difference between fitting in and belonging. With the mortals, you will always be fighting a war within yourself, trying to be one of them. But here, in Elfhame, you *belong*. Just as you are." He leaned down to kiss her again and her heart bloomed for him and his words.

This was all she'd ever wanted. She had locked away the half of her that was Fae—the half that called to Elfhame and yearned for freedom—because it had been the only thing she could think to do in order to find happiness. But what he was offering her was something more than that. It was a chance to not only be herself, but to embrace it fully without reservation.

She tangled her fingers in his hair and kissed his neck. If Adrastus, a Prince of Unseelie, was willing to accept her and offer her a place here, then why should anyone expect her to turn that away? His leg made its way between her thighs and she let out a soft moan as the heat of her magic flooded her. Even her power was responding to his touch.

His hand roved down her body, taking its time to reach her thighs. He kissed her deeply, then paused before his hand went any further. "Is this what you want?"

Kelera could hardly keep track of her racing thoughts. Was he still talking about staying in Elfhame with him? Or was he talking about the two of them, here and now?

His fingers gripped her legs, and she parted them slightly. Definitely here and now. Her fingers ached to touch him as he was touching her, but she hesitated. She was a virgin. Untouched and untainted. But here in this magical forest, beneath the stars of Elfhame with Adrastus, the thought of allowing him to take her didn't seem wrong. Instead, there was beauty in it. In allowing herself to do as she pleased without worrying about what anyone else would think. *I could love this man*, she thought to herself. Not in the way she'd believed she could love Alexander. Adrastus wasn't a stranger to her. He'd let her see the worst and best parts of him. Even in his darkest moments, she cared for him and understood him. She could truly love him if she allowed herself. And that was the only truth that mattered right now.

She nodded. "This is what I want." Then she kissed him fiercely and without reservation.

His hand slipped beneath her feathered dress and met her bare flesh. His restless fingers trailed up her skin, reaching the place that her undergarments should have been. He stopped, allowing his fingers to rest in place with a look of pleasant surprise on his face.

Breathlessly, Kelera said, "I didn't have anything clean to change into."

"It seems fate knew what would happen tonight, even if we didn't." He leaned down, planting soft kisses along her collarbone.

His fingers moved again, reaching the place where no man had ever touched her before. The intensity when he stroked the most sensitive part of her left her breathless. Her body shuddered under the touch, and she ached for more. As if reading her mind, Adrastus slid his fingers inside of her, navigating a part of her body that not even she had been brave enough to explore.

His other hand came to her breast, grazing them under the light fabric of the dress. She ran her fingers along his scarred back, pulling him closer to her. Her hands drifted over the puckered skin, wishing she could take away all the pain he had ever endured.

He brought his lips close to her ear and whispered, "I want to be the man you believe I can be. And you give me the courage to try. Stay with me, Kelera."

This time, there was no question. He was pleading with her to stay with him. And this time, there was no hesitation in her mind. She would. To hell with Samael and the mortals in King Tristan's court who had scoffed and turned up their noses at her. To hell with what everyone thought. She had made a vow on the day that Samael had scarred her face to never cower before anyone again.

She couldn't forget that. And Adrastus would help her make sure of it. He took his hand away and her body screamed in the absence of his touch. He kissed her on the mouth again and his body nestled between her legs.

She reached down and fumbled at his pants, drawing them down around his thighs. He was tender as their bodies melded together. She cried out at the momentary pressure and sting of him entering her.

He stilled and between heavy breaths, asked, "Are you alright, Kelera?"

She kissed him softly. "Yes, I'm more than alright." She pulled him closer in a silent signal for him to keep going. She'd crossed into uncharted territory, but there was no shame or guilt. Primal instinct took over as she moved her hips with his. Each movement brought on a tantalizing pleasure that threatened to consume her. She was so engulfed in the sensation building in her that she called out his name.

It seemed to fuel him as he pushed deeper. The binding ceremony had brought their power together, but now it was as if their bodies were one as well. When they both reached the peak of their ecstasy, Kelera swore the stars above them glowed brighter. And in that moment, she wondered if she, too, would forever shine a little brighter.

Chapter Ten

Kelera was back in the Unseelie Palace, running through the halls in a deep blue velvet gown and laughing. The hallway shifted with each command she gave it, taking her exactly where she wanted to go. To Adrastus. When she reached the throne room, he was waiting for her and beside him was a second throne... Her throne. He was dazzling in his black jacket, donning the Unseelie crest. And a crown of silver glinted atop his head with a blood-red stone in the center. She reached for the top of her own head and her fingers met cool metal. Pulling it from her neatly styled hair, she studied it. A stone and crown that matched Adrastus'.

Her stomach fluttered like the wings of a thousand pixies. She bounded up the steps to get to him, but to her horror, they continued to grow. Step after step, she could never quite reach him.

Sweat beaded down her back as she relentlessly struggled to ascend the steps. After what seemed like forever, she reached the *top of the stairs and held her hand out to Adrastus. Sparks flew as their fingers met. Before she could fully take hold of his hand, his skin turned to ash, and he blew away. Terrified, Kelera turned to where the courtiers stood. Among them were her father and Cierine. They smiled sadly at her as they burst into flames and faded away with nothing but embers and drifting ash left behind.*

She woke with a start and the subtle scent of a smoldering fire filled her nose. The hair on her arms stood on end. A dying fire like the one in her dream. She tried to ground herself. The Unseelie Palace was gone. She was in the Spring Court with Adrastus.

She sighed with relief as she settled into his arms. The heat from his body shielded her from the crisp morning air. Memories of her night with him replaced the horror of her nightmare, though the smell of fire still lingered. She tried to reassure herself. It was likely from the Beltane fire that would finally be dying down.

She buried her face in Adrastus' bare chest, willing herself to stay in the present moment. After the passion they had shared, she'd fallen asleep in his arms, content to rest her head on his chest and drift off into oblivion.

She inhaled the familiar scent of him, reminding herself that the dream likely meant nothing. He was still there, sleeping peacefully, with no knowledge of the horror she had witnessed. The sun was beginning to rise, which meant Bothwell would be waiting for them. It would be best not to mention the dream to Adrastus for now. He would have enough to worry about today.

Kelera's troubles would have to wait. She'd had plenty of nightmares since Ammon's death and since this particular one didn't have any magical repercussions like she'd experienced in the Summer Court inn, she chalked it up to being nothing but a bad dream. It was likely just her anxiety about the shift in their relationship playing itself out in the depths of her subconscious.

Adrastus groaned, stretched his arms out above his head, then ran his hand through her hair. He stroked it gently and kissed the top of her head. His voice was husky as he said, "Good morning, little thief."

Their naked bodies were pressed together and warmth crept into her like the night before. She looked up at him with a blush. But before she had the chance to respond to him, the Guardians came stumbling into camp. Jinx whistled. "Looks like someone embraced her Beltane duty as the Goddess last night."

Kelera buried her face in Adrastus' shoulder to hide her flushed cheeks. She was incredibly grateful for the blanket of furs he had draped over them before they fell asleep. Adrastus threw a rock in Jinx's direction, and he frowned as he hopped out of the way.

Kelera chided them, "If you gentlemen don't mind, I would like to get dressed now."

Now it was Jinx's turn to blush. "Of course, Milady." In perfect sync, the Guardians turned their backs to Kelera and Adrastus, facing the forest.

They waited patiently as Adrastus handed Kelera her a set of travel clothes. The dirt and grime of their journey from the Winter Court had been washed away, and she looked at him questioningly.

Adrastus pulled his shirt over his head and explained, "I washed them in the spring while you were asleep."

"I appreciate that."

He grinned. "I made sure to wash your delicates as well. Can't have you out running around without your unmentionables." He winked.

"There's a reason they're called unmentionables, Dras. As in, don't mention them," she scolded, but couldn't help smiling back at him.

She dressed quickly and cleared her throat, letting the men know it was safe to turn back around.

Adrastus sidled up to her then announced, "Pack quickly. We are to meet Bothwell and go with him to the palace. He was clear that we would have that amount of time to convince him to vouch for us."

The Guardians were no longer in a joking mood. They must have known the severity of this goal. Ragnor threw his pack over his shoulder as he said, "Understood."

Jinx had drunk entirely too much the night before. Kelera was forced to spend the better part of the morning hanging back with him while he got sick behind various bushes and trees. Up ahead, Bothwell and Adrastus led the way, with Tepin and Ragnor following close behind. She didn't mind bringing up the rear of their little band, though. She trusted Adrastus to know how best to convince their new acquaintance that the safety of the entire realm rested on their collective shoulders.

And the distance from Adrastus allowed her to collect her thoughts about what had happened the previous night. She had never really thought about her virginity before. It wasn't uncommon for young men and women their age to engage in pre-marital acts in the mortal court. But she had always done things by the book. She had always imagined it would be something she would experience with the man who would be her husband.

Jinx dry heaved beside her and she patted him on the back. When he was able to walk again, he whined, "I'll never see her again."

Here we go again, Kelera thought with annoyance. He had been droning on and on about the mysterious woman he had met at the revel. *The great love of his life,* as he called her. Though he hadn't gotten her name. Kelera reassured him, "If it's meant to be, then your paths will cross again."

"I hope so." He sniffled. "Love doesn't come easy."

"No," Kelera mused, "it sure doesn't." She watched Adrastus walking ahead of her, out of earshot. "Can I ask you something, Jinx?"

"Of course." He wiped his nose with his sleeve, and she fought back the urge to cringe.

"How do you know when it's love?" Her mind drifted to the way she had completely and utterly lost herself with Adrastus. It had felt so right. And even now, she craved his touch again.

"Easy. It's when you can't possibly imagine yourself with anyone else in the world. I like to think of it as *souls* binding. Sort of like the way your magic is bound to Prince Adrastus."

Bound. Was that how she felt in her heart? It was true that she could no longer imagine going home to Nevene to marry Alexander. She'd believed she could come to care for him, but she hadn't felt as if she could never live without him. Adrastus, on the other hand... it was hard to imagine being apart from him. He understood her and supported her. Her feelings for him were something she couldn't put into words.

But she couldn't shake the nightmare. He had burned away at her touch. They all had.

Bothwell announced from up ahead, "Nearly there!"

Kelera questioned his definition of nearly. They were approaching an opening in the trees, but she couldn't see anything but a river. The water was dark and seemed too deep to wade across. She grabbed onto Jinx's sleeve. "Are we going to swim across?"

She was a decent swimmer, but the river was wide and the water was rushing faster than she was comfortable with. Jinx scratched under his eyepatch and yelled to Ragnor, "I'm in no shape to be swimmin' boss."

Ragnor rolled his shoulders back. "Aye, I'm feeling the same way." Then he turned to Tepin. "Care to get us across?"

Tepin cracked his knuckles and grinned. "I'll see what I can do." He raised his hands above his head and Kelera's jaw dropped when she saw the water shift.

She jogged to catch up to them at the bank and took her place by Adrastus. "Is he stopping the water?"

Adrastus sounded just as awestruck as she was. "Looks like it."

Jinx chuckled. "Just wait for it."

As if in response, Tepin closed his hands into tight fists. The water began to part, allowing a glimpse of the wet earth underneath.

Jinx puffed out his chest. "He's a master river wielder."

"Jinx," Ragnor growled in warning.

But it was too late. Tepin buckled under the pressure and the river crashed violently back together. She gasped. No way was she going to put herself at the bottom of a raging river.

Ragnor glared at Jinx, who dipped his head in apology.

Tepin shook out his hands with a pained frown. "Well, that's rather embarrassing. I admit I'm not quite myself after a night of reveling."

Adrastus crept close to Kelera. "Do you think you could help him?"

"No." Kelera's answer came out before she could really stop to consider it. She wasn't familiar with water magic, but she had been able to call upon the sea when they were in the Summer Court. She wiggled her fingers at her side. Her magic had been overtly present since coming to the Spring Court. If it was stronger in the land where she had been born, then would it give her the ability to call on any element she wished?

Her voice shook as she said, "I can try to help."

Tepin smiled at her gratefully as she took her place beside him. He took her hand in his, raising it in the air and extended his other hand. Kelera followed suit and stared down at the water. She pictured what she wanted it to do, imagining it stopping and spreading wide enough for them to pass through.

It was as if the water itself was rushing through her veins as Tepin's magic flowed through their locked hands and out to the river. The water parted, leaving them a narrow path, just big enough to walk through one at a time. Kelera took a step back, still holding onto Tepin's hand. "Are you certain it will hold?" If their power faltered for even a split second, it could send the water crashing down on them. The pressure would be their end.

"We are the water's master. Believe that, and it will hold."

Jinx swatted a hand in the air. "Tepin does this all the time."

"Shut up, man." Ragnor shook his head like a frustrated father.

Jinx jumped down the bank and stood between the parted river. "I'm just explaining to our friends here that his mom was a river sprite."

Kelera looked at Tepin and his broad frame. "Aren't river sprites very small?"

Adrastus chuckled as he jumped down from the bank. "Can't believe everything you hear in the mortal books, little thief." He held out a hand to help her down, and she took it.

Once she was standing on the bottom of the riverbed, she began to sweat. She followed behind Adrastus and tried not to think about how their fate was in the hands of her—a halfling who had only used water magic once before—and a man who had drunk until the sun rose just a few hours ago.

The water was still around them, but she could spot colorful fish swimming wildly around. She and Tepin had disrupted the natural flow of the river, and the wildlife was no longer sure of where to go. One small fish with golden scales swam along the water's wall, keeping pace with her. She was so amused by the little fish that she didn't realize they'd already reached the other side of the riverbank. Adrastus gave her a hand and pulled her up.

She was glad to have changed out of the white dress from the previous night. The thought of the delicate swan feathers being coated in mud made her sad. She wanted to remember that dress just as it had been when Adrastus had made love to her on the forest floor. Her fingers fumbled as she straightened her vest and remembered the way she'd dug those very fingers into his back the night before.

The vest and the rest of her clothes smelled much better than they had when she'd changed out of them in the Summer Court, and she was grateful that Adrastus had taken the time to wash her them in the spring. His attentiveness astounded her. As a prince—especially one of Unseelie—washing someone's clothes like a lady's maid was the last thing she would have expected.

The sound of water crashing startled her, and she turned to see the river running its natural course. Tepin wiped away the sweat on his face with the back of his sleeve and began to walk as if nothing had happened. His strength was impressive, and she was proud of her part in helping him. She wondered if he could teach her more.

Bothwell patted her on the shoulder. "Well done!" He tilted his head and his eyes danced with curiosity. "You're quite powerful."

Kelera beamed with pride. She had used her magic with no negative consequence and it felt amazing. To top it off, she had impressed the emissary. Perhaps that would earn them a few points when it came time for him to make his decision.

Adrastus nudged her in the shoulder and pointed ahead to large rocky mounds in the ground. "The Seelie Palace is just past here."

Kelera clenched and unclenched her fists in nervous anticipation. By dinnertime, they would be in the heart of the Seelie Court. That was how long they had to sway Bothwell to their side if he hadn't made up his mind already. They were so close to the safety they'd been hoping for. There, they would be surrounded by the palace guards, near an army that would hopefully stand between them and Samael. But it would all come down to him.

Her heart raced at the thought of their journey coming to an end. Last night she had been so committed to the idea of staying in Elfhame, but first she would need to get word to the mortal court. She needed to make sure her father was safe before she truly made up her mind on what she was going to do with the rest of her life.

Adrastus slowed to keep pace with her. "Wait until you see the palace. There's nothing like it."

Kelera grabbed hold of his sleeve to stop him. "Listen, Dras, once we reach the palace..."

He looked away, avoiding her eye. "You have to leave."

"I have to go warn my father. If the Queen can give me a guide, then I can go to them. Explain what's happening. They need to know that there is a traitor working with Samael."

Adrastus looked back at her and sighed. "I know. I said I'd help you and I meant it. But you'll be back, right? After you warn them."

"I would like to. But I have to speak to my father first... and Alexander."

"The fiancé. Right." Adrastus pursed his lips. "Then we'd better get moving." His mood had shifted, reminding her of the indifferent version of himself that he had shown her in the Unseelie palace. His own sort of mask.

Kelera didn't push the subject any further as she followed him to the mounds. From a distance, she had thought they were rocks left to erode over time. But now that she was close enough to touch them, she was stunned. They were shaped like enormous men laying curled up on the ground. Massive beasts, like the giants she had read about in children's stories. They were hunched over and covered in moss.

Astonished, she asked, "Are these sculptures?"

Adrastus shook his head. "No one really knows. Legend says they are giants who long ago roamed Elfhame. As they grew old, they became very tired. So, they decided to rest here. The stories say that they will sleep here until a time when Elfhame needs them again."

"That's quite a tale." It wasn't hard to believe here in a realm where skeletal men rode in the sky and powerful Fae parted rivers. But if there was ever a time that Elfhame needed help, it was now. Why not wake from their slumber?

They wove their way between the resting beasts. It was unsettling to think that creatures this large may have once roamed the land. Ragnor led the way, sure of his ability to navigate the familiar territory. But when a cool breeze brushed through Kelera's hair, he raised his hand, bringing them to a halt.

A wind swept by again, this time from the other direction. It made the hairs on Kelera's arms stand on end. Adrastus grabbed her roughly and threw her to the ground. She yelped in shock as something slammed into him. That would have been her. She shot up to her feet and ran around one of the boulders to find Adrastus alone on the ground.

He shouted to the men, "Get eyes on it!"

The men drew their weapons and Kelera regretted not making them give her one of her own. Adrastus strode over to her with blood running from his brow. She reached a hand up to his face. "You're hurt."

"I'm fine." He moved his head away from her and his eyes roved over her. "Are you alright? I saw her coming. I didn't want her to grab you."

"I'm okay, I promise." Kelera looked around the clearing. "What was that thing?"

"Some sort of wraith. I've only seen one like that before." He positioned himself in front of her. "One of Samael's playmates."

Her imagination took her to a place she really didn't want it to go. Wandering to the dark depths of what Samael and his so called playmates could possibly like to do together. She shivered. That meant the wraith was there to collect them. "Can't we make a run for it?"

"The palace is too far. We might not all make it."

"Okay, so we stay and fight, then. You can draw on my magic."

A screech tore through the air and a tall figure appeared from out of nowhere. It wore long, willowy robes and seemed to float above the ground. The wraith's skin was gray and sagging, like loose leather. Her lifeless eyes met Kelera's, and it summoned her with a wag of its long bony finger.

Adrastus pushed Kelera further behind him. "Not a chance."

The wraith's mouth elongated to reveal rows of dagger sharp teeth. The scream that came next was like a thousand panes of glass shattering all at once. It clouded Kelera's vision, and she covered her ears.

When the screaming stopped, there were no sounds around them. Kelera couldn't even hear the sound of her own breathing. For a moment, she thought the wraith had deafened her until she heard it speak. The sound came from inside her own mind and she turned to Adrastus to see if he could hear it, too. He gave her a curt nod and took her hand in his.

The wraith spoke with a scratchy voice, "Children of spring. I am here to collect what is owed to the King of all realms. Come with me now, and I will not harm the Guardians or the Queen's man."

Kelera looked at Ragnor and the others who stood with their weapons drawn. The hard determination in their eyes told her that they wouldn't back down. Bothwell, on the other hand looked shaken, with wide eyes and trembling hands. *Good,* she thought. *Let him see firsthand what sort of threat Samael poses to his people.*

The wraith cackled at them. "So, you intend to fight me? You are more foolish than you look." Cloudy magic crept from her hands, bringing with it a putrid smell. She cooed, "Very well."

Kelera's vision darkened and the beautiful, lush, green landscape around them turned to fire. She could feel the heat of the flames and something told her this was no ordinary vision. Fear swelled in her and she gripped Adrastus' hand as tightly as she could.

The wraith sounded pleased as the words rolled off her lips, "I can taste your fear like rotting fruit, halfling. You've seen this before, haven't you? In your dreams, perhaps?"

Adrastus looked at Kelera with confusion and she kicked herself for not telling him about the nightmare from the night before. He asked, "What is she talking about, Kelera?"

The wraith answered for her. "She saw what will happen if she stays. Didn't you?"

Kelera stood her ground. "It was nothing but a nightmare."

The wraith floated closer to them, her ragged robes flowing around her. "Stupid girl. What you saw was so much more than that. It is what will happen when your magic consumes you. You will destroy everything you hold dear and be left with nothing but ashes to tend to. Come now, dear, you know I speak the truth. Embers and ash with nothing more to fight for." She paused and grinned to reveal black, broken teeth. "Unless..."

"Unless what?" She couldn't help herself. If the wraith was telling the truth, then Kelera would do anything to protect Adrastus and the people she loved from the fate she saw.

"Give your fear to me. Think of how much happier you could be if you released it to me so that I might devour it. You would never have to be afraid again."

No fear. There had been many times when Kelera wished she would stop letting her fear stand in her way. Would it be so bad to live a life without it?

Adrastus' voice was firm. "Don't even think about it, little thief."

"But without it—"

"Without it, you will lose all sense of self preservation." He turned to the wraith. "Isn't that right? Without fear, she wouldn't know when to hold back. She would put herself and everyone she loves at risk."

The wraith shook with anger. "*Bastard.*"

Adrastus raised his hands and with it, shadows rose around him and Kelera. An icy chill filled the air, and she knew this was his Unseelie magic. He bared his teeth at the wraith and said, "Why don't you go back to the hole you crawled out of?"

His shadows shot out at the wraith, catching her off guard and pinning her to the ground. Ragnor jumped at the opening and took his knife to her throat. He began to cut into it.

The wraith thrashed around the ground and sent a wave of magic into Adrastus and Kelera. Adrastus' eyes went white as he fell into a fit on the ground. He yelled out in pain and a jolt of adrenaline shot through Kelera. What was the wraith doing to him?

Ragnor was still sawing into the wraith's neck. But it was taking too long. Adrastus could be dead before they removed the wraith's head. Kelera pushed past her fear and called on her magic. Using the link between her and Adrastus, she allowed her magic to flow into him.

There was something different this time, too. Power was emanating from every part of her body, flowing up from the tips of her toes to the crown of her head. It was as if the very magic from the land was surging through her and making her power whole.

She could see her magic through his veins, turning golden and cutting through the darkness around them. He closed his eyes and when he opened them again, they were the familiar green that Kelera loved so much. With a roar, he pushed the wraith's magic from him. Just as it snapped away from him, Ragnor tore the wraith's head from its body. He threw it to the side and wiped the sweat from his brow.

Jinx kicked the head further away and snarled, "That was one nasty bitch."

Kelera ignored them and ran to Adrastus. She knelt to the ground and checked him over. She ran her hands over him, looking for any sign of injury. He grabbed her hands gently and held them still. "I'm okay. I shouldn't have let her get the jump on me. I—"

Kelera cut him off with a kiss. She tore her hands away from his and placed them on his cheeks. "You scared me."

"So, it seems that fear does come in handy after all," he joked. More seriously, he said, "You did good, little thief."

He was right. There had been no casualties—no one caught in the crossfire this time. The clearing was back to normal, with the setting sun casting soft light on the healthy green grass. There were no fires or other signs that her magic was out of control. She was proud of herself. The confidence gave her newfound courage as she kissed him again, more deeply this time. The thought of losing him was almost too much to bear. Maybe Jinx had been right after all... maybe this could be love.

Chapter Eleven

K elera's heart was still racing as she and the others gathered up their things. The wraith had slowed their pace down considerably, and there wasn't a moment to spare. She wasn't the only one who was still recovering from the attack. The men's exhaustion was plain as day in the way their shoulders slumped. The palace still wasn't within sight and they had lost daylight.

Bothwell was silent for a while before he spoke. "Samael's reach is further than I had wanted to believe. It is worse than any of us on the council thought."

Adrastus said through clenched teeth, "If you believe nothing else that I say, do believe me when I say this: Do not underestimate my brother."

Adrastus had a slight limp as he walked behind Kelera. Though he didn't say it, she knew he was hurting after the altercation with the wraith. She wished Gadreel had covered more on healing magic when she had trained with him in the Unseelie library.

Worried for Adrastus, she asked, "Are you sure you're alright?"

He ignored her question, asking one of his own, "Why didn't you tell me about the dream?" He stopped walking and winced as he rubbed at his leg.

Kelera wrapped her arms around herself. "I wasn't sure what to make of it. After what happened between us, I didn't want to ruin anything or make you think that I regretted it."

"Do you regret it?" His eyes were searching her as if he was hoping to read her thoughts.

"No," she answered quickly. "Not at all." She took a step closer to him, wanting to bridge the distance that the wraith's foreboding words threatened to create between them.

Adrastus pushed a strand of hair from her face and cupped her cheek. "Good. Because I need to say something while I still have the chance. Maybe I should have said it long before now, but I didn't think you were ready to hear it."

Kelera's heart skipped a beat. What could he have possibly been keeping from her? She nodded cautiously. "Go on."

Adrastus let out a big breath. She couldn't remember ever seeing him this nervous. He stepped close enough that she could feel the heat of his body as he said, "I've grown up in a family where violence is strength and selfishness is common. I've done all the wrong things. I failed to protect you, left you to the whims of my brother..."

"Dras, we've already talked about this. You were doing what you thought would protect your people."

He grimaced, then continued, "I should have trusted you from the beginning. You are so much more than anyone could have imagined—than *I* could have imagined."

Heat flooded her cheeks. The look in his eyes mesmerized her. No man had ever looked at her like this before. Like she was the center of the entire universe. She had to admit, he was more than she imagined, too. He made her feel like the person she was always meant to be. When she was with him, she felt *seen*. It was a feeling she had only ever experienced with her father and Cierine. It was hard to imagine any other man giving that to her.

But the wraith had known about her dream. And that revelation made the images of Adrastus and everyone she cared about turning to ash feel very much *real*. What if returning to Elfhame to be with him after all of this was over meant his downfall? Was she willing to risk everything to find out?

Adrastus sighed. "What I'm trying to say is, I love you, little thief. I have for a while now. And after last night, I think you could love me, too."

It was like the breath had rushed out of her. Her hands began to tremble at her sides. "You love me?" The words felt strange on her tongue. This should have been a beautiful moment. But the fear was too overwhelming. What if loving her destroyed him?

So, she argued, "You can't, Dras. The dream... I watched everything around me burn. Fire consumed you, my father, Cierine... and it was all because of me."

Adrastus' eyes darkened. "It was a dream, nothing more. The wraith was trying to use your fear of it to manipulate you." He gritted his teeth as he said, "It meant nothing."

"We can't know that. Please, just listen. When we reach the Seelie palace, I have to go back to warn the mortals. And maybe it would be safer for everyone if I just—"

"Stayed," he interrupted her, "in Nevene? For good."

She nodded slowly. "At least until we can know for sure that the dream was just that."

"You would give up your chance at true happiness for *them*," he spat.

Kelera flinched at the obvious disdain in his voice. How easily she forgot where he had come from. He was Fae through and through. She tried to reason with him as she said, "This isn't about the mortals. It's about doing what's right for everyone. Including you. I care for you, Dras, I do." She reached for him, but he pulled away.

"Don't pretend this is about protecting me. You're afraid." He snarled, "The mortals do not deserve your loyalty when they have never given it to you in return."

His words stung. She clenched her fists. "That's not fair."

Adrastus opened his mouth to say more, but Ragnor drew their attention as he shouted, "Riders approaching!"

Kelera spun around to see a banner donning an image of a delicate crown laden with whitish-pink flowers—hawthorns. It was said that the hawthorn held strong magic that promised cleansing, guardianship, and fertility. She reflected back to the Seelie books she'd read in the library with Gadreel. The hawthorn represented the Seelie Queen.

Kelera stood silently beside Adrastus as the riders approached. His declaration of love hung in the air between them. She wanted to reach out to him, but stayed where she was. The Queen's guard was the more pressing matter at hand.

Oliver rode at the head of the small band. He was clothed in bark-colored armor that looked lovely against his golden-brown skin and wore a quiver and bow on his back. He smiled widely when he spotted her and bowed to her from his horse. "Lady Kelera, Prince Adrastus. We've been waiting for you." He then tipped his head to Bothwell and said, "I see you found each other."

Bothwell raised his chin. "I see you did not exaggerate in your claims, Lord Oliver."

Kelera sucked in a sharp breath. "Does that mean you will help us?"

He nodded. "You and your band appear to be pure of heart. I trust your intentions. And after the attack back there, I do believe, should the Seelie Court sit idly by, then danger will befall our land."

Kelera grasped his hand. "You have no idea what this means to us."

Bothwell patted her hand, his kind eyes meeting hers. "I cannot promise you an army. I can only promise that you will be heard by our council."

"That is something." Kelera knew from her own experience in King Tristan's court how difficult it could be to sway an entire council of men. But it was comforting to know that they were garnering support slowly but surely.

Adrastus sounded strained as he addressed Oliver, "What are you doing here? I thought we were to meet you at the palace."

Oliver looked around nervously. "You were. But when you didn't show before sunset as planned, we were worried you might have run into trouble."

You have no idea, Kelera thought with exasperation. She was glad to see him and the armed men who had ridden in with him. When Adrastus made no move to respond, Kelera stepped in and said, "We appreciate your concern." She noticed the way the Queen's guard eyed Ragnor and the others. "May we introduce you to Ragnor, Jinx, and Tepin? Guardians of the Wildwood."

Oliver's eyes widened in surprise. "It is an honor." He and the Queen's guard bowed their heads with respect. Then Oliver continued, "I admit, our arrival isn't wholly out of concern for your well-being."

Kelera's heart pounded in her chest. Oliver's frown told her whatever news he brought wasn't good. "What has happened?"

Oliver twisted his horse's reins in his hands as he said, "Someone has raided the armory. Uniforms and supplies are missing."

Kelera didn't understand how someone could steal such valuable supplies from a place so heavily guarded. "Do you think Samael had anything to do with it?" She thought of how easily he had broken into the Nevene palace and taken the servant girl and Cierine from right under their noses. Whatever he was up to, it wasn't good. Things were escalating if someone had been bold enough to break into the Seelie Palace.

"Perhaps, but the guards saw and heard nothing..." Oliver shifted uncomfortably. "There's something else."

Bothwell barked, "Well, spit it out then."

"We have received word from Prince Gadreel. He says that Samael has amassed a force larger than we expected. He has aid from the mountains and has called upon any man or woman fit to fight in both Autumn and Winter. With the threat he poses to their families, they're all too afraid to deny him. Gadreel says that with such a force, he will have the ability to split them up." Nausea rolled in her stomach as Oliver finished, "He believes Samael plans to hit the mortal realm and the Seelie Court at the same time."

Kelera's head was reeling. "No. When?"

"Soon."

She turned to Adrastus. "I have to go to them."

Adrastus cursed under his breath. "I don't know what my brother is up to, but I can say with some certainty that I don't believe Samael would split his forces. There is no way he would march on the mortal realm until he had control over the Seelie Court and its forces."

"*Some* certainty. That means there's a chance my father and Cierine are in danger as we speak."

Adrastus growled. "It's not safe. The mortals don't stand a chance against Unseelie forces. And *if* what we're hearing is true, then you wouldn't make it in time. You would be walking into occupied territory. I will not have you caught up in that."

Oliver chimed in, "He's right, Kelera. We would need the council's permission before taking any of our soldiers over the border. And even if you got there to warn them in time, the chances of your people defeating a Fae army are slim."

"So, what would you have me do? Sit by as the mortal court is ravaged?" She couldn't let that happen. Her pulse raced as she struggled to think of something, *anything*, that would help her save the mortals. "If you cannot send an army, then send just a few men with me. I will lead them there. We can help the mortals defend themselves."

Oliver and the others waited awkwardly as she and Adrastus faced off with one another. Tension clung to the air, but Kelera didn't care. She had to get to her father.

Adrastus' nose flared. "Even if we had the Seelie army's support—which we do not yet—we couldn't afford to send any of the men away. Between Samael's army and the Night Riders he's created, we can spare no able bodies. We have to defeat Samael here first."

"You promised." Angry tears welled in her eyes and her magic stirred in her like the first signs of a storm.

"If I have to choose," he paused, taking a deep breath, then continued, "if I can only save one, then it will be Elfhame. You must understand that." His eyes were pleading, but all Kelera could focus on was the stab of betrayal that accompanied his words.

This is what she had feared all along. As much as she cared for Adrastus, they would never work. When it came down to it, his loyalty was to his realm—to Elfhame—while her loyalty was to the mortal realm. She owed nothing to Elfhame, even if she had grown to love it. She owed nothing to him.

Kelera raised her chin in defiance. "Then you will understand that I must choose as well." She turned to leave, but his magic wrapped around her wrist. She looked down to see shadows gripping her tightly. The knife of betrayal dug into her heart and twisted. It was almost too much to take, and a small, horrified sob escaped her. He couldn't keep her there. He wouldn't, would he?

His eyes were hard as he said, "I cannot protect you if you go to them."

"Then I release you from your promises."

Adrastus flinched at her words. He spoke slowly, "You are bound to me."

Was that a threat? Kelera tried to pull away from the shadows that were holding her in place. It was no use. Anger began to boil in her. "You promised we'd be equals."

"You just released me from my promises." Softer, he said, "I will do whatever it takes to protect you, Kelera, especially if you are not willing to protect yourself. You're not thinking clearly. If we can defeat Samael here, then we can go to Nevene just as I promised. My brother would not be so foolish as to split his force. If he truly is sending his men into the mortal realm, then it would only be a small party. Surely, your father and his knights are capable of holding them off."

"How can I believe anything you're saying when you don't truly know what Samael is doing?" Her magic flared like crackling flames and his shadows snapped away from her arm. She used the chance to put more distance between them. But the sudden burst of her magic set small fires around her. The flames were low and sputtered in the grass. Oliver and the Queen's guard backed their horses away, glancing at one another nervously.

Adrastus raised his voice. "I have done nothing since our binding, other than try to keep my promises. For star's sake, *I love you!*" His shadows reached out for her again, and she took a few strides back.

"If this is your idea of love, then I don't want it. Love is not a means of control and possession." She felt like someone was sitting on her chest as she tried to get control of her magic. But anger was clouding her mind, making it difficult to hold on to the power threatening to burst from her.

Adrastus looked like she'd punched him in the gut. "That's not fair."

She was hurting him, but she couldn't stop. Not if she was going to get him to let her go. It was clear that he was willing to hold her there by force. She needed to get to her father and if Adrastus would keep her from doing so, then she would need to say something to cut him deep. Something that would make him turn away from her. So she said the one thing she knew would break him. "It's not your fault. I should have known a son of Unseelie could never be capable of understanding what true love means." The words were like acid as they left her mouth, and she hated herself for saying them.

Adrastus' mouth dropped open. His face crumpled for a moment, and Kelera knew she had broken his heart. She stepped further out of reach, but this time he made no move to stop her. Anger replaced the devastation on his face as he straightened and said, "And you do? To you, love is *conditional.* You think if you don't behave a certain way, then people will never love you. I thought we were past all of this, but it appears not."

Her resolve softened, and she went on the defensive. "None of that matters now. I know I shouldn't ask you to put Elfhame at risk. But my position is the same as yours. You believe you must stay and protect Elfhame, and I feel I must go to Nevene and do whatever I can to help."

"You will fail." His words were harsh and his eyes were cold. She'd hurt him, and now it was his turn to do the same.

With her fists balled at her sides, she raised her chin and said, "I will not."

He pointed north. "Go then. Run to the mortals. Give everything you have to offer them. And don't bother returning."

Hot tears streamed down her face. She wiped them away bitterly with the back of her hand. He was letting her go. No. He was *sending her away*. Forever. She wanted to take back the things she had said and beg for his forgiveness. But instead, she turned on her heel and ran as fast as her legs would carry her.

Chapter Twelve

The cold night's breeze swept past Kelera's face as she ran. It occurred to her how irrational it was of her to run off like she had. The Spring Court was unfamiliar territory to her, but she knew if she continued north, then she would eventually reach the blackthorns.

The fight with Adrastus kept replaying in her mind. She regretted the hateful things she'd said to him, but she couldn't take them back now. All she could do was push forward.

If Samael's forces were already marching on Nevene, then she would never make it in time. And what would happen when she did? Without Adrastus to tame her magic, she would be a danger to everyone, not just Samael's army.

"Shit." Kelera cursed out loud as she slowed to a walk. "What am I doing?"

She'd acted out of fear back there with Adrastus. Fear for her father and the place she had called home. Why hadn't he just listened to her? She was only asking for a small force to take with her, after all. She knew he had a duty to the people of Elfhame, and she didn't blame him for needing to make sure they were protected. But why couldn't he understand her side of things? How dare he judge her for choosing her people when he was doing the same?

She ran her hands through her hair, pulling it away from her face. Her hands brushed against the points of her ears and her knees weakened. Emotions were getting the better of her. It was like being caught in a snowstorm. Thoughts and feelings were flurrying around and making it hard for her to focus. She fell to the ground. Her mind was reeling with all the choices she had made up to this point. This wasn't like her. She had always known what to do—sure of the path she should follow.

She took a steadying breath. There was no turning back now. Was there? It was true that she could go back and apologize. She could beg Oliver to help her send a message to her father. Surely, there was a way to warn the mortals. Maybe if she spoke to the Queen herself, then she could plead for a small group of men to accompany her over the blackthorn veil.

But what if they didn't listen? What if going back wasted precious time, and the mortals suffered for it? Her resolve hardened. Going through the veil was the only way.

She stood, determined to face this all with a level head. There was a path ahead cutting through the tree line. Looking up at the stars to check that she was still headed north, she cursed under her breath and said, "Here goes nothing." She veered onto the path, ducking under low-hanging branches filled with lush green leaves.

By now, she had grown accustomed to walking in the thick brush of the Spring Court. It was as if the ground shifted, allowing her to pass freely without fear of tangled roots and rocks beneath her feet.

The further she walked, the more her magic began to dim. Perhaps she was nearing the blackthorns and her magic was weakening because of the proximity to the mortal realm. Kelera grumbled to herself, "Now is not the time for the fire to go out. I'm going to need every ounce of power I can get."

The only comfort was the constant presence of Adrastus' magic flowing through her—dancing with her own. Hopefully, it would stay with her when she crossed the veil, giving her the edge she needed. Her hands were as cold as Adrastus' ice magic, and she blew into them. It helped only for a moment, but soon her entire body was shivering.

The strength of his magic only brought back the pain of parting with him. Shaking her head, she looked up at the trees above her and swore again, "Dammit." The trees were devoid of the lush greenery she had been passing through only moments ago. The path may have been leading her north to the blackthorns, but it had also taken her to the Autumn border. To Samael's territory.

Stopping in her tracks, she whipped her head around, hoping for another way through the forest. The path was the quickest way. Who knew what sort of shrubbery or wildlife awaited her in the thick of the woods?

Picking up her pace, she continued to follow it. Each step held purpose. Get to Nevene. Warn King Tristan. Stop Samael. It played like a mantra in her head, distracting her from the terror and heartache that threatened to slow her down. If she allowed the dark thoughts to creep in or the regret at leaving Adrastus the way she did, then she'd fall apart.

A man's voice echoed through the trees, "This way, men. The High King's orders were clear. Every inch of the border needs to be checked for weakness."

Kelera stilled like a deer that had caught a hunter's scent. She backed slowly into the brush and ducked behind a few bushes that were still holding their brownish-green leaves.

Another man grumbled, "Can't he just tear the damn forest down? It would be a helluva lot faster."

The first man chided him, "And I suppose it's you who would volunteer for such a task?"

Before the other man had a chance to respond, more shouts came from down the path. Kelera's path. The one that was apparently crawling with Samael's men.

She took a step back, and a twig snapped under her foot. She froze. The men did too.

The first man spoke slowly with caution, "You hear that?"

The other grunted in response.

Kelera's heart thundered in her chest. She had to move. Now. She spun on her heel and started east. If she lost them through the dense forest of the Spring Court, then she would be safe. Then she could find her way north again.

Branches snapped far behind her. It seems they had hesitated to investigate the noise, giving her the head start she needed. Soon she could no longer hear the men. Praying that they had given up, she ducked behind a tall evergreen. She steadied her breathing and strained for any sound indicating that they were still following her.

Just when she thought she was safe, a branch snapped behind her. When she spun around, nothing was there. Something snickered, and she stilled. From the corner of her eye, a shadow rose up beside her. For a moment, she feared Samael and his men had finally caught up to her and her blood ran cold. But as she turned her head slowly, she realized the demon was not Samael or the men from the path.

Its pitch black mane of feathers was slick and full, around what should have been a face. It was like nothing she'd ever seen, even in storybooks with one enormous eye and an arm protruding from its chest. A crackling laugh escaped it as it licked its cracked, dry lips.

Before she could react, the beast was upon her. It clawed at her and snapped sharp fangs at her neck. Her magic pulsed into it, throwing it off of her. She called on it again, relishing in the comfort of Adrastus' power combined with her own. But as she attempted to hit it with another magical blast, the creature ducked low, kicking its leg out and knocking her to the ground.

Her head slammed against a rock, blurring her vision. She threw her hands out to shield herself from the attack as the beast climbed on top of her. Razor-sharp pain shot through her arm as the beast's teeth sliced into her.

Blinded by pain and unable to control her magic, flames flooded from her fingertips and onto the creature's feathery mane. Once the fire caught onto a handful of feathers, there was no stopping it. The beast leapt from her, flailing wildly around the brush. Kelera could do nothing but sit by, horrified as the fire engulfed the creature. It let out an ear curdling screech as the flames consumed it.

Once it was gone, ashes drifted down into Kelera's hair. Embers and ash, just like the wraith foretold. She dusted it out of her hair with trembling hands and gasped in pain as she moved her arm. Bile rose in her throat as she tore her jacket off. The flesh around the wound was green like ivy and her blood dripped on the forest floor.

Her teeth chattered from the pain, but she tried to quiet herself. Had Samael's men been close enough to hear the attack? Had they seen the flames? She needed to move, but she couldn't travel like this, and she wanted to kick herself for storming off without her pack. Definitely not her brightest idea. Though, if she was being honest, taking off without any Fae to help her also wasn't the most brilliant thing she'd ever done.

The sun would be rising soon, and she hadn't realized how much time had passed since she'd left Adrastus. As she scanned her surroundings, she spotted a faint orange light in the distance. It was settled snuggly between a small copse of evergreens. That meant it was in Seelie territory. And that it was her best bet in finding a path forward. The residents might be able to help her with her wound, and if they were familiar with the forest, then they could help her get to the blackthorns without venturing too close to Unseelie land.

Hopefully, Samael's men wouldn't venture this far from the Autumn border, even if they had noticed the commotion.

Adrastus would be saying "told you so" right about now for her foolishness of stumbling upon the enemy and letting that creature get the jump on her. She shook her head, hoping thoughts of him would dissipate. He had told her to leave. And that's what she'd done. After the things she said to him, he'd probably get a kick out of her predicament.

She tied her jacket sleeve around the gash on her arm and followed the light, trampling over the overgrown thicket. A branch scraped across her cheek, cutting over the puckered flesh of her scar. Hissing in pain, Kelera pushed forward, determined to make it to the house before the sun fully rose.

She leapt over a fallen log and into a modest, neatly kept garden. She kept her eyes on the orange glow of a lantern hanging on a covered front porch. It was a modest home—a tiny cabin much like the one she'd been taken to when she had first arrived in Elfhame. The one where she had first met Adrastus. She held a hand to her chest, feeling a slight pang at the memory. She'd had no idea then that a stranger in the woods would leave such an impact on her life and her heart.

Pushing past the guilt and regret, she rapped her hand on the door. It opened right away and Kelera jumped back a step. A tall man with olive eyes so piercing that they nearly glowed as bright as the lantern stared back at her. He had two small horns protruding from his head that looked as if they were made of bark.

She fumbled for her words, "I-I hate to bother you, but I'm afraid I got a bit turned around. And I'm hurt. I was trying to head north, you see... to meet a friend. But I wound up on a path that took me west. A-a, well, I don't know exactly what it was, snuck up on me. If you could offer me aid, I would be incredibly grateful."

He looked her up and down suspiciously and began to shake his head in answer. But before he could shut the door in her face, a stout woman stepped into the doorway at his side. She yawned, rubbing the sleep from her eyes and chided him with a raspy voice, "You know better than to turn away a lost soul. Move aside." She pushed him gently out of the way and opened the door wide. She whistled when she saw Kelera's arm. "Looks like you found yourself a *fachan*. Nasty little buggers."

Kelera laughed awkwardly. "This one wasn't so little."

The woman gave her a sympathetic pat on the shoulder and said, "Come in dear, will you? We would be happy to fix you up and point you in the right direction."

The man's voice was firm with warning. "Elra."

But the little woman waved him off and said, "Let's get you a spot of tea first to warm you up. Gets brisk in these parts with Autumn so near."

Kelera's mind immediately went to the Elfwine, and she declined, "No, I couldn't put you out. Please, I'm rather in a hurry to meet my friend." There was no time to linger when she had no idea how far she still was from the blackthorns.

Elra smiled broadly, her eyes crinkling at the corners. "I insist. It's not often we get travelers through here." She gestured for Kelera to step inside. "Come now, come now." Then she ordered the man, "Ansel, go and pack her some fresh fruit from the garden to take on her journey. Poor thing looks rather famished."

Kelera smiled at the kind gesture but stood awkwardly near the doorway. Elra seemed nice enough, but it would be best to remain wary. Especially since she was now traveling through Elfhame on her own. She'd only run into trouble in doing so in the past.

Elra waddled over to the small fire and grabbed a kettle while her companion went outside to the garden. Kelera watched closely as she poured steaming water over a net of herbs. It smelled divine and made her stomach rumble. It had been a while since she had eaten or drank anything.

Elra handed her a teacup, and she took it graciously, but didn't drink from it. Elra busied herself with searching for supplies to tend to Kelera's arm and said, "Don't pay Ansel any mind, dear. He's been nervous as a bee in a rattled hive since the frost."

Kelera set the teacup down on the table beside a green sofa. "The frost?"

"Yes, been creeping over our garden for the last week or so. Ever since his royal majesty was killed. Nasty business all that." Elra motioned for Kelera to take a seat on the sofa. She talked as she got to work rubbing a salve on the wound. "Until now, the frost never ventured further than the Autumn tree line. But a king's magic is powerful and all that power returning to the land... It's surely enough to stir up some trouble with the seasons." She finished off with a bandage wrapped tightly around Kelera's arm.

The world will succumb to frost. Kelera was tired of those words echoing in her mind. But what if they were no longer just words? What if it was the prophecy coming to fruition?

The sounds of hoofbeats roared through the quiet stillness of the cabin. Kelera's heart skipped a beat. "Elra, are you expecting anyone else this morning?"

Elra looked just as shocked as Kelera. "No."

The word rang in Kelera's ears. The symphony of hoofbeats told her there was more than just a travel party outside. Elra ran to the window and moved the floral curtain aside. Kelera towered over her and peeked out at the intruders.

A frightened whisper escaped her, "Night Riders."

The horses stamped their hooves into the ground, tearing away at the beautiful, lush grass in the garden. Their rotting flesh was festering with blood and pus, and their bones were visible beneath the spiked metal armor they wore. The Night Riders were exactly as she'd remembered. No one could forget what death looked like when it stared them in the face.

The door swung open to reveal Ansel. He slammed it behind him and twisted his hands together. His chest was rising and falling heavily. "They're here for the girl."

Elra studied Kelera, stepping away from her slowly. "You're the one they're looking for?"

Ansel's voice shook as he said, "I knew she looked familiar to the likeness on the posters. If we don't give her up, they'll kill us, my love."

Kelera turned back to the small framed window, shoving the curtain aside just enough so she could see into the front yard again.

The Night Riders each let out a horrendous screech and when the sound faded, a familiar voice as smooth as honey called out from behind them, "Well, this is quite the scene. The all-powerful halfling, hiding in a hovel."

Kelera shuddered, and it took everything in her power to stay calm as the man who had started all of this stepped into view. Samael.

Chapter Thirteen

K elera's heartbeat drowned out Elra's frantic cries. *It was all for nothing,* she thought. She let go of the curtain and took a frightened step back from the window. After all the running and all the sacrifices, Samael had found her. There was no telling what he would do to her or the innocent, terrified couple beside her. Would they give her up? Would she blame them if they did?

Elra's firm hand on her arm drew her attention. This couple didn't know her and they certainly didn't owe her their loyalty. But Elra had let her—a stranger—enter their home and had tended to her injury. She never imagined that she would bring danger to their doorstep. She'd trusted that she was safe, even if only for a moment.

How wrong she had been. She pleaded with the couple, "You have to run. Whatever he promises you, he won't keep to it."

Elra's eyes were filled with frightened tears as she clung to Ansel's shirt. "They say you killed Prince Ammon. And that you played a role in the King's demise."

"The first part is true. But it was an accident. Truly. And as for the King, it was Samael who committed the traitorous act. My friends are at the Seelie Palace as we speak, trying to set the record straight. Trying to stand against Samael."

Elra's nose flared. "I have no cause to believe you're lying."

Ansel added, "Or that she's telling the truth, Elra. We cannot make an enemy of the King of Unseelie."

Kelera argued, "Samael is already your enemy. He is an enemy to all of Elfhame. Please, go to the palace."

Samael's voice sounded closer as he announced, "Time is running out."

Elra ushered Kelera further into the house toward the kitchen in the back. "We will help you."

"No," Kelera urged, "you must go. I never meant to put you in danger. I saw them on the border, yet I came here anyway. My desperation has put you at risk."

Elra gave Kelera a sad smile. Before anyone could say anything more, hoofbeats thudded on the ground in the backyard. Kelera ran to the kitchen to look out the back window. Several Night Riders in untattered capes sat on horseback. Their horses appeared healthier than the others she had seen, with more flesh still clinging to their bodies. These must be the new Riders Samael had made after the battle with the Wild Hunt. There was an alarming number of them. More than she had anticipated. How many poor souls was Samael going to destroy in order to get what he wanted?

Her stomach somersaulted as she scanned the tree line where the Night Riders sat. There was no way out of the cabin. She and the innocent couple were surrounded.

She grabbed hold of Elra's hand. "Is there anywhere you can hide? A cellar, perhaps?"

Elra whimpered as the front porch creaked under the weight of heavy boots. "The bedroom. It is spelled for protection, and there are no windows."

Kelera took a deep breath. If she could slip out of the house somehow, then maybe she would be able to lead Samael and his men away from the cabin and the frightened couple. She urged them, "Go there. Now. And do not come out until they're gone."

Elra clung to Kelera's uninjured arm. "You must come with us. You must. The spell, it can keep you safe."

Ansel argued, "Elra, they will kill us all."

Elra snarled at him. "We will not turn her over to that *beast*."

Kelera grabbed hold of both of their hands as footsteps entered the home. "There is no time to argue. Let's go."

Kelera fled to the room, allowing Ansel to slam it shut behind her. The sound of wood splitting filled the air as Samael blasted his way through the front door. His footsteps were heavy and determined as he stalked toward the bedroom.

The space was cramped and modest, with a four-post bed and handmade furniture laid out carefully. It was obvious that this was a home that had seen many years of love and care. And now it was going to be destroyed, all because Kelera had brought trouble to its doorstep.

Ansel and Elra were arguing with one another in hushed tones. Elra stormed across the room, putting space between her and her husband. Ansel called out to her with open arms and regret filling his eyes. They had dimmed considerably since the first moment Kelera had seen them, and she wondered if it was a reflection of the fear and emotions he was feeling inside.

His voice broke as he said, "There is nothing else to be done, my love. If he realizes that we are harboring the fugitive halfling, then it will be our death."

Samael cooed from the other side of the door, "We can still remedy this. Open the door and I will allow you and your wife to live out the rest of your days here in peace."

Kelera paid close attention to his words. The rest of their days could consist of only one... or two, if they were lucky. He wasn't truly guaranteeing their safety. She snarled at the door, "You are full of sly promises, Samael. We both know you care nothing for these people. How can they be sure you will not find a way around those words?"

Samael chuckled. "I suppose you must have faith." The door creaked as he pressed against it. "Come now, Kelera, open the door. I understand you're frightened, but once the ceremony is complete, there will be nothing left to fear. I can offer you a place beside my throne."

"You mean at the foot of it." Kelera spat.

Samael's power pushed against the door like a low tide, but whatever protection spells the couple had put in place, held. Kelera shook, afraid of what would happen if he broke the defense. As if responding to her panic, Adrastus' magic began to creep from her palms and up to the door. The shadows that derived from his Unseelie power danced around the frame, shielding them from Samael.

She could picture Samael's slender face twisting into a sneer as he tried to coax her out. "Kelera, I can assure you that if you do not do as I say, then things will get much worse for both you and the two innocent Fae you have ensnared into your web of trouble." He lowered his voice, so that Kelera had to take a step closer to the door to hear as he said, "It seems to be a habit of yours. First your precious Cierine, then my poor brothers."

His words were like a punch to the gut, but Kelera didn't let it show as she narrowed her eyes and warned, "Adrastus will come for me. He will not allow you to claim Elfhame as your own." Even through her facade, she despised the way her voice trembled. Samael thrived on fear, and she was giving him exactly that.

"Ah, yes, my brother, the fierce warrior prince, has found love. Who would have thought it would be with a mere halfling?" The floor creaked and moaned as Samael stalked in front of the doorway, as if searching for a weakness in the protective shield. "I shouldn't be surprised. He always did fall short of his potential. Not to worry, though, he'll have no use for you once I'm through with the two of you."

Samael's magic pushed against the shield, causing it to buckle slightly. The door cracked under the pressure. Kelera ran to one of the dressers and slid it to the door, pressing it against it in a fruitless attempt to put more of a barrier between them. Even with the strength of her bond to Adrastus, she doubted her ability to stand against Samael's power of the crown and the cursed Fae who waited patiently outside.

Samael growled in frustration as his magic slinked along the barrier. She could almost picture the shadows he wielded searching for weakness in the spell. He mused, "It seems your control over your magic has improved since we last saw one another." He continued to pace outside of the door. "It's a shame you didn't have that sort of control when you were in my room of shadows."

As if it had been summoned by Samael's words, a vision of Ammon appeared in the corner of the room. Kelera's eyes darted to the couple, wondering if they, too, could see the apparition. It was clear they did not, as they held one another, listening to the exchange.

Kelera eyed Ammon. His corpse-like face was looking directly at her with haunted eyes. It had to be another one of Samael's tricks. She bristled. "Ammon wouldn't have been in that room if it weren't for you. His blood is on your hands too." She would live with the guilt of Ammon's death and the memory of his lifeless eyes staring up at her. But she was not the only one to blame. Samael had pushed her, tortured her, and he would have killed Adrastus if she had not acted. Saving him was something she would not feel sorry for.

Calling on the blanket of magic she had used against the siren, she draped it over her mind in an effort to block Samael out of her head. The vision of Ammon drifted away in a cloud of dust, banished along with her lingering regret. At least for the moment.

Samael tsked. "Yes, poor Ammon." Samael's magic pulsed against the door again, splintering the wood so that he could see inside. His cold, frost-colored eyes bore into hers. He ran a hand through his icy white hair and smiled slyly as he asked, "How did it feel to kill such a powerful being?" When she didn't answer, he continued to goad her. "Admit it. It was satisfying. Imagine feeling that rush of divine power all the time. That's what I can give you."

Kelera's magic felt like a storm brewing. Sweat beaded on her forehead as she tried to contain it, worried that it would consume the entire cabin if unleashed. Her words were underlaid with a deadly threat as she said, "Do not do this, Samael. Do not push me."

He didn't balk. "I'm here for you and you alone. Your power belongs to me, and I mean to claim it once and for all." He whistled between his fingers and footsteps approached from the front and back doors of the home. Kelera couldn't make them out through the small hole in the door, but there were too many footsteps to count. It was impossible to know how many men he had called into the cabin.

There was no way the spell would be able to hold against all of their magic. Worried that Ansel and Elra would become yet another piece of collateral damage in her mission to defeat Samael, she conceded, "Fine, I will come out, but Ansel and Elra must be released first. You and your men must let them leave, untouched and unharmed, and I will come out." *Though that does not mean I will leave here with you,* she thought to herself.

"Deal." With Samael's word of agreement, the footsteps receded out of the cabin.

Kelera began to shove the dresser away from the door, but Elra grasped onto her wrist. "You can't." She leaned in to whisper into Kelera's ear, "I don't know who you are exactly, but I do know that if your power is desired by a king, then it must be kept from his hands."

Kelera whispered back, "Go. And do not slow until you reach the Seelie Palace. Tell them what's happened here. And don't worry. He will not be getting what he wants today." With a reassuring smile, Kelera gently removed Elra's hand from her and slipped out the door.

Behind her, Elra and Ansel scurried from the room. Ansel gave Kelera a small regretful smile as he opened the back door and stumbled out with his wife's hand in his. Samael nodded to one of his men, and Kelera's breath caught in her throat. She stood unmoving and watched through the kitchen window as the man shouted something to the Night Riders. To her relief, the Riders moved aside, allowing the couple to pass.

Only once they were out of sight did Kelera turn back to Samael. He stood smugly to the side with his arm extended in an invitation for her to pass by. "After you."

She turned her nose up at him, brushing past him and up to the front door. She paused in the doorway when she saw the horde of Night Riders and the Unseelie Fae waiting for her. She couldn't see the Night Riders' faces well enough to get a read on their emotions—if they had any, that is. But the Unseelie soldiers were a mixture of curiosity and nerves. They gripped their weapons tight—swords made of sleek, dark steel.

Some she recognized as Fae from the Winter Court, with a blue pallor to their skin and horns or tusks. Others were pale, with hair the color of leaves in the fall. All looked as if they would rather be anywhere else. She scanned the crowd for any familiar faces from the palace and saw only one.

Kane stood at the head of the small army. The most brutish of the brothers grinned at her. "Miss me?"

Kelera spat, "Don't flatter yourself." It wasn't surprising that Kane was here to stand with Samael. He was the muscle behind the brains. She'd witnessed first-hand the savagery Kane delighted in when he was in the pits and there wasn't a doubt in her mind that he was eager for a war if only for the bloodshed he would get to take part in.

Samael pushed her forward. She stumbled over the threshold and to the edge of the porch. She had no idea what they had planned now that they'd gotten her right where they wanted her. Before she could put up her defenses, Kane and Samael raised their hands in unison and a blast of snow hit her like a blizzard. It knocked her from the porch and onto the ground, rendering any shield she was preparing to raise useless. She rolled on the grass and a light frost crunched beneath her weight.

She moaned from the impact and could see her breath in the air. The Seelie Court shouldn't be experiencing such cold weather. She gasped. The Seelie Court. She was on Seelie soil! It made her magic stronger. *And Samael doesn't know I am bound to Adrastus. I can use that to overpower them.* Kelera dug her hands into the earth, welcoming the fresh wave of power flowing into her.

Samael looked like a fenrir—the massive wolf-like creatures that Kelera had read about—preparing to pounce as he stepped down from the porch and said,

"It's in your best interest not to try anything stupid. Come with me and I will show mercy."

Though Adrastus was not there with her, his magic spun around hers, making her shiver and sweat all at once like a fever coming on. Distraction would work in her favor, giving her enough time to muster every ounce of power she could, so she said, "You don't know what mercy is, Samael. Don't bother pretending that you do."

"It's clear you've grown to care for my brother and the pathetic Fae of this land, though I can't imagine why. What if we made a deal?"

A deal with Samael would be like playing with fire. There was no doubt she would get burned. She scoffed, "I'm not the fool you believe me to be."

Samael tsked at her. "That's why I know you'll take it. My Night Riders have located my brother and are hunting him as we speak. It seems he was coming after *you*. It's too bad he was not fast enough."

Kelera's heart leapt to her throat. He'd tried to follow her. But why? Was it to drag her to the safety of the Seelie Palace walls? Or was it to help her on her mission to save the mortals? Either way, he had come. The horrible words she had spoken to him hadn't made him stop caring for her. Her mind was racing so fast that she almost missed what Samael said next.

"Do the ceremony that will bind your power to mine *willingly* and I'll let Adrastus live."

It was a payment she couldn't make. What leverage did she have if she could not bind herself to Samael? *He never said it has to work.* The revelation echoed faintly in her mind. It was true. If she agreed to the binding, then he would have to uphold his end of the bargain, even if the ceremony did not work.

Samael thought he had her right where he wanted her, but he was mistaken. "Deal," she said, praying to the stars that she was not wrong about this.

"Smart choice." Samael extended his strong, slender hands. He would have her stand to face him rather than meet her at her level. So different from Adrastus, who had knelt in front of her on the dunes for their ceremony.

The sun had risen over the horizon now. It was full and beamed down on them, highlighting Samael's ice-colored hair. Kelera took his hands and stood, ignoring the aching pain in her arm from the fachan attack.

Samael squeezed her hands with malicious strength, and she bit the inside of her cheek to keep from crying out. He closed his eyes as his magic crept along her fingers, to her palm, and then slinked around her wrists. It tightened around them for a moment, then moved on, sliding further up her arms. It poked and prodded at her skin, as if trying to find a way to enter her body. But it was useless. The bond between her and Adrastus held strong, locking out any outside force that wanted to threaten it.

Samael furrowed his brow. "Stop resisting me."

"I'm not. I swear it." It was the truth. She remained relaxed and open, confident that she could uphold her end of the deal to allow him to bond with her—knowing that the bond with Adrastus would never allow it.

Samael pulled her in close to him and, hissing in her face, said, "Then why isn't it working?" He shouted to Kane. "Figure it out!"

Kane pulled a book from his pack and flipped through it. "I don't understand. There's no reason for it not to have started merging. Could be that we don't have the power of the full moon."

Samael's voice was thunderous, "With the full power of the crown, I do not need it. I have the power of the ancestral Kings."

Kane shrugged. "Maybe a protective block of some sort?"

Samael twisted her arm, sending a scorching sensation through the fachan bite. His words were venomous as he said, "You've tricked me."

She knew she should have been frightened by his anger. But it didn't matter anymore. There was no way around the truth. She supposed she had let this go on long enough. And she'd made a vow to herself. She wouldn't show weakness. He deserved nothing but her wrath.

The twitch in his jaw and the red rims around his eyes told her just how distraught he was becoming. Kelera laughed at him. "You simply said that I had to agree to the binding. You said nothing of it being a success. It seems I have picked up a few tricks during my time here in Elfhame. How to twist an agreement, for example."

The pressure of her magic rose to the surface, intertwined with Adrastus'. It fueled her as she pulled her hands from Samael and raised them. She blasted the magic in the garden in a flurry of light, knocking Kane and the other men into the tree line. It even rocked the Night Riders back. She didn't bat a lash as she heard them and their horses clatter to the ground. Horses whinnied in pain and the Night Riders lay crumpled under their robes. She hoped it hurt.

Samael cursed under his breath and Kelera basked in the satisfaction of seeing the revelation dawn on his face. She said, "I'm already bound. To Adrastus."

A dark fog rose from the ground around Samael as if his anger was taking a corporeal form. It swept into her with a flick of his wrist. The fog wormed its way into her nose and mouth, threatening to suffocate her. She looked back at the men who were dusting themselves off from her blast of power. It was obvious she would receive no help from them. So instead, she focused on Adrastus' magic pulsing in her veins, still bound to hers, but she couldn't find the strength to unleash it.

She tried to speak, hoping to reason with Samael before it was too late. "Sam—"

His jaw twitched, and he pulled the fog from her lungs. She gasped for air, but the fog still held her in place. It seeped into her very marrow, smothering her and Adrastus' magic into submission.

There was no way to access her magic now, and he knew it. In his classic arrogant manner, he shrugged. But she knew it was a facade. The twitch of his eye told her as much. There was no hiding the hatred he was feeling for her right now, after realizing he couldn't have the power he'd been longing for.

He slicked his hair back as he said, "I am incredibly disappointed in you, Kelera. But don't be so smug. You didn't honestly think that I would rest the entirety of my plans on your shoulders, did you? My ascension will happen, with or without your power. With the force of my Night Riders and the Unseelie Court fighting for me, I will still succeed. It is true that your magic would have made things much easier for me to take the Seelie throne—to give me power that matches their own. But it will have to be done without you. You have already lost. As we speak, my men are preparing to wreak havoc in your precious mortal court. They will tear your people apart with their bare hands and feed them their entrails." His mouth widened in a genuine smile. "And as for your father..."

Kelera's stomach somersaulted at the mention of him. "What have you done, Samael?"

He stalked over to her. Reaching down, he wrapped her hair around his hands and pulled her up. Her scalp screamed as he jerked her up, careful to continue holding her magic in place with his fog. "I had planned to use your father as last resort leverage to make you come willingly to me. But unfortunately, you are no use to me now. *What is bound may not be broken except in death.* Perhaps, instead, I can present you a different deal."

Thinking of her father made her dizzy with worry. What was Samael getting at? She struggled against the fog, trying to call on magic—any magic that could help her break free. Her breathing was ragged as she said, "How do I know you truly have my father? It could be a trick of some sort."

"Would you like me to show you?" Samael swept his hand through the air with a flourish and a tall shadow began to form. She watched in horror as darkness turned to flesh. Dark brown hair that matched her own, and warm, dark eyes that she'd spent her life looking into for reassurance. Her father, Sir Aldric, stood before her as real as Samael and the men surrounding her.

Hot, angry tears welled in her eyes, but she forced them back, determined not to let him see her cry. Her voice, however, betrayed her. She sounded like a child as she said, "Papa?"

Another shadow rose behind her father, slightly taller and broader in build. As the shadows faded, raven hair and forest green eyes were revealed. Kelera shook her head. Adrastus wasn't here. "This is one of your tricks."

Samael hummed, "Is it?" He snapped his fingers and blood began to seep from her father's stomach as Adrastus plunged a sword through his back.

She couldn't stop the gasp of horror that escaped her or the sob that followed as her father fell to the ground. His armor clattered and then there was no more sound, only the beating of her heart in her own ears. She knew this wasn't real—that it was Samael's magic—but that didn't make the pain of seeing the man she cared for murder her father in cold blood. It looked so real, and even through her tear-filled eyes, she could see the blood pooling around her father's unmoving body.

Samael pressed himself against the back of her and she could feel his arousal against her. She struggled to move away in disgust. He was enjoying this. Having her and her mind at his mercy. It reminded her of the monster he was.

He brushed her hair from her neck and let his lips linger over it as he said, "Doubt me all you want. But my men *will* find Adrastus. And when they do, I will make the unimaginable become reality. You will lose everything. Starting with him." He pointed to her father's corpse, then, using his free hand, he pulled a sword from the scabbard on his back. Steel with a custom-made hilt flashed before her eyes and she knew without a doubt that the sword before her was her father's. It had been commissioned to match the one he'd given her, only larger in size.

She hated how weak she sounded as she said, "What have you done with him?"

"My men are holding him near the veil, awaiting my command."

"What do you want, Samael?" Her heart raced, and she stopped struggling against his hold. With the threat of her father's life, she had no time for games.

He released her hair and took hold of her chin. He pointed her face at the illusion of Adrastus, forcing her to look him in the eye. Samael drawled out his words as he said, "Leave here. Turn your back on my brother and his cause and I will allow you and your father to live." Samael put the blade of the sword to her throat and her heart stilled. Kelera glanced at the sharp steel and caught a glimpse of something dark and rusty-brown on it—blood.

Her heart ached with worry for her father, but if Samael was telling the truth and his men did in fact know where to ambush Adrastus, then she would be leaving him to fend for himself against them. Samael truly had her at a disadvantage now. The magic he was using to hold her in place was powerful. More powerful than his magic was before, and she wondered if it was because he had bound Kane's magic to him or if it was magic inherited with the Unseelie crown.

Her heart felt as if it were splitting in two, but she found just enough strength for her voice. "I will not allow you to destroy them, either of them." She wanted to reach for Adrastus, but knew he wasn't really there. Regret threatened to consume her. She shouldn't have left him in anger. That shouldn't have been their farewell.

If she chose to save her father and return to Nevene, would her magic still be able to ground Adrastus' power? If it didn't, then he risked losing control. He risked becoming something dark and sinister, or worse... he risked not using it and losing to his brothers.

She swallowed her uncertainty as she spoke. "If I agree, then I want your word that you will not lay a hand on Adrastus."

Samael kissed her on the neck, sending a wave of nausea rolling through her stomach. He spoke in her ear, "Very well. I will include him in the deal. I will allow you, your father, and my bastard brother to live. All you have to do is walk away and never return."

"Why not just kill me?" Kelera had to tread carefully where Samael was concerned.

He rolled his eyes. "Because I made a deal with someone."

"Who?" She thought of the mortal traitor. She had suspected the greedy Duke Cunningham and his mercenaries, but there was no way he would have spoken on her behalf to ensure her safety.

Samael sneered at her. "Do we have a deal or not? Time is not on your side. Should I not send word by the time the sun begins to descend, then my men will finish what I started." He gestured to the blood on the sword. Her father's blood?

Samael lowered the sword and stepped around her as he extended his hand to shake. He grabbed hold of

Kelera's shirt, pulling her into him. His hand snaked around her waist and she could still feel the arousal between his legs. His lips lingered over hers as he taunted her, "Decide swiftly, halfling, or I may decide to forgo my mercy. I may take my brother's little pet right here in front of my men before I rid this world of you completely."

Kelera tried to catch her breath, but couldn't gain control. Her magic was running wild in her veins, still stifled by the power Samael was wielding to hold her at bay. It felt like razor blades beneath her skin. Without her magic, she would die here, leaving her father and Adrastus to Samael's twisted ideas of mercy.

She turned her face away from him and her eyes met "shadow Adrastus'" as she said, "You have..." Tears spilled down her cheeks and lips, leaving a salty taste in her mouth. "A deal."

Annoyance flashed in Samael's eyes. Was he angry that she had bartered for his brother's life? Or still mad that he had lost his chance at claiming Seelie magic for himself? But taking this deal *was* costing her more than he could imagine. It was something Samael would never understand. Returning to Nevene forever meant giving up on Elfhame. Giving up on any dream she'd had of returning to Adrastus to make things right.

Samael wasn't able to take her magic, but he was taking everything else from her. The choice between the life she longed for and her father's safety was an easy one. She would not claim freedom at the expense of her father's life, and Samael had known it.

Well played, she thought as she reached her hand out and placed it in Samael's. It was not lost on her that she was also giving up the chance to warn Adrastus of an ambush or of helping him defend himself against anything Samael had in store. Before they touched, Kelera drew back slightly. "You swear that you give your word that neither you nor your men will lay a hand on Adrastus? That you will allow him to live."

"You have my word." He took her hand and squeezed so hard that she cried out. Shadows and ice flooded through her fingers and into her wrist, a sign of Samael's magic binding the agreement. She glanced back at "shadow Adrastus" and mouthed the words *I'm sorry*. Samael dropped the sword and grabbed her chin roughly. His fingers dug in as they had many times before in the Unseelie Palace.

His irritation was obvious as he spoke through clenched teeth. "Adrastus will live. Now go. And do not think of returning."

She gulped. *Adrastus will be okay*, she told herself. Oliver and the others are close by. They'll come for him. She locked the thoughts firmly in place. Determined not to waver in the belief for fear that she would lose her nerve, thus condemning her father to a sure death.

Her voice sounded small to her as she said, "Take me to my father now."

She willed herself to start walking toward the tree line and not look back for fear she would change her mind. Every step she took toward the trail felt like another stab in the heart. She thought of her father's sword in Samael's greedy hands. The blood on the blade was the only thing fueling her forward.

Samael shouted to Kane, "Take her to the veil! Allow her and her father to pass through unharmed." He smiled viciously at her. "It's been a pleasure, Lady Kelera. It pains me to think of the havoc we could have wrought in the world together, but I am confident that I'll be able to go on without you."

She took the opportunity to have the final word. She looked back one last time as she said, "You are *nothing* without the power of others."

To her satisfaction, Samael's smile faltered. It was short lived, though, as Kane grabbed her by the collar of her shirt and dragged her away. She stared straight ahead, guided by the sun and Kane's rough grip.

Behind her, she heard no sounds of struggle, only Samael's victorious laughter. *Please forgive me, Dras*, she thought as her heart shattered into pieces.

Chapter Fourteen

Kane shoved Kelera forward, nearly knocking her off her feet. She stumbled and looked up at the sky to check the position of the sun. It would be descending soon, and she feared they wouldn't make it to the blackthorn veil before it was replaced by the rising moon. She had once loved to gaze at the night sky in Elfhame, delighting in the beautiful twinkling stars and the constant glow of the moon. But now her father's life hung in the balance of its appearance.

That made it her enemy at this moment. Just as much as the barbaric man walking beside her was. Kane had been no friend to her during her imprisonment at the Unseelie Court. He had spent his time tormenting servants, always unnaturally close to his mother's side. Or in the pits, condemning innocent Fae to their deaths for affronts to the royal family. Slights that the Unseelie royals had masked as crimes.

Tired, hungry, and in pain from the fachan bite, she was unable to hold her tongue and spat, "You are vile."

Kane simply chuckled and shrugged his broad shoulders. "Your point?"

"Wasn't there ever a time in your life when you wanted to be someone people would respect and not just fear?"

Kane grabbed her by the back of the neck, jerking her toward him. He narrowed his eyes and sneered. "Now, why would I ever want such a thing?"

She held her gaze steady as she answered, "Because there is more to life than playing the brute and making mommy smile."

His face hardened at the mention of his mother. Queen Beatrice was as bad as the rest of them. She thrived on cruelty and it was no surprise that Samael, Kane, and Ammon had grown up to be vicious monsters. The true wonder was how Gadreel and Adrastus had not.

Kane's voice trembled with anger. "You know nothing of mothers and sons." He paused and smirked hatefully. "Come to think of it, you know nothing about *mothers* at all, do you?"

Kelera gritted her teeth. "If my mother was anything like yours, then it is a blessing that she abandoned me." The words turned to ash on her tongue. Truthfully, he was right. She still knew next to nothing about the woman who gave birth to her. But she had to hold on to the belief that her mother had left her with her father for her own good. She wouldn't allow herself to believe that her own flesh and blood could be as manipulative and horrible as the Unseelie Queen was.

Kane released her neck and shoved her forward. As they walked, he mused out loud, "It's a shame, really. That you weren't raised in Elfhame. I saw what you did to Ammon. To think, the eldest Unseelie Prince, left in a crumpled heap at the hands of a mere halfling."

The laugh that escaped him as he thought of his own brother's demise gave Kelera goosebumps. Had anyone mourned Ammon's death?

Kane sounded impressed as he continued, "The court healers say every bone in his body was broken, you know."

Kelera swallowed the bile that threatened to rise at the memory of Ammon's lifeless eyes staring up at her in the cavernous room of shadows. She felt a tremor in her hands and focused on steadying them. Adrastus' power was still flowing through her veins and caressed her own now, as if it was trying to steady her.

He clucked his tongue and added, "Makes one wonder what you would have been like if you'd been trained to wield your power as a child instead of being raised alongside the weak mortals. Did you enjoy learning their pretty dances and how to step aside demurely when your betters passed by you?"

"My father loved me and gave me a good life," she said, though there was no use arguing with Kane. He would never understand. The Princes of the Night had been taught to look down upon anyone with weaker magic than them. Mortals, having no magic at all, made them completely insignificant in their eyes. The mortals were merely there to serve or entertain in the Unseelie Court.

Kane finally let go of her once the blackthorn veil came into view. It was much closer than she had expected. The overgrown brush of trees tangled with thorns brought a sense of dread to her. It was so different from the last time she had seen it—when it had been a promise of her and Cierine's freedom from the clutches of Samael. Now, it felt like the gates to her prison. An entryway back to a life of oppression and unfulfillment.

Why did it feel as if she were making the biggest mistake of her life? She slowed and Kane turned to her with irritation. He tapped his foot on the ground impatiently. "Your father is waiting."

She looked Kane up and down. She hadn't spent much time with him in the Unseelie Court, and had certainly never been alone with him like this. Though he was just as savage as Samael, she didn't see him as a particularly ambitious man. He had always appeared happiest when fighting in the pits or whispering secrets into his mother's ear. Was the freedom to do as he pleased what had enticed him to take Samael's side over Adrastus'?

Attempting to plant seeds of doubt in his mind, she said, "Samael will never value you. He *takes* from others like a leech with no intention of giving anything in return." She put a hand on her hip. "What has he promised you?"

Kane moved so quickly it stunned her. She never expected someone of his massive size to be so lithe. He wrapped an arm around the small of her back and yanked her into him. Fighting his brute strength was useless, and Kelera was forced to press her body against his. He leaned down, his lips grazing against her ear as he whispered, "Blood."

He drew away and grinned at the disgusted look on her face. He put his fingers between his lips and let out a loud whistle. Two armed men appeared, dragging a cloaked figure with them. Kelera's heart skipped a beat, and she moved to run to them, but Kane's arm stopped her.

He looked her up and down with hunger in his eyes. "Samael was a fool to let you go when we could have found other uses for you. Perhaps I will pay you a visit once we've taken your realm." He licked his lips. "Think of the fun we could have."

"I'd rather not." Kelera shoved him aside and ran to the guards. They dropped the person between them on the ground and sauntered away without a care in the world. She sank to her knees and tugged the hood from the person's head. Her father's eyes crinkled at the corners as he smiled at her. He didn't speak, though. As hard as he tried, opening and closing his mouth with frustration, no words came. It had to be a spell. Finally, he embraced her, squeezing her tightly in his arms.

The guards took a step toward them as if they would attempt to separate them, but Kane stopped them. "She has a deal with the King." Reluctantly, the men backed down.

Kelera rose, still holding onto her father's arms, unwilling to let go after being apart from him for so long. She shot a look of daggers at Kane. "What did you do to him? Why can't he speak?" Magic crackled beneath her skin. All she had to do was release it, and these men would regret ever laying a hand on her father.

Kane sighed with annoyance. "He'll be fine once you cross the veil."

"You're all monsters."

He snickered. "That's the idea."

Fury nearly blinded her, and the heat of fire licked at her ankles. She and her father jumped back away from the flames that had sparked with her anger. Avoiding her father's eyes and what horror she imagined them to hold, Kelera held her gaze on Kane.

He was watching the fires with fascination. There was no fear in his eyes. Perhaps he thought it was too insignificant of a demonstration. With a shrug of his shoulders, he said, "You'll have to do better than that if you want to impress me."

Impressing him was the last thing on her mind. But her father's presence beside her made her think twice before calling on her magic again. There was no reason to frighten him. And she had made a deal with Samael after all. If she hurt Kane or the guards then he would likely retaliate by hurting Adrastus. She closed her mind to the pain she craved to inflict on the Fae standing before her and her magic settled back beneath the surface in response.

Kane turned away, but before he could disappear into the forest, she called out. "What will happen to Adrastus if Samael succeeds in capturing him?" As much as she wanted to believe that Adrastus was capable enough to evade Samael's minions, she knew better than to underestimate them.

Kane grinned at her. "He is no longer your concern."

"He's the best of you and you know it."

"For now," is all Kane said as he turned and walked away.

She shook away the doubts in her mind. Adrastus had always taken care of himself. He would figure a way out of the mess she had left him in. She closed her eyes and focused on the familiar strum of his magic running through her veins. Distance couldn't break the power of the bonding ceremony—only death could do that. He was alive. Which meant he still stood a chance of defeating his brothers.

She felt a horrible longing in her heart to return to Adrastus as she led her father to the blackthorn veil. Ignoring it the best she could, she said, "Let's get you home."

He slipped from her grasp and shook his head. She didn't know what he was getting at, but every moment he stood on this side of the border put him at risk. Before he had a chance to stop her, she grabbed hold of the thorns allowing them to slice into her skin. Then she clutched her father as tightly as she possibly could and pulled him with her through the veil.

This time she used every ounce of concentration she could muster to make sure she didn't leave her father behind like she had before. The magic drew her in more gently than the last time she had passed through, but the same sensation of being sucked under water hit her. She tried to call out to her father to reassure him, but her voice was muffled. Darkness enveloped them and in her mind, she tried to picture the gardens of the Nevene palace. Perhaps imagining their destination in her mind's eye would ensure they did not end up turned around and back in Elfhame.

The immense magic of the veil pulsed around her, but she didn't fight it. She allowed it to draw her through to the other side. Bright light stunned her eyes and she squinted as Nevene came into view. What she once remembered being a lush field looked dull in comparison to what she'd grown accustomed to in Elfhame. Everything seemed to be dimmed here and a small part of her wanted to cry or turn back. She hadn't taken more than a step into the realm that she had once called home before realizing how much she would miss Elfhame.

Chapter Fifteen

Kelera choked back tears as she glanced around the field. The colors here in Nevene were drab and dreary compared to that of Elfhame. Even her magic had dimmed, leaving her feeling unfulfilled. The only thing comforting her was the calloused hand holding onto hers. She turned to her father and leapt into his arms. Tears spilled down her cheeks as she buried her head in his shoulder. "Papa."

He held her tight. "My girl." A sob escaped his throat, and Kelera's heart hurt for him. She couldn't remember the last time she had seen her father cry. His voice was a mixture of rage and relief as he said, "I thought you were lost to me."

She pulled away, looking at the bruises on his face and the cut on his lip. "Did they hurt you, Papa?"

He glared over her head at the blackthorn veil. "They tried." He bared his teeth in a defiant smile. When he looked back down at her, his face softened. "Oh, my dear girl, what have you done?"

His words wounded her. Was he ashamed by the display of her power? Did he think she had been the one who betrayed the mortal realm? Memories of the way the council had looked at her when Cierine had been taken flashed in her mind. They'd been wary of her then and who was to say that suspicion had not grown since she'd been gone?

"I had to come back, Papa. To warn you. Samael—"

Her father cut her off. "You shouldn't have come. You need to run. Now. And don't look back."

"I can't leave. The Unseelie Court plans to attack Nevene, and soon. You have to get your men ready. You must warn King Tristan."

"King Tristan is no friend of yours right now." He grasped her shoulders, and she was reminded of the time before, in this very spot, when she was a child and he had made her promise not to use her magic ever again. His voice trembled as he continued, "When you left the rescue party at the border, some of the council members claimed it was proof that you were, in fact, working with the Fae. You are wanted for treason, my girl."

It was like a knife to the gut. They thought she had left the men behind intentionally. Anger rose in her like a wildfire. Her magic flared in response, but she shoved it back down, gritting her teeth as she said, "That was an accident. I didn't know what I was doing then. King Tristan can't possibly believe that I would have ever put Cierine in danger." Her heart skipped a beat. "Oh stars, Cierine did make it back, didn't she?"

Her father gave her shoulders a reassuring squeeze. "Yes, she is safe. She has pleaded your case, but the council is in the King's ear. If they find you here, then you will be tried."

Tried? Samael had tricked her. He must have known from his mortal ally that she would be placed under arrest if she returned to Nevene. If she was found guilty, she would be executed—there was no mercy for traitors here—and she would no longer be able to stand against him. And Adrastus would no longer have her power linked to his. Without her magic anchoring his, and with Samael wielding the crown's power along with his own, then Samael would be the more powerful of the two.

Clever bastard.

She had to fix this. "Papa, listen to me. There is a traitor in the court. Someone who really is working with the Unseelie. If I can figure out who it is, then I will be able to prove that it wasn't me. I'm stronger now. My magic it—"

"Unseelie? Magic? Kelera, these are the things I warned you about." Her father dropped his hands from her shoulders and took a small step back.

"I'm learning how to control it. I can help defend Nevene. I'm stronger now, Papa. I can't just run away when you are all in danger. I came back for you. For *all of you*." She was out of breath when she finished. She was here to help them. Surely, once she explained everything to King Tristan, he would understand. They would all understand. They had to, or else all she had done to get back to them would be for nothing. She would have left Adrastus to fend for himself for *nothing*.

She cursed under her breath as her magic built like a firestorm. Her father rushed back to her, but she stopped him. "No, Papa."

He ignored her, pulling her into him, and she felt her power calm slightly. It still pulsed in her veins and she focused on the cool flow of Adrastus' magic wrapping around it.

Her father cradled her in his arms as he had done many times when she was a young girl as he asked, "What happened over there, sweetheart?"

Where should she begin? So much had transpired in such a short amount of time. And how could she possibly make him understand that it wasn't all bad? Saying it out loud to her mortal father, who had raised her and sacrificed so much for her, felt like a betrayal.

She peered up at his battered face—a face wounded because of her, because Samael had wanted to hurt her in the one way he knew how—and shook her head sadly. She didn't want to lie. Her father deserved the truth, at the very least. "I learned how to use my magic. It was..." she corrected, "it is, unstable. So I took part in a ceremony to control it. I'll explain the rest later, but right now, we need to find the mortal who is working for Samael. I thought for a time that it might be Duke Cunningham, but I'm not sure anymore, and I have no proof."

"Kelera, you said the Unseelie plan to attack?"

"Yes, Prince Samael, I mean, King Samael plans to take Elfhame before moving onto the mortal realm."

She saw the gears turning in her father's mind as he scratched at his beard. He shook his head in confusion. "But the Unseelie Court has promised to stand with us." He mused more to himself than to Kelera, "He explained it all, that the Unseelie Court was framed for the kidnappings. That it was the Seelie Court that had been behind everything."

"Who explained it all?" Kelera clutched her locket nervously. "They're lying."

"My dear, it is why the King and his council were so quick to believe that you were working with them. Because your mother was Seelie... because *you*, my girl, are Seelie."

"It's a trick, then. Who told you this?" The Fae couldn't lie. How had Samael been able to misdirect the mortal court?

Something rustled in the tall grass. Kelera's father grabbed hold of her wrists as he urged her, "We're out of time. We'll fix this. Together. But you can't go back to the palace. We need to find you someplace safe to hide."

A bitter voice boomed in the clearing. "You wouldn't be trying to aid a fugitive, now would you, Sir Aldric?" Duke Cunningham and his men had snuck up on them. His vicious-looking henchmen positioned themselves around her and her father like a pack of fenrir ready to go in for the kill. Their weapons were already drawn, making it clear to her that they would be happy to take her in with a fight.

Duke Cunningham laughed arrogantly. "You are outnumbered and out armed. Come with me now, Lady Kelera, and you will find yourself in a cell rather than six feet under the ground."

Kelera's nose flared in anger. Here was another man who thought her weak. One who thought he could make her cower with his threats. Magic prickled at her senses, and she knew she would be more than capable of unleashing it on them. Imagining a slow, stable stream, she released the magic. A warning for Cunningham and his men to stay back. She expected her father to back away from her in fear, but he stood firm and steady.

Cunningham's men, however, watched with horror-filled eyes as a soft glow of firelight and shadows drifted from her fingertips. Their faces paled, and they bumped into one another, trying to put distance between her and themselves.

A building pressure filled her senses. The magic wanted to be set free, to wreak havoc on the men who dared come between her and what she'd risked everything to come to Nevene to do. But what of her father? He could be caught in the crossfire. Images of Ammon's body being thrown against the cavern wall clouded her thoughts. The memory of his eyes staring lifelessly up at her made her breath hitch in her throat. She couldn't risk it.

With a great deal of control, she pushed the magic back in and locked it up tight, picturing an impenetrable door.

She raised her chin. "I will come with you peacefully, but I wish to have an audience with the King."

Cunningham scoffed. "You are in no position to make demands."

Still, Kelera could see the slightest twitch of his jaw that told her he knew for a fact that she was. His men were no match for the magic of Elfhame.

But she didn't have to point that out as her father stepped forward and declared, "But I am. I have served his Majesty and his father before him with loyalty. I have shed blood, sweat, and tears for this kingdom."

Worry flashed across Cunningham's face, and Kelera felt a semblance of satisfaction. Her father was the commander of the King's Knights. He wasn't like the scarred and dirty mercenaries surrounding them now. No. He was a true warrior. And here in the mortal court, that meant something.

Cunningham offered, "I will grant you an audience with the King to speak on your daughter's behalf. But she has to come with *us*."

Her father opened his mouth to argue, but Kelera stopped him. She spoke softly so the men surrounding them wouldn't overhear. "Go, Papa. Find Cierine. She may be able to help talk sense into King Tristan. Tell him what I've said." Her father nodded, and she added, "Do it quietly. We cannot let the traitor know that we are onto them."

Her father gave her one last hug. "I will fix this. Don't worry, my girl."

Duke Cunningham signaled to one of his men, and the beast stepped forward, taking hold of Kelera's arm. He tore her away from her father and twisted both of her hands behind her back. It took every ounce of self-control to hold back her magic. She closed her eyes, trying to picture something to calm her mind. It was Adrastus' face that she saw. Beneath the Elfhame stars as his deep green eyes bore into hers. Eyes that were full of promises.

Kelera grunted as the man's rough hands on her brought her back to the present. Another man with dirt smeared across his face handed him a rope twisted with a thin strand of iron. They tied her arms with it so tight that it cut into her. She hissed with pain, though it was not for the reason they thought. Mortals had the misguided belief that iron would hinder the Fae. She tried not to tug at the ropes in an attempt to keep them from biting into her skin any more than they already were.

She caught a glimpse of her father as they began to drag her away. His fists were clenched tightly and his jaw was set. She prayed to the stars that he would keep his temper at bay. Her life depended on King Tristan listening to them. All of their lives did.

Cunningham walked beside her. He brushed her hair from her ear to reveal the point at the top and leaned in to whisper venomously, "Lady Kelera, daughter of Sir Aldric, you are under arrest for the kidnapping of Princess Cierine, for colluding and conspiring with the Fae against the mortal realm. You will be tried for treason against your king and your country. Should you be found guilty, you will be executed by beheading."

Kelera shivered. He was getting pleasure from this. Did he hate her that much for simply existing? She'd never done anything to cause him insult or injury. They'd only ever met a few times in passing. Or was he happy that she would take the fall for the crimes he himself had committed? He was mortal, which meant that he could have been the one to feed the lies to King Tristan. As a respected member of the court, he would easily be believed.

"Perhaps you should be reading these rights to yourself." She side-eyed him, trying to gauge his reaction.

His face revealed nothing. Instead, he picked up his pace, leading the way to the palace. Guiding her to her prison. His men pushed her roughly through the small village that was settled near the palace gates.

Villagers were gathered in the street, giving her and Cunningham's men a wide berth as they passed by. Even with the setting sun, she could see their faces clearly. Soft shadows were cast along them, but the bitterness and unease were as clear as day. Some, who were not brave enough to stand in the crowd, craned their necks as they hung out their window. They were all there to get a look at the supposed traitor and her walk of shame.

A few cursed and spat at her feet, calling her a monster and a whore. Others threatened to come close, waving white-knuckled fists in the air. Cunningham's guards were determined to get the prisoner into her cell and thrust the enraged villagers back.

Murmurs in the crowd soon turned to shouts. One man yelled, "Take the beast's head!"

Others cried out, "She has brought death to us all!"

"The King never should have let her stay!"

"Should have smothered her in her cradle!"

"Fae whore!"

Kelera remained stone-faced as she walked. She would not allow their words to sting. They were afraid and ignorant of what was truly going on. It wasn't their fault. They were facing a threat they didn't understand, and it was easier to have someone to blame than to wonder why all of this was happening to them and their families.

It was only when she spotted a few women from the palace that her heart ached a little in betrayal. Drisella was at the front of them, not a hair out of place on her head. She raised her regal nose in the air, looking down on Kelera as if she were nothing more than a piece of dirt under her silk slippers.

Kelera had never liked Drisella and her friends. They'd shown her nothing but cruelty. But they had grown up together in the palace. The fact that these women could stand here and watch Kelera suffer as if it were the newest form of entertainment struck a chord within her. How many others in the palace would be thrilled to see the "villainous halfling" brought to "justice?"

Kelera refused to allow anyone to see the effect this was beginning to have on her, so she locked her eyes on the gates ahead and counted each step she took. One, two, three, four... if she could just focus on her steps, then she could suppress the heartbreaking betrayal that threatened to take her determination to save them away.

Something hit her in the leg and she looked down to see a rotten beet. It left a reddish-purple stain on her pants. Shouting erupted in the crowd where the beet had come from, and she spotted Dodger's large frame. Her friend and her father's right hand. Her heart fluttered at seeing a friendly face in the angry mob. Well, friendly for her... not so much for the fruit thrower. Dodger slammed his head into a villager holding another piece of rotting fruit and blood began to pour from the man's broken nose.

Dodger nodded to Kelera and held a hand to his heart. "We stand with you, Pipsqueak. Stay strong!"

Cunningham shouted to his men. "Get him out of here!"

Before she could see where they were taking him, Cunningham shoved her through the gate. She glanced back one last time, hoping to catch another glimpse of her friend, but all she was met with were resentful, frightened faces staring back at her.

Chapter Sixteen

K elera rubbed her arms to stop the shivering. She'd never been in the dungeons that were hidden in the depths of the Nevene palace before. When she and Cierine were young, they tried to sneak down to catch a peek at the infamous criminals who resided there. It all seemed very entertaining at the time, but now that she was here, she could think of no place worse to be. Even the pits in the Unseelie palace didn't compare to the damp walls in the mortal dungeons that dripped with water.

She shifted on the mold covered mattress in a hopeless attempt to get comfortable. The cramped cell smelled of human filth and she wondered what happened to the poor soul who had been here before her.

Prisoners rattled against their bars, shouting profanity at the guards, who sat at a cramped table playing cards. The guards would occasionally shout back, but judging by the slur in their speech, there was something stronger than tea in their cups.

Kelera leaned her head against the stone wall and looked up at the narrow window above her. It was so small that even a child wouldn't be able to slip through, but the soft moonlight that drifted in gave her a reprieve from the darkness of being partially underground.

Once upon a time, patience had been something she'd had plenty of. She had worked hard to be tolerant of those who treated her like an outsider in the mortal realm. And she'd been vigilant when she had worked at becoming the perfect lady of court in the hopes of one day getting her happily ever after.

But that girl was gone. That version of herself was replaced with a raging fire. She was a woman now with responsibilities that far surpassed table manners and holding her tongue when someone made a snide remark about her ears or her mother.

It occurred to her that the first version of herself was never real. Her time in the Unseelie Court showed her that she'd been wearing a mask her entire life. Trying to hide who she really was. And now that she knew that, there was no going back. Her time with Adrastus had taught her that.

A lump in her throat formed as the thought of Adrastus crept in. She'd been so consumed with fear for her father and the relief that came with getting back to the mortal realm, that she hadn't fully contemplated what might have happened to Adrastus after she'd left him with Samael's men hot on his trail.

She shivered. Loneliness was something she'd been used to all her life. Aside from Cierine and her father's men, she'd been an outcast. Tolerated, but never truly accepted. But that had all changed with Adrastus. Even the Guardians had been quick to accept her. Many in Elfhame had. The absence of them was suffocating now.

She balled her hands into fists, digging her nails into her palms.

If she could take back the horrible things she'd said to Adrastus, then she would. If she had spoken out of logic rather than fear, then maybe she could have reasoned with them all. Maybe they would have come with her. But what was done, was done. It was time to face up to the consequences of her actions. And to pray that everything she had done would not be in vain.

She shut her eyes, trying to drown out the sounds of the prisoners and the dripping water around her. Instead, she concentrated on the buzz of her magic, intense and inviting in her veins. And with it came the icy chill and warm embrace of Adrastus' power that was still entwined with her own. He was still alive. Of that, she had no doubt. What would it feel like if that changed? If the familiar sensation of their bound magic was broken suddenly. The possibility made her ill.

She slid down on the mattress and laid on her side, hoping the nausea would soon pass. She would never forgive herself if something happened to him. But there hadn't been any other choice. Adrastus was capable of defending himself against his brothers' magic. He had proven that in the pits when he had won Kelera from Samael. Her father, on the other hand, was no match for that sort of power.

As gifted of a fighter as he was, if she had not made the deal with Samael, then it would have cost her father his life. She wouldn't blame Adrastus if he hated her—if he never forgave her for not choosing him. *I did what I had to do. There was no other choice.* She repeated this thought to herself until a commotion at the guards' table startled her.

She groaned as she sat up on the stiff mattress and craned her neck to see through the bars on her cell door. One of the chairs was lying on its side and the guards were shouting at someone.

"You can't be down here!"

"I can do as I damn well please. Now *move aside*."

Kelera smiled to herself despite her bleak circumstances. She would know that commanding voice and fiery red hair anywhere. She stumbled up to the bars and pressed her face between them as she shouted, "Cierine!"

Cierine spun around with a look of fury on her freckled face. The guard moved to grab her arm, and she swatted him away. "Don't you dare put your hands on me, you buffoon!" He grabbed at her arm again and she reared back, slapping him hard in the face. He stumbled back with his mouth gaping open, and Kelera felt just as stunned as he looked.

Cierine had always had a fiery spirit to match her flaming hair, but when Kelera last saw her in the Unseelie Court, she'd been defeated. Abuse at Samael's hand had dimmed her a little and Kelera had worried she'd never quite recover from it. Seeing her now, like this, washed away all of those worries.

Cierine ran to Kelera, reaching her hands through the bars. Kelera took hold of her soft, delicate hands and held tight, afraid if she let go, then her best friend might slip away as quickly as she had come.

Cierine was breathless as she asked, "Are you alright? They haven't hurt you, have they?" Her eyes were dark with concern as she looked Kelera over from head to toe.

"No. I'm okay." Then, in the next breath, Kelera said, "You made it home. I was so worried it might not have worked when I pushed you through the veil without me."

The guards were standing by the table, looking unsure of what they should do. The one who had been slapped finally sat down in his seat, clearly not wanting to call upon the Princess's wrath again. The other followed suit, allowing the women a moment to talk.

Cierine gave her a wicked grin. "Of course I got through. You think a magical veil is enough to hold me back?" she joked. Then, more seriously, she added, "It was chaos when I returned. They were trying to blame everything on you. I told them what really happened and tried to make them understand, but they wouldn't listen. I even tried amassing a search party with my own money, but no one would take it. They were afraid my uncle would punish them if they did." She furrowed her brow. "I'm so sorry I left you there, Kelera. I'm so, so sorry."

Kelera smiled softly. "Don't be sorry." She peeked at the guards to make sure they weren't listening. "Did my father talk to you?"

"He did. He told me everything. But," she bit her lip as if afraid to ask, "what happened to you there? He said you seemed... different."

"Different?" Were her father and Cierine doubting her now, too? She bit the inside of her cheek to distract herself from the heaviness in her chest.

Cierine studied Kelera's face carefully. "He said you were talking about using your magic and how you had performed some sort of spell."

What would they think of her if they knew she had bound herself for life to a prince of Unseelie? She released Cierine's hands. "There was a ceremony."

Cierine raised an intrigued eyebrow. "What sort of ceremony?"

Perhaps it would be best just to come out with it. "I bound myself to Prince Adrastus." She held her breath in anticipation of Cierine's response.

Cierine's eyes widened, and she gasped. "What does that even mean?"

"It means our magic is linked." Of course, it meant far more than that. But she wasn't sure how to explain it to someone like Cierine. Even if she was her best friend, she was still mortal and had suffered at the hand of the Unseelie.

"Did he force you?" As Cierine asked, Kelera was reminded once again of how fierce and protective her friend could be.

"No. We each had our reasons. But he's not what you think. He's different from Samael."

The corner of Cierine's mouth perked up in a sly smile. "You care for him."

"I do," Kelera admitted, though she couldn't bring herself to voice just how much.

"Where is he now? Why didn't he cross the veil with you?"

"We had a... disagreement. I went off on my own and was ambushed. Samael forced me to choose. Adrastus or Papa." She pushed past the lump in her throat as she continued, "I had to save Papa. I needed to come back to warn you all. Samael's army is—"

"Not coming, according to my uncle." Cierine's face hardened. "But something *has* happened. Not long after your arrest, men carrying a banner with light pink and white flowers attacked one of the southern villages. They claim it is retribution for taking a Seelie Fae woman hostage—for taking *you* hostage. Whoever is behind this is setting you up. Families are already gathering at the palace gates. They're in rough shape."

Kelera's knees went weak, and she grasped hold of the bars. Men carrying the Seelie Queen's banner? It didn't make any sense. It had to be another one of Samael's tricks. How could she have been so foolish? Thinking that anything she had done thus far would have made a difference. People were suffering because of her.

Her voice shook as she said more to herself than to Cierine, "I was too late. I should have come back sooner. I shouldn't have let myself fall for..." She couldn't say Adrastus' name out loud. She was second guessing every decision she had made, questioning if she had done even one small thing differently, if it would have changed the course of things. Her chest rose and fell with quick breaths as she said, "I have to get out of here, Cierine."

"I'm working on that. Sir Aldric is in Tristan's chambers now. If anyone can make my uncle listen, it would be your stubborn old papa." Cierine wrinkled her brow. "Perhaps if I can get to Alexander and ask for his help, we could get you out of here faster. I hate the thought of you being trapped in this place."

Kelera felt ill all over again at the prospect of seeing Alexander. Would he even agree to help? Or did he, too, believe the lies that were being told about her? If he came for her, then that would mean that he hadn't given up on her as she had on him. After all that she had done—after her night with Adrastus under the Elfhame stars—she wouldn't be able to give her heart to Alexander. Would he come to her if he knew that truth?

Cierine's voice was heavy with concern as she asked, "Kelera, what's wrong? You're as white as a wraith."

"It's nothing." She collected herself and reached for her friend through the bars. "You have no idea how glad I am to see you."

"Not as happy as I am. And not as happy as we'll both be once you're out of this horrid place." She wrinkled her nose. "Can you believe we *wanted* to see this place when we were little? Some things are best left to the imagination."

They both laughed. Cierine always had a way of making Kelera feel better. It was a short-lived reprieve, though, as the guards snapped at them. "Time's up! The King was clear. There were to be no visitors."

Cierine whispered, "Should I hit him again?"

Kelera patted her on the hand. "You've done enough for now."

"I *will* find a way to free you. After all, I do owe you a rescue." Cierine turned on her heel and brushed past the guards with an air of confidence.

The one she had struck flinched as she slammed the door to the stairs shut behind her.

Once again, Kelera was left with the excruciating task of waiting. She stared down at the plate the guards had brought to her. It was a sad excuse for a meal with a piece of stale bread and something gray and lumpy beside it. Even if she hadn't been experiencing constant waves of anxiety accompanied with nausea, she still wouldn't have eaten it.

She curled into a ball on the mattress, trying to focus on the warmth of her magic and not the chill in the cell. She would wait to be rescued as Cierine had suggested. If she used her magic to escape, then it would only give the tribunal more evidence to use against her. Instead, she would wait for her father and maybe even Alexander to talk some sense into the council. They respected Alexander and if anyone could secure her release, it would be him. Then she would have a chance to set things straight. To tell them that the Seelie had nothing to do with the attacks. That it was all happening because of the Shadow King of Unseelie.

Exhaustion soon crept in, clouding her guilt and she hoped it would send her into a much needed sleep. Her magic draped itself over her like a warm blanket, shielding her from the cold. As she began to drift off, she settled into that warmth. With all the emotions she was experiencing since her arrest, she expected to fall into a fit of nightmares. But instead, the constant flow of her magic dancing with Adrastus' kept her grounded.

She whispered quietly, wishing he could hear her, *"I'm so sorry, Adrastus. I thought I would be okay with the choice I made, but I've made such a mess of things."* She longed to see his face, to be wrapped in his arms again, and to feel his lips on hers. She never should have let herself care for him the way that she did. Then her heart wouldn't be breaking in two at this very moment.

Tears spilled onto the mattress as she thought, *I did this to myself. I am the reason Samael took Cierine. I am the reason the rescue party never made it through the border. It was my fault that I wasn't strong enough to contain my magic. If I hadn't felt the need to bind myself to Adrastus, then I could have gotten here sooner to warn them. This is all my fault.*

Adrastus' magic tightened around her own, jolting her, and throwing her onto her back. She stiffened from the strength of it, and every muscle in her body went rigid in response. She tried to move, but was frozen in place.

Panic coursed through her as her vision went white. She attempted to call out to the guards, but her voice wouldn't come. Adrastus' magic snapped at hers, nipping at it like a rabid animal. Voices filled the cell, but it wasn't the familiar cries of the prisoners or the snarling guards.

Samael's voice was filled with malice as he said, "Father had such high hopes for you. Just think of how disappointed he would be if he could see you now."

It felt as if Kelera's heart had stopped completely as her fear slithered around her like a snake about to devour her. Her vision cleared and she could see Samael in front of her. She tried to move her arms, but they were tied into place by chains frosted with a thin layer of ice. It shimmered with magic. There was no use trying to struggle. He was wielding the power of a king now.

Kelera was dizzy. How had she gotten here? Her gaze darted around the room. There was a massive wooden desk to her right, and the walls were painted with beautiful fall foliage. Leaves danced along the walls in bold oranges and reds. Or was it just from her spinning head?

Samael continued to taunt, "Unfortunately for you, *brother*, he is no longer here to protect you. Wait until you see what I have in store."

Adrastus snarled, "Do your worst. Getting me out of the way will not win you this war."

His voice sounded close. As if it were coming from her own throat. Startled, she looked down again at the hands restrained by the chains. They were large and strong. Not her own. She was seeing through Adrastus' eyes. She wasn't really here at all.

Relief hit her like a tidal wave. He was alive. But it was quickly replaced with horror. Samael had been right. His men had known exactly where to find Adrastus and had taken him as soon as they found the chance.

She continued to watch the scene unfold from his point of view. His magic had brought her here for a reason, whether he realized it or not. She tried to reach out to him in her mind, *Dras, can you hear me?*

Nothing.

Dras. I'm here. I'm right here with you. You need to hold on. Please.

Still no response.

Samael rubbed his hands together and a burst of snow flurries formed between them. "You wouldn't believe how intoxicating the power of the crown is. I had known it would be worth all the bloodshed and sacrifice, but I had no idea it would fill my entire being with such indescribable power." He sighed and took a step closer to Adrastus. "You see, brother, I want more. I want the stars themselves to kneel before me." His grin was filled with promises that he had yet to fulfill. The promise of pain and disaster.

The world will succumb to frost. And be reborn in fire. Who would be the fire that would stand against him?

Samael extended his arms and the flurry of snow wrapped itself around Adrastus.

Kelera wanted to flinch, but Adrastus held steady as he said, "Kill me if you wish, but it will not give you the power you crave."

Samael laughed. "I cannot kill you after the promise I made to that little halfling bitch of yours."

Adrastus fought against the restraints and Kelera hissed in pain as the icy magic bit into her own skin. He snarled, "Kelera is capable of so much more than you give her credit for."

Samael's shadows balled into dark clouds and slammed into Adrastus' face. The magical punch came as a shock. She felt the impact on her own face and shook her head, stunned. He smirked as he stared into her eyes—into Adrastus' eyes. "Kelera betrayed you. She left you behind. But not before leading me right to you."

"Liar," Adrastus snarled.

Don't listen to him, Dras. Samael was trying to use Adrastus' love for her to break him.

"All my Riders had to do was follow the path she'd taken. I'm embarrassed for you that you weren't powerful enough to hold them off." Samael smiled and the candlelight dancing across his face made him look as if he were wearing a mask of light around his eyes.

When Adrastus said nothing, Samael continued, "She chose *them* over *you*. Do you see now that she felt nothing for you? You were a means of survival and nothing more. And now she is facing death as we speak." Adrastus gripped the arms of the chair, digging his fingers in until they turned white. His contained anger only fueled Samael, as he continued to taunt Adrastus, "You didn't honestly think I would allow her to come out of this unscathed? Those mortals are going to do what they do best. They are going to turn on her and make her pay for *our* sins."

He's baiting you, Dras. Do not lose your hope! Kelera was shouting, but Adrastus still could not hear her.

Samael tilted his head as he continued, "You never were good at looking at the bigger picture, were you? Moment by moment, the mortals are rallying to my side. Stupid oafs. It was much easier than I expected. All it took were a few whispers that the Seelie were planning to take down the blackthorns. That it was they, with the help of their halfling Seelie pet, who kidnapped the women." He shrugged. "And now it will be *I*, the merciful King of Unseelie, who will swoop in to offer them help. To infiltrate their ranks and claim their kingdom as my own." His smile was sly as he finished. "They will hold the doors open for me. And with their very own army, I will claim both them and Elfhame."

"You son of a bitch." Adrastus tried to call on his magic. Kelera felt it tug at her own, but it was frozen in place. Was it because of the restraints? Or because it was using its strength to keep her here? She focused, trying to call on it herself. A blast of their power would be enough to incapacitate Samael long enough for Adrastus to escape. At least, she hoped it would.

The power began to rise, but just as she took a breath to release it, Samael wrapped his shadows around Adrastus. Her magic was snuffed out like a candle, and she clenched her teeth in frustration.

Samael cocked his eyebrow. "Interesting. Her magic is still bound to yours. I expected a quick trial and swift death."

Adrastus' voice was filled with satisfaction as he said, "As I've said before. You underestimate her."

"I did hope to have her out of the way before we proceeded, but I'm growing rather impatient."

His shadows slithered around Adrastus, tangling around his arms, legs, and neck. They shifted and moved as if they had a mind of their own, and Kelera held her breath, waiting for the worst and wallowing in desperation. She'd never felt so helpless in her entire life.

Samael stalked around him. "Did you ever have the pleasure of seeing father cast his curse?"

Adrastus grunted in response. But Kelera wasn't sure where this was going. She listened carefully, hoping that the bond would be strong enough to hold her there with Adrastus.

Samael spoke with child-like awe as he said, "I never saw true power until I watched our father destroy a man's very soul. The Night Riders truly were his greatest masterpiece." He shook his head as he mused, "And it's not easy, let me tell you. It comes at a cost—darkening a piece of your own soul in the process. I suppose that's why father only ever made a handful of them." He raised a hand in the air and small, dark shadows swirled around his fingers.

These were different from the ones Kelera had seen him wield many times before. As she peered into them, she saw true darkness. It was a void of nothingness, and just looking at them gave her a sense of pure emptiness. Was that what death would feel like?

Adrastus was silent as Samael continued, "I, however, wish to have an army of them. My own Night Riders, utterly devoted to me. And you, my brother, are going to make quite the addition."

Kelera screamed when Samael grabbed hold of Adrastus, placing his hand over his heart and burrowing the empty shadows into him. Pain seared through Kelera's chest and she thrashed to escape them.

Her vision went black, and she was sure this was the end of both her and Adrastus. She was still thrashing when her sight slowly began to clear. She fought against the firm hands that were pinning her down. Trapping her on a hard mattress.

Her vision returned, and she looked around in confusion to see the stone walls of her prison cell. Her chest still ached from the ambush of Samael's shadows, and she clutched at her heart as a cry tore from her throat. The hands released her and she rolled to her side, curling herself into a ball.

Samael was destroying Adrastus' soul, and she was stuck in a dungeon miles away. He was lost to her, all because she had abandoned him. She shuddered as she cried out his name. "Adrastus."

A man's voice echoed in the small cell. But it wasn't the voice she longed to hear. "Kelera, it's me. It's Alexander."

Chapter Seventeen

K elera tried to stop the flood of tears flowing from her eyes and sat up. Alexander was here. In her cell. Doing her best to collect herself, she wiped at her face and took a deep breath in. The dungeon was as dark and cold as it had been before the dream. It was as if a part of her had never left at all. She cleared her throat and returned her gaze to Alexander. At one time, she would have been relieved to see him, but instead, she felt as empty as Samael's shadows.

Alexander's sandy brown hair had grown longer in the time that she'd been gone. His face was covered in stubble and there were dark circles around his brown eyes, as if he hadn't been sleeping well. She could only imagine how much he and the rest of the realm had been through, knowing that the Fae were lurking in the shadows.

He sat beside her on the small bed, moving carefully as if she were a wounded deer he'd found in the woods. His eyes lingered over the scar on her face longer than she was comfortable with. He reached out to touch it, but she drew away from him.

His voice was calm and soothing as he said, "You are safe here, Kelera. You're home now."

Home. It was a word that had new meaning to her now. There was a time when she couldn't imagine calling anyplace but Nevene home, but now she longed to return to Elfhame. More than anything, she wanted to go back to save Adrastus.

She sat up abruptly. "Are you here to set me free? Has King Tristan agreed?"

Alexander was thoughtful for a moment before he answered, "We are still trying to make him see reason. But Cunningham says he witnessed you using magic. Is that true?"

Once again, she had doomed herself. "It is."

A glimmer of fear flashed across Alexander's face, but he didn't move away from her as she might have expected. Instead, he spoke low enough that the guards wouldn't hear. "Listen to me very carefully. I can fix this. But I need you to do exactly as I say."

She would do anything if it meant getting out of this cell and going to Adrastus. The pain that Samael had inflicted on him was unbearable and there was no telling how long she had before he was too far gone. She nodded eagerly, "Yes. Anything."

He grasped her hands, and she fought the urge to pull away. They were softer than Adrastus' and didn't feel right around her own.

Alexander leaned in close and his breath was warm on her face. "I can break you out. And together, we can cross the veil."

"The blackthorn veil?" She furrowed her brow. Alexander had been accepting of her as a halfling, but had never indicated any interest in the Fae. In fact, he had gone after them when the woman at Cierine's wedding reception had been taken. She shook her head, struggling to understand as she asked, "You mean take you into Elfhame with me?"

"Yes. We can still be together, don't you get it?"

Kelera's stomach turned at the thought. She wouldn't go back to pretending and hiding who she was. Alexander could never give her what Adrastus had offered—unconditional love. She tilted her head and looked at him with guilt eating at her. "I'm sorry, but I can't."

He insisted, "I know you're afraid, but you don't have to be. We can be happy there. We will go back and you will perform the spell that King Samael has requested."

"*Samael*?" She didn't understand. "You want me to *bind* myself to that monster?" She tore her hands away from him and leaped from the bed, putting as much distance between them as she could. "Are you insane? Do you have any idea what you're saying? Do you know how much pain he has caused... how much agony he plans to inflict on the world?" She was too stunned to think straight.

Alexander stood and took a step toward her. She backed into the corner of the cell and looked for the guards, but they were gone. A shiver crept up her spine as she prepared to ask a question she dreaded to hear the answer to. Her words were slow and deliberate as she asked, "How do you know about Samael and the binding spell?"

He held his hands out innocently. "It's not what you think."

"What I think," she continued to speak low and concise, "is that you are the traitor. The one who has been working with him all along. The traitor who has been spreading whispers through the council that Seelie is the threat when it is quite the opposite." She couldn't have believed it if he weren't standing before her saying the words. He knew about Samael and his plans to take her power from her. He was the mortal traitor—the man whom the council trusted enough to take his word as he misdirected them.

Alexander looked down at his boots, avoiding her eye. How could he have betrayed his own people? Trying to come to terms with the realization, she muttered under her breath, "They trusted you. King Tristan, my father... and you sold them out. The people of this realm are counting on you, and you want to feed them to the dogs?"

"I didn't mean for it to get so out of control. But you and I can fix it. We can repair what's been broken."

Fury nearly blinded her as she spat, "You mean repair what *you* have broken."

He ran an exasperated hand through his hair. "You don't understand. My family coffers were empty. Samael paid me to look the other way, promising that no one would be killed in the process. I didn't think a few villagers would be missed." He started speaking quickly, and Kelera struggled to digest it all. He stuttered, "A-and he assured me once he was king, the Fae would pass through Nevene to the northern countries."

As Kelera's anger rose, so did her magic. It was pulsing in her palms, begging for her to unleash it on his traitorous face. "He outwitted you, Alexander. He never said Nevene would remain untouched when they passed through to Amaran and Marenth. He played you for a *fool*."

Alexander's cheeks reddened, and he shouted, "I am nobody's fool!"

Kelera jumped back at the sudden madness in his voice. His body trembled under the dusty light shining through the narrow window. Was it really already dawn?

How much time would it take until Adrastus fell to Samael's magic?

He argued, "He promised to return you to me, and he followed through on that. He will honor the rest of the deal we have made."

Kelera laughed in his face. "He knew there would be no saving me from my fate once I returned. He did not send me back here to be with you. He sent me here to *die*."

Alexander slammed his hand against the wall, jolting her back to the present danger she was in. But she did not cower as she said, "You have betrayed your own people. And for what? The lavish lifestyle that you are accustomed to? There was truth when Samael said the humans he took would not be killed, but I've seen his alternative to death. And it is so much worse." She recalled the screams coming from Samael's room of shadows and the long, icy blades he liked to play with. Like the one he'd used to mar her own face.

Alexander faltered for a moment, and she could have sworn she caught a glimpse of remorse. But then his face hardened as he said, "There is no use dwelling on what is already done. What matters now is that you and I end up on the winning side of this." He grabbed hold of her arms and gave her a small shake. "You will bind yourself to Samael. You and I will marry, and together we will have a place beside his throne."

"Don't you see? Samael will never honor any deals he has made with you. The kidnappings were meant to rock the kingdom, to distract King Tristan and his forces while he planned his ascension to the mortal throne as well as Elfhame's. If he can make them believe that it is the Seelie Court that is coming for the mortal realm, then King Tristan will stand with Samael against them. Samael will claim Elfhame, and then he will take the mortal one."

"Samael would have taken what he wanted either way. I've seen his magic. Our armies wouldn't have stood a chance. King Tristan never would have agreed to work with him if he knew the truth. I am protecting all of us. And Samael's price is simple. Allow him to use your power and you and I will be safe, Kelera. With our position, we can protect your father and Cierine as well!"

She pushed him off of her. "Is that why you asked me to marry you?"

"No. I-I mean, not at first. I had no idea Samael would be so interested in you."

"Then why? You owe me an answer to that, at the very least." She stood her ground, though she wanted to tear his eyes out.

Alexander hung his head in shame. "Because I thought that marriage to a Fae would solidify any alliance I had with him." When she scoffed, he looked up and reached for her again. "But I can make you happy. You believed it once. Please believe it again."

She couldn't contain her rage any longer. She slapped him in the face and sparks flew from her fingertips. "You are asking me to sell a piece of myself for your own happiness. Do you not see that? Or do you just not care as long as you get what you want?"

Alexander stumbled back in surprise. He had the good sense to look nervous as he glanced down at her hands and then back up at her. She stepped forward to strike him again, but his narrowed eyes gave her pause.

His face darkened as he said, "Look around. You are out of options. You can either go to Elfhame and do as I command, or I can leave you to die at your beloved king's hand. And don't think for a moment that he'll stop there. Your father was seen trying to help you escape."

"Don't you *dare* threaten my father." Magic seeped through her skin, heating up the small, damp cell.

Steam lifted from the walls and Alexander reached for the dagger at his belt.

"Do the right thing, Kelera."

She snarled, "You and Samael are too late. He knows that. It is why he sent me here to face execution."

Alexander gripped his dagger, but did not draw it. "What do you mean?"

"I am already bound. To Prince Adrastus, the *rightful* heir to the Unseelie throne." Kelera raised her chin triumphantly.

Alexander's face turned white as he spat, "You're lying."

"Would you like to see for yourself?" With a sly smile, she called upon Adrastus' Unseelie power that had been entwined with hers since the ceremony. It was magic that she had never dared to touch herself. But now, here in this cell beneath the place she had once considered home, she no longer felt the need to hold back. This time, someone would cower to *her*.

Kelera released the magic with full confidence. It effortlessly drifted from the tips of her fingers, filling the already dark room with shadows that threatened to smother everything within sight. She had seen what Adrastus' power could do to a man and if Alexander was determined to stand in her way, then he, too, would see.

"Open the cell, Alexander."

"I cannot do that." He drew the dagger from his belt, but she noted the way his hand trembled. He was frightened. And for once, it didn't bother her.

She raised her chin. "I am going to tell King Tristan of your treachery. Everyone in this palace will know what you have done. You cannot stop me."

His voice shook as he spoke. "You can't."

She snapped the shadows at his feet, forcing him to take a step back toward the bars of the cell. Her lip curled as she said, "All my life I have heard what I can't do. Perhaps it is time for me to show everyone what I am truly capable of."

A rush of heat coursed through her body—her magic spinning itself with Adrastus'. It twisted through his shadows, casting a glow through the cell. She took another step, causing Alexander to press himself against the cell and said, "I am done taking orders from all of you. I have spent my entire life trying to trick others into loving me by being what they want me to be, and I am sick of it. I didn't even know who I was until..." *Elfhame.* Until Elfhame showed her everything she was capable of. Power, strength, and *love.*

Alexander held the dagger out in front of him, pointing it at her heart. "I can't let you leave here. I can't let you tell them. Believe me when I say I didn't want to kill you, but I will do what I have to in order to protect my family's name."

"Your family name will mean *nothing* if Samael succeeds in his plans. You will mean nothing!" The magic stayed under her control, bending to her will as it slithered around Alexander. She held it back just enough so that it would not touch him. As hard as his betrayal was to swallow, she wouldn't hurt him unless he forced her hand. She took a deep breath. "Come with me. Admit to your crimes and perhaps King Tristan will show you mercy."

Alexander laughed bitterly. "You think the council will believe you? If you tell them that I, a loyal member of the court, a son of one of the oldest, most prominent families in all of Nevene, am a traitor? They will never trust someone like you."

Kelera flinched. His words stung, but he was right. The mortals were never going to accept her. No amount of perfection was going to make a difference. It didn't matter that she had learned their silly dances or that she knew which fork to use for each course at their big, fancy dinners. She was never going to find her happiness living amongst them.

She expected to feel rage at the idea that she had wasted years of her life trying to make them happy. They had used and oppressed her and made her believe she had to prove her loyalty. But instead of grief or anger, she felt relief. There was no reason for her to lie to herself any longer. It was freeing.

She shook her head and smiled softly. "You may be right. But it doesn't matter anymore. I have people who care for me." She thought of Gadreel, the villagers in the Winter Court, the Guardians of the Wildwood... and Adrastus. "People who have never tried to change me or use me to their advantage." She shrugged. "I'll be fine. But you, Alexander, are finished."

She raised the shadows, intent on pushing him aside and leaving this prison behind. But Alexander lunged first, with his dagger aimed at her heart. She blocked herself with her hands and the sharp steel cut into her arm, slicing through her jacket. She hissed in pain and the shadows snapped at him. They sizzled as they struck him and the smell of burning flesh filled the air.

Alexander's eyes, which Kelera had once considered beautiful and kind, were now full of malice. "I offered you the world. I was willing to take you when no one else would."

He lunged at her again, but she was ready this time. She cast the shadows down on him, pushing him to his knees. Focusing on the frost in her veins, she drew it out and directed it toward Alexanders arms and legs, freezing him in place.

It was his mistake for thinking that she was the same girl who had walked with him in the gardens. The girl who had believed that he was the answer to all her problems—the man who would give her the happy ending she had longed for. If she hadn't been so stubborn and determined to fit in, then she would have seen what had been in front of her all along. The mortals had turned on her before and they were turning on her again. It was something that Alexander had come here thinking he could use to manipulate her into doing what he wanted.

She sneered down at the deceitful, weak mortal man at her feet. Had she really given up on Adrastus, just to be executed by the very people she was trying to save? Just to be accosted by the man she'd been betrothed to?

Alexander stuttered, "W-what are you doing to me?"

Kelera circled around him slowly, basking in the enjoyment of seeing the traitor at her mercy. "It is one of the benefits of being bound to the Bastard Prince of Unseelie." She leaned down to speak into his ear, "You see, his magic dances in my blood with my own power." She stood and walked in front of him so he would have no choice but to look her in the eye. "You underestimated me. And you underestimated Elfhame. They will stand against Samael and they are stronger than even he anticipates. It seems you chose the wrong side, after all."

Alexander opened his mouth to speak, but the door to the stairs slammed shut. Kelera's shadows covered his mouth to keep him from calling out, but it was too late. Cierine rounded the corner with a familiar face in toe. Gadreel.

Adrastus' older brother slicked his frost-colored hair back and whistled. "This is quite the scene. Here I was expecting to see you in desperate need of assistance and a bath." He and Cierine halted to a stop when they reached her cell. He wrinkled his nose at her. "I suppose I got the bath part right."

Looking incredulously between Kelera and Alexander, Cierine shoved her mass of red hair out of her face and cried out, "Kelera! What are you doing?" Her eyes flitted around the cell and back to them.

Kelera stood tall. "Shall I tell the Princess of your treachery?" Alexander was trying to speak through the shadows, and his muffled grunts grated on her nerves. She snarled at him, "It is time that you come clean."

Cierine narrowed her eyes as she watched the exchange. "Come clean about what, exactly?"

Kelera straightened as she said, "Lord Alexander is the mortal traitor. He made a deal with the King Samael and planned to trade me and my magic for his own gain."

Cierine's face turned as red as her hair and she raised an eyebrow. Kelera waited for her to doubt her or to try to argue on his behalf. It was, after all, a shocking truth. But instead, she said, "Do you confess to these allegations, Lord Alexander?"

Kelera removed the shadows from his mouth with a flick of her wrist and they drifted closer to her, hugging her body. She looked down her nose at Alexander. "Confess to your crimes."

He spat on the ground at her feet. "Never."

Gadreel balled his hand into a fist. For the first time since meeting him, he looked every bit the Prince of Darkness that he was as he said, "It *was* you slipping out in the night to meet my brother, wasn't it?"

Alexander widened his eyes in surprise. He sputtered as he denied it in a fruitless attempt to save himself, "I do not know you or your brother. She is a liar and a traitor. She will say anything to save herself."

Realization dawned in Cierine's eyes. "When my uncle ordered a curfew for all the court, you were caught sneaking out. Of course, they all thought perhaps you were just having some fun in the brothels—trying to drown out the sorrow of losing your betrothed. But that wasn't the case, was it? My uncle and his council allowed your status to cloud their judgment." She leaned in close to the bars, staring daggers at Alexander. "You may have been able to fool them. But you will not do the same with me."

Kelera recalled the night when she had run into the field, following the screams of the helpless mortal woman whom Samael and his minions had kidnapped. Alexander had been firm in trying to get her to stay behind while he followed the screams into the tree line.

She'd been blind too. She whispered in disbelief, "The truth was in front of us from the start. At Cierine's reception, in the field, you were stalling for time so that Samael's men could get the woman over the border. You wanted me to stay where I was so I wouldn't see."

Alexander bared his teeth. "I will admit nothing." He looked directly at Cierine as he said, "I demand to be taken to the king."

Kelera's nose flared in anger. He still expected to talk himself out of the mess he had made. Magic burned in her veins, and it felt as if her blood was boiling. How many of the helpless mortals in Samael's room of shadows were there because of this man and his greed? How many had been brutalized and tortured, all in the name of keeping his family coffers full?

Her control slipped and with it, so did the Unseelie power she was wielding. It slammed into Alexander so hard that she heard the crunching of bones. He cried out in agony, but that only fueled the magic. Her Seelie power pushed Adrastus' shadows forward, burrowing into Alexander's mind.

The images of Samael's shadowy cavern were still playing out in her memory. The flash of icy steel, and the cries of tortured souls calling out to her in the dark.

She felt the images flow from her and into Alexander's mind. It was like slipping a letter beneath a door.

Alexander writhed in agony, straining against the magic she was still using to hold him in place. "What are you doing to me? Make it stop!"

Coolly, she said, "Admit to what you've done."

The power flowing from her was dizzying. It filled her entire being with a satisfaction that threatened to consume her. The fire was building within her. Magic that was wild and not meant to be contained. He was at her mercy. They could all be at her mercy if she chose it. There was no one to stop her. Her eyes darkened around the edges until all she was left with was the immense power engulfing her.

Images of the nightmare she'd had in the Spring Court blazed to life. The visions of a world consumed by destruction and fire flowed from her to Alexander. She would share her terror with him.

She ignored his horrified screams. *Embers and ash*, she thought to herself, *perhaps the wraith was right and that is my fate.*

Without her sight, she could feel every fiber of the magic of Elfhame. Her nerve endings buzzed and crackled from the heat of her Seelie magic, but she shivered from the chill of Adrastus' Unseelie power. It was like being trapped inside of a storm with no escape to be seen.

Is this what Adrastus feels when he's losing himself to the combination of his Seelie and Unseelie power? This is why he needed my help to ground him, she thought with a start.

"Kelera! Stop!" Cierine's words were a distant echo in her mind, but there was no mistaking the terror in her voice. It was impossible to tell how long she had been entranced by the power, or what she was doing to those in the prison cell with her.

Kelera felt for her magic with her mind and took hold of it. Like a rope attaching a boat to an anchor, her magic settled Adrastus' Unseelie power. As it calmed, her vision returned to reveal the destroyed cell. Weak spots in the stone walls had crumbled, and the bed was popping with a dying fire.

Alexander was lying unconscious on the floor, his chest rising and falling steadily. There was no sorrow in her heart at the sight, not after all he'd done. He was lucky she'd left him alive. She turned to Cierine, fearing the terror she thought she would find in her eyes. Her hair was ruffled and there was a hole in her dress where it had been singed.

Kelera gasped, "Oh stars, did I do that?"

Cierine raised her eyebrows as she answered, "Yes. Have you always been able to-to…" she fumbled for the words to finish. She had never seen Kelera use her power like this. When they were children, Kelera had attracted magical creatures and perhaps had used a sliver of magic here and there in games. But never to this extent. She wasn't sure that Cierine would have even remembered it.

"I have always had magic, but not like this." She paused for a moment, trying to read her. Would she hold this against her? Would her best friend fear her because of what she could do? Kelera bit her lip. "I'm so sorry, Cierine. I didn't mean to hurt you. I'm still learning to control it."

Cierine embraced her in a tight hug. "You need not apologize to me." When she pulled away, her eyes were bright. "I'm rather impressed."

Kelera laughed with relief.

Cierine took hold of Kelera's hands and sighed. "I suppose I should go to Tristan." She glanced down at Alexander. "I will tell his Majesty that Lord Alexander here has revealed himself as the traitor and to warn him of what is coming."

The adrenaline from the confrontation with Alexander was wearing off. She followed Cierine out of the cell and they locked it behind them. It would hold Alexander there until the King decided what to do with him.

Kelera turned to Cierine to face her. "What are you doing here, anyway?"

Cierine put a hand on her hip and gestured to Alexander's unconscious body. "I could ask the same of you. Here I am, playing out my heroic fantasies to come and rescue you, only to find that you've already saved yourself." She blew air through her lips, making a funny sound.

Kelera laughed and turned her attention to Gadreel. "And you. How are you *here*, of all places?"

He smiled broadly at her. "Oh, how I have missed the way you wrinkle your nose when you're surprised."

Cierine stepped aside and Kelera threw herself into Gadreel's arms. He rested his chin on her shoulder and spoke into her hair, "I thought you could use a friend. Though I did not expect to run into this beautiful vixen." He gestured to Cierine, who blushed at the compliment. "I didn't realize you already had someone planning your escape."

Cierine chimed in, "I was looking for Alexander so I could ask for his help." She shot a seething look at his unconscious body, then continued, "Instead, I spotted Gadreel sneaking through the gardens. I thought he was one of Samael's men, so I hit him with a rock." She gestured sheepishly toward the minor cut on Gadreel's hairline.

He laughed that beautiful, lighthearted laugh that Kelera had grown to love during her time in the Unseelie palace. Then he said, "She has quite the arm. But once I kindly explained who I was and what I was doing here, we decided to be in cahoots."

Cierine stared down at Alexander in disgust. "I can't believe it was him all along."

"I couldn't believe it at first either. I guess I was blinded like everyone else." Kelera grabbed Cierine's arm. "Listen, I need you to gather as many men as you can who are willing to fight. If King Tristan won't listen to you, then I need you and my father to be ready."

Cierine nodded. "Francis will help. He's believed every word I've told him since my return." Her face glowed as she spoke of her husband.

Kelera, however, had her doubts. Lord Francis' knight, Sir Jacome, had accosted her at the King's Tournament before Cierine was taken. All for being Fae. Kelera hesitated, then asked, "If the Seelie come to aid the mortals, will his men stand with them?"

Cierine nodded again with her usual air of confidence. "They will once I reveal the treachery that has been at play here. Sir Jacome still doesn't understand what came over him that day at the King's Tournament. Kelera, there are still people here who will stand by you." After an uncomfortable beat, she said, "Though, it will take some convincing where the King is concerned. Villagers continue to spill in from the south, claiming that it is in fact a Seelie raid party that has murdered their fathers and brothers. It's not good."

"Then we will make do with whatever force you can muster. The truth will reveal itself in time. Let's just pray to the stars that it won't be too late when it does."

Gadreel bit his lip. "Kelera, you need to know that things have escalated in Elfhame as well. The Seelie Queen is fading fast, meanwhile the frost is spreading. And Samael now has the forces he needs to storm the Spring Court. If you factor in the mortals, then I fear we really are in peril."

Kelera rubbed at her temples. "Surely the Unseelie Fae will not stand with him after what he's done to them in the pits."

His voice was filled with disgust as he said, "Rumors say he has killed women and children from the villages in Unseelie to set an example for anyone who would dare think to stand against him. Between his growing army of Night Riders and calling forth every Unseelie man and woman fit to fight, he has the numbers he needs."

The villagers weren't warriors, but they did have magic gifted to them from the land. If he was forcing them all to stand with him, then their combined power could be strong enough to take down the Seelie defenses. She gritted her teeth as she said, "Then there isn't another moment to waste." She grabbed Gadreel's hand and began to pull him toward the door.

Cierine called out to ask, "What are you going to do?"

Kelera looked back at her, then at Gadreel, grateful for his presence. "I'm going to go home—to Elfhame."

Chapter Eighteen

Kelera was grateful for knowing King Tristan's palace like the back of her own hand. She'd spent her life exploring these halls and had memorized every twist and turn. And thankfully, these walls, unlike the ones in the Unseelie Palace, did not have a mind of their own. She could easily escape this one and reach the blackthorn veil. She only hoped that once she was back in Elfhame, she would be able to find where Samael was holding Adrastus. It was clear from the vision that he was in a manor of some sort. Perhaps in the Autumn Court, judging by the fall foliage painted on the walls.

Gadreel followed silently, allowing her to guide their way. The halls leading away from the dungeons were quiet. This wing of the palace was often avoided. It was where the King's storage and archives were located. The lights were dimly lit, casting foreboding shadows across the carpets. They reminded her of the ones she had called on in the cell. Adrastus' magic had been present and that must have been a good sign, right? That meant he had to still be fighting to hold on to his humanity.

They cut around a corner, heading to a small servant's entrance that would lead down the stairs and into the side of the courtyard. She and Cierine had used it many times before as children when they didn't want to be caught exploring this part of the palace.

She took to the steps as quickly and quietly as possible, following the curve of the stairwell. Before she could catch herself, she slammed into someone. The force knocked her back and into Gadreel's arms.

"Cunningham." Kelera choked back the lump in her throat as his weasel-like face came into view. If he called for the guard, they would come running. And as hurt as she was by her recent treatment, she didn't want to punish them for following orders as they'd been trained to do.

Duke Cunningham's eyes narrowed, reminding her of a skeleton with the sharp angles of his face. He put his hand on the hilt of his sword, but as he gripped it, ready to draw, Gadreel blew a swift breath in his direction. A frost formed around Cunningham's hand, freezing it in place.

"Nice," Kelera whispered to him. She'd only seen Gadreel use his magic for more... pleasurable reasons. This was the first time she'd seen him use the shadowy ice magic shared by the sons of King Cyrus.

She leveled her gaze at Duke Cunningham, whose eyes had gone wide in surprise. He likely hadn't expected another Fae to be lurking within the palace walls today. With a firm and steady voice, she warned him, "We do not want to hurt you. But we are leaving this palace one way or another. If you go down to the cells, then you will find Lord Alexander. *He* is the real traitor, not me."

Cunningham gave her a sly smile, shocking her into silence. "You are quite impressive, I must admit. The King and council were wrong to underestimate you."

She had no time for compliments, nor did she want anything of the sort from someone like him. Gritting her teeth, she repeated, "It is Lord Alexander who is your enemy, not I. Now, will you allow us to pass or will you force my friend here to freeze you permanently?" She wasn't sure if Gadreel was capable of such a thing, but judging by the way Cunningham was eyeing him, he believed it.

Cunningham tilted his head as he studied her. "I do not know whether you are telling the truth. But I am curious to see how this will all play out. I'd be inclined to put my money on you."

Rumors of his gambling were spread far and wide in Nevene. His response shouldn't have come as a total surprise, but still, it wasn't the answer she wanted. Impatience was building as she clenched her hands into fists at her side. She needed to get to Adrastus. If there was any chance of saving him from the fate Samael bestowed upon him, then she needed to go now and she'd be willing to take Cunningham down as she did so.

Cunningham shrugged his shoulders. "It seems the prisoner escaped while I was out patrolling. I would imagine by now, she has sought sanctuary across the veil." He gave her a wink.

Kelera nodded slowly in understanding. It was difficult to tell whether he was letting her go for fear of what she and Gadreel would do to him if he tried to stop them or if it was for some unknown reason he didn't want to share with them. Either way, this was their chance to escape. She grabbed Gadreel's hand and hurried down the stairs. Before they reached the bottom, she called up to Cunningham, her voice echoing on the stone, "I will not forget this."

"See to it that you don't. I don't offer my help for nothing."

Cunningham was the last man she would have expected to find an ally in, but she would take any support where she could get it. They fled to the landing of the stairwell and bounded out of a small door leading out of the servant's entrance. She was ready to leave the palace far behind her—thinking, now, only of the man who she had left behind in Elfhame.

Please don't let me be too late, she thought to herself as she and Gadreel ran as fast as their legs would carry them. She had no idea how long it took for the Night Rider curse to consume a man's soul, but she was willing to do everything in her power to reach Adrastus before that happened.

***

Urgency pushed Kelera forward. They'd slipped out through the palace gardens without anyone else catching sight of them. Once free of the palace grounds, Gadreel took the lead easily with his long, graceful legs. Kelera, on the other hand, struggled to keep up. Her legs ached from being stuck in the cramped cell after such a lengthy journey back to Nevene on foot.

Kelera had told him about her dream in between heavy breaths. He'd listened carefully, not revealing much of his reaction with his face. Only once she had finished completely did he respond, "I should have known what he was planning."

"You couldn't—"

"It was my only job. It was the reason I stayed behind instead of going with the two of you. The reason I was not with Oliver when..." He slowed to a walk and wiped at his eyes with the back of his sleeve.

"When what, Gadreel?" Kelera put her hand on his arm.

"When they came for Adrastus. Oliver and your friends from the Summer Court were with him. They were coming to help you. But," his voice cracked, "they were all ambushed. That's when Dras was taken."

Kelera's stomach did a flip. They were coming for her? All of them? In the end, they had all chosen her. Her eyes prickled with tears. "And the others?" She dug her nails into her hand, fearful that all of her friends were dead because she had left them behind. The gratitude she'd felt a moment ago knowing that they had come for her dissipated, replaced with guilt that threatened to rock her to her core.

"Wounded. *Alive*, thank the fates, but wounded. Oliver sent word to me about you and Dras. But the point is that I should have been there. I should have been there to protect you all. Or at the very least, I should have gathered the right information to keep you safe."

"It is not your fault." It was hers, but she couldn't bring herself to voice that part out loud.

"Do not act like you're not carrying guilt as well. I will forgive myself if you do." He gave her a sad, lopsided smile.

"Let's get home first, then we'll work on ourselves." She smiled and patted him on the arm.

They picked up their pace again, but just as they came into view of the blackthorns, they were met with unfamiliar faces. There were at least fifteen that Kelera could count, each armed with steel blades and each donning the Seelie Queen's crest over their ill-fitted armor.

Bodies littered the ground at their feet. None of them had been armed to defend themselves. Nor had they been dressed for battle. Nausea came in waves and Kelera trembled. This had been a massacre.

The Fae before her didn't deserve to call themselves soldiers. They were murderers. And they were standing between her and Elfhame.

Gadreel groaned. "This is definitely not good."

Kelera didn't hesitate to summon her magic. There was nowhere for her and Gadreel to go but forward. These were no Seelie soldiers. She'd spent enough time in Elfhame to recognize Winter and Autumn Fae when she saw them. These were Samael's men, and she would take them down without mercy or die trying. A man with wild white hair and icy eyes blew a horn and the small force turned their attention to her and Gadreel. There would be no turning back now.

"Get ready," she warned Gadreel.

He scoffed. "You sound like Dras."

Kelera smiled to herself and allowed Adrastus' shadows to flow from her palms along with a whirlwind of power—her power. The men paused, startled by the sight of Unseelie magic coming from her. It seemed Samael had not let his men know that the halfling wielded the magic of one of their own princes.

Their hesitation gave her the advantage that she needed. She sent a wave of shadows into them, rocking them off their feet and into the dirt. Gadreel joined in, calling on a flurry above that sent hail raining down on them.

One of the Unseelie men ducked away from the stormy attack and beelined for Kelera. She let her anger drive her and Adrastus' shadows, but just as the man reached her, the magic buckled. The shadows blinked out. The man tackled her to the ground and snapped his sharp fangs at her neck. She struggled under the weight of him.

Where was Adrastus' magic? The power was still there, but it had dimmed significantly. All she felt were subtle traces of it. Like the thin smoke from a dying fire. She was losing it. She was losing *him*.

Panic coursed through her, distracting her long enough for the man's teeth to puncture her just below her artery. Searing pain shot down through her shoulder and she screamed with a fiery rage. The man gasped as her Seelie magic smoldered in her veins. The heat raced along her skin, burning the man where he touched her.

He threw himself from her, crying out in agony and trying to use his ice magic to offset the burns. It was useless. Any frost that he tried to form on his skin sizzled and melted. Steam rose from him as he screamed for help.

Gadreel shouted to her, "I can't hold them all off!"

Heavy footsteps sounded from behind her, and she spun to face whoever was coming to join the Unseelie. But her heart soared when she saw the flash of familiar armor. Dodger stood at the head of the knights. Her father's knights.

He shouted to Gadreel, "Perhaps we can help!" The knights wasted no time in advancing on the Fae, stepping into a formation that came with years of practice. They clashed with the Unseelie, slicing through flesh with effortless precision.

Dodger grabbed hold of Kelera's arm. "I told you, Pipsqueak, we stand with you."

She whipped her head toward the knights and Unseelie. A few of the mortal men went down at the mercy of the Unseelie's magic. She shook her head. "You don't stand a chance against their magic."

"We will do what we can to give you the upper hand."

She nodded but couldn't ignore the growing pit in her stomach. "Okay, go."

Dodger ran to join his men. They were quick and that would work in their favor, allowing them to evade some of the magic that the Fae were trying to hit them with. Still, it wasn't enough. Knights were falling left and right. She tried to call on the shadows again, but instead felt her own magic raging. If she released it without Adrastus' power to ground it, then it could be a catastrophe. She could wound her father's knights in the process.

Something sharp hit her from behind. She spun around to drive her magic into the attacker but stopped dead in her tracks. The horned man held a tiny girl, who couldn't be more than four years old, in front of him. His gray clawed hands seized the girl by the neck, threatening to puncture her delicate flesh.

Kelera could still hear the cries of the men behind her as Gadreel and the knights continued to fight them off. But all she could focus on was the sweet, innocent face looking at her with pleading brown eyes. Kelera held her hands up in a sign of truce, showing that she would hold off her magic, and said to the man, "Let her go."

He snarled at her. His voice was thick with an accent she didn't recognize as he said, "How is it that you wield the magic of our land?" His grip held firm on the girl and she whimpered.

Kelera's heart hammered in her chest. She couldn't count on this man to release the child. The only way was to catch him off guard. And she couldn't rely on Adrastus' power to do it. Instead, she recalled a time, long ago, when she was a young girl chasing a bogie through these very fields. It was the last time she had used her magic before promising her father to lock it away.

Rather than calling on the fire she so often wielded, she allowed her magic to burrow into the ground, feeling for the roots under foot. In an effort to keep the man talking, she explained, "I am bound to Prince Adrastus of the Unseelie Court, and I must demand that you release the girl. She poses no threat to you and your men."

He raised an eyebrow. "But you do."

Her nose flared as she said, "Yes. I do."

Her magic found what it was searching for. Just as it had done when she had wielded her power to trap the bogie, a thick root began to form from the earth and she tugged it up with her mind. Far more than a hair ribbon was on the line this time.

The root answered her call, bursting through the hard packed earth. She wrapped it around the man's throat. He was so stunned that both of his hands went to the root, trying to tear it off of him. Kelera motioned for the girl to come to her. The child did as she was bid, wrapping her tiny arms around Kelera's leg. She pulled the girl into her so she wouldn't see what came next. With a flick of her other hand, she commanded the root, snapping the man's neck.

He fell to the ground. Without a second thought, Kelera turned to the battle raging behind her. She held the girl tight, keeping her tiny, innocent face from looking in the direction of what she was about to do.

Kelera closed her eyes and drove her magic under the men's feet. Careful not to allow it under the knights, she chose the Unseelie, who weren't directly engaged with the mortals. The land answered her as roots shot up from the ground and into flesh. Fae cried out in shock and pain as the roots burrowed through their armor and into their bodies.

Dodger and the other knights leapt back from the Unseelie, giving Kelera an opening to finish more of them off. But as she called on more of the roots, the Unseelie raised their hands in surrender. Their eyes were all on her and a shudder wracked her body as she eased her magic to a stop. She waited, seeing if the Unseelie would accept her mercy or continue their attack. She didn't want to kill them if they were willing to concede.

An Unseelie boy, no more than a teenager, knelt to the ground and whispered under his breath, "By the stars." He lowered his head to the earth in submission, and soon the others followed. Kelera released the roots, but did not send them back into the ground. Not yet. Not until she knew this wasn't a trick.

Gadreel's voice was thunderous as he said, "Samael has led you all astray. But we will show mercy. You will leave this realm or pay for your crimes." He sounded every bit the Prince that he was.

The boy, who had bowed first, rose. He spoke to Gadreel, but his eyes were on Kelera. His accent was similar to the man who had held the little girl hostage. "We want to accept your mercy, Prince Gadreel. We have known it well throughout the years in the mountain villages. But we also know King Samael's wrath. If we do not do as we are bid, then he will destroy everything we hold dear."

Gadreel's voice was softer as he said, "I can assure you that any defectors will be protected in the Seelie Court. If you denounce Samael, then we will offer you forgiveness for the crimes you have committed here."

Kelera shot Gadreel an incredulous look. "Look at what they've done." She pointed to the bodies of the mortal villagers. The little girl's family was likely among the dead. They had never stood a chance. This was brutality. Her magic burned and sweat beaded on her forehead as she tried to contain it.

Gadreel shook his head. "I am heartsick, Kelera. What happened here was a tragedy. But do you really believe these men had a choice?"

She looked at the boy. His face was covered in dirt and blood, but she recognized the terror and sadness in his eyes. She'd seen that look on Adrastus' face before, when he'd taken down the rogue Fae in the Winter Court. Gadreel was right. These men were not the enemy. It was Samael. Could she blame them for trying to protect their families at the cost of their own innocence? Samael had turned them into soldiers against their will.

"Mercy, then." She bent down to pick the little girl up. "Go. Before I change my mind."

The boy bowed deeply to her and when he rose, there was a glimmer of respect in his eyes. He turned to go, and the others followed without a word. Only when they were out of sight did she turn to Dodger and the knights, who were left standing.

She held her breath, bracing herself for the fear she expected to see in their eyes. But instead, they too had soft expressions. They bowed their heads in a silent show of respect. Dodger approached without hesitation.

"Kelera, you need to go." The use of her name in place of the nickname he'd called her by since she was a child caught her off guard, letting her know just how serious he was. "Go, knowing that when the time comes, we will stand with you."

He reached out to take the girl from her arms. The terrified child clung tighter to her, and she whispered in her ear, "Dodger will take care of you. He is the second bravest knight in all the land." Reluctantly, the girl let go and allowed Dodger to take her in his arms.

He raised a cocky eyebrow. "*Second* bravest?"

"Watch out for my father. If you find yourselves across the veil in Elfhame, then go east. Come to the Seelie Court and ask for Gadreel or Oliver."

He nodded in understanding. "What about you?"

She looked at the blackthorns. "I have something I need to do first."

Chapter Nineteen

Kelera shivered, but she wasn't sure if it was the adrenaline from the fight leaving her body, or the chilly autumn air. The sun was barely visible behind thick, ominous clouds, making it seem much later than it really was.

Her mood reflected the gloomy weather. She trudged through the field of dead grass, determined to get to the house from the vision. Adrastus' power had failed her back in Nevene and that could only mean one thing. She was dangerously close to losing him.

Gadreel stumbled behind her. "Slow down! You can't simply knock on the door and ask if you can come in. And after what I witnessed back in Nevene, your power may need time to recharge. You are going to wear yourself out if you're not careful. Even magic as powerful as yours has its limits."

Honestly, she wasn't experiencing any fatigue at all. If anything, she felt stronger than ever before. They were in the Autumn Court now and though it wasn't as fulfilling as it was in the Spring Court, Kelera's magic was dancing beneath the surface. It was as if it were celebrating her return to Elfhame.

She shook out her arms, trying to rid herself of the feeling of being pulled under by the veil's magic, and rolled her eyes at Gadreel. "I am aware of that. But you weren't there. You didn't feel what Samael was doing to him."

"You weren't there either. Need I remind you?" Gadreel strode in front of her, forcing her to stop in her tracks, and crossed his arms over his chest. "It could have been a dream. Samael is a monster, but I can't believe that he would curse our brother to that wretched existence."

Kelera gritted her teeth. "It was not a dream. I'm telling you, the binding spell allowed me to see through his eyes. He's in trouble and it's all my fault. I will do whatever it takes to get him back."

"As will I." He rubbed the sides of her arms gently, reminding her of the kindness he had shown her since the moment she opened her door to him at the Unseelie Palace. "But I will not put your life at risk in doing so. That is the last thing Dras would want."

"And I suppose you have some sort of plan?" she asked. Gadreel was clever. He had been working with Adrastus from the very start to protect the people who resided in the Unseelie territories. All the while keeping Samael's trust—enough so that he'd been tasked with watching over her during her time in captivity by the royal family.

"Samael would only know of one place in the Autumn Court to take our brother. It is a family home of sorts. In truth, it was just the place where we stayed during my father's inspections, as he liked to call them. I know every way in and out of that place. If we are going to get Adrastus out of there without a confrontation with Samael, then you need to slow down and follow my lead." He cocked his head to the side. "Can you do that?"

She let out a frustrated breath. "Of course I can."

He raised an uncertain eyebrow at her, but said no more as they began walking again. Kelera tried to focus on the small but steady hum of Adrastus' magic winding its way around hers and not the large pit in her stomach.

When they had first performed the binding ceremony, the presence of his power had been unsettling. She had never experienced anything like it, and it had taken time to grow used to it. But now, as it continued to fade, it felt as if she was losing a piece of herself. She couldn't imagine what its absence would be like. Or worse, what it would feel like for Adrastus to no longer belong to this world.

Her throat was dry as she asked, "What will happen if the curse is successful? Is there any way to reverse it?"

Gadreel stared straight ahead as he answered, but she could see the tension in his shoulders. "I don't know. Father created his Night Riders long before I was born and none had ever been defeated before you came along."

Right. Her run in with the treacherous skeletal rider in the Winter woods. How would she ever be able to forget the way his rotting corpse had threatened to end her life? She hadn't known then what she was capable of. But if Adrastus turned, she knew deep in her heart that she wouldn't be able to bring herself to hurt him.

With desperation, she insisted, "Surely, there must be a way to cure him." Leaves crunched beneath their feet as they walked, and Kelera shivered from the cool autumn air.

Gadreel's voice was grave as he said, "There is a lake in the Seelie Court. Blessed by the elders and claimed to be guarded by the Lady of the Lake."

Images of an ethereal woman rising from the water with a sword in her hand flashed in Kelera's mind. She'd seen the painting in the Unseelie ballroom on the night of the King's revel. Was it a myth, or did she truly haunt the waters of Elfhame?

She supposed they would soon find out. "So we take him to the lake and it will heal him?" It sounded far too simple and if there was anything she'd learned since her time in Elfhame, it was that nothing was ever as it seemed.

Gadreel flashed her a hopeful smile that didn't quite reach his eyes. "That's the hope. But truthfully, we need to prepare ourselves for the worst."

"I can't lose him."

Gadreel chuckled. "It seems I have missed much since I parted with you both at the Summer border."

Kelera's mouth perked at the corner. "You have no idea." The memory of Adrastus proclaiming his love for her and the way his hands had felt when he'd touched her sent a shiver down her spine. She couldn't let the last words between them be the ones she'd spoken out of fear and anger. She picked up her pace, forcing Gadreel to jog to keep up with her.

"Come on, you've got to give me more than that. After all, I am the one who..." He trailed off and held an arm out to slow her down. He pressed a finger to his lips in warning for her to keep quiet. Whispering, he said, "We're not alone."

The sky was as gloomy as a brewing storm, and Kelera squinted into the shadows it was casting. Samael had a way of lurking in them. Magic flared at her fingertips. If he was here, there was no way she would let him best her this time. Gadreel swatted at her hand and she scowled as she said, "Ow. What are you doing?"

He pointed up, and that's when she heard it. Thunderous hoofbeats echoed through the dark sky. Something that resembled starlight twinkled in their wake as monstrous, midnight black horses stampeded toward her. The leader of the herd lowered his head, veering down to the ground.

As they neared, the riders came into view. They were broad men with braided beards and determined eyes. The leader spurred his steed, and it snorted as it jumped onto the ground. The horses that followed danced around, trying to get their footing on the rough earth.

Kelera marveled at the strength of the horses. They were hard muscled, with sweat dripping from their velvety fur. Very unlike the rotting steeds that the Night Riders rode. And the men who sat upon them were not skeletal monsters, but rather men of flesh and bone.

The only thing that set them apart from the living were their mysterious pooled eyes. At first glance, Kelera mistook the color around their pupils for black, but as the leader jumped down from his horse and walked closer to her, she could see that they were a brilliant purplish-blue, like the night sky when the stars were at their brightest.

Gadreel dropped to his knees and bowed so low that his forehead touched the ground. Kelera, on the other hand, stood frozen in place. She couldn't stop looking at the man. Staring into his eyes was like gazing into the heavens.

His voice was just as thunderous as his horse's hoofbeats when he spoke. "Kelera of the Seelie Court, we have heard whispers of you in the wind." The title he used to address her was surprising, but she didn't interrupt as he continued, "The land has been calling to us and we are here to answer."

"And what exactly is it that you are answering...?" He seemed to know her, but she had no name for him.

He introduced himself, "I am Woden." The name was familiar. She'd heard the Guardian's use it when they lost Chaz to the sand wielder.

"You are the leader of the Wild Hunt."

He smiled in a way that was so human and mundane that it caught Kelera off guard. This man was a legend, but here he was smiling at her as if they were two strangers passing on the street.

"I am many things, Milady. But right now, I am your friend."

Kelera would take all the friends she could get. But what she really wanted to know was whether her new friend and his men would stand with the Seelie Court against Samael. She raised her chin and took a step closer to the leader. "Will you fight with us, then?"

Woden chuckled in response. "We will be there when you call."

He grabbed hold of the saddle and swung himself up, whistling to the rest of the Wild Hunt. Kelera shouted to him, "How do we call upon you?"

But rather than answer, he gave her a fearsome smile. This one was the very opposite of mundane. It was a smile that spoke of mysteries undiscovered and questions unanswered. And with that, he led the hunt off the ground. Her hair whipped around her face as they galloped by. Just as they began to ascend into the sky, she caught sight of a familiar face. It had been sickly and green the last time she'd seen it staring up at her from the sands of the Summer Court. Only now, his face was glowing like starlight and his eyes were vibrant, dark hues of purple and blue.

"Chaz," she whispered. She ran a few steps forward, as if to stop him, but she wasn't fast enough. He gave her a wink as his horse jumped from the ground and into the air. She shuddered, and a sob escaped her. It was not from heartache and guilt, but instead it was relief. He had made it to the Wild Hunt, after all. She couldn't wait to tell the Guardians.

"Shit," Gadreel said breathlessly. "I've never in all my life seen the Wild Hunt with my own eyes. It was..."

"Remarkable," Kelera finished for him. They had speculated that the Wild Hunt would aid them in their battle against Samael, but having it confirmed changed everything. Now they could only hope that they would know how to call on the Hunt when the time came.

She grabbed hold of Gadreel with newfound hope. "Let's go get Adrastus."

They didn't have to travel far to reach the manor. Gadreel was familiar with the territory and navigated with perfect precision. They'd avoided the main roads leading to it, cutting through barren fields and empty villages. Each one was raided, left with barren food stores and broken boxes on the ground. Samael had left nothing for the Fae who had resided there. He was going to starve them all to feed his army.

The villages were like ghost towns, with no sign of its residents. Kelera had asked where they had all gone and the regret in Gadreel's eyes had told her enough. Samael had gotten to them. They had either been so afraid that they had fled—perhaps to the east, seeking salvation in the Seelie Court—or they had been forced to join his army.

Now she and Gadreel were approaching a tree line. Wildlife startled her as they scurried over fallen branches to hide. Her heartbeat was pounding in her ears as Gadreel pointed ahead to a small light behind a copse of trees and said, "We're here."

Kelera balled her hands into fists and her magic pulsed like a beating heart. They continued toward the light and a large manor came into view. It was simple in comparison to Cierine's childhood home, Rose Manor.

But it was elegant in its own way, with its smooth stone walls and intricately carved gargoyles positioned on high stoops.

She followed Gadreel to the side of the home, where a small door led into the cellar. It felt as if eyes were on her and she looked up at the statues as he unlatched the door. The gargoyles seemed to watch her, staring down with steady eyes. It sent the hairs on her arms standing on end, but she ignored it as Gadreel signaled for her attention. She crouched down beside him and gazed down into the pitch-dark cellar.

His face was paler than usual as he turned to her and said, "Are you ready?"

Without missing a beat, she answered, "Absolutely."

She *was* ready. Ready to choose love over fear. Love for the people who had stood by her—who had shown her kindness without any expectations. Ready to accept her role in this war against Samael. A role that called her to Adrastus' side. She had been too weak to admit it before, but she was strong enough to know now that she'd had the power all along to make herself happy and she was prepared to act on it. She was ready to save the man she loved.

Chapter Twenty

Cobwebs clung to her clothes and her hair. The cellar was as dark and damp as the dungeons she had just escaped from. Worse was how eerily quiet it was. There were no footsteps above, or muffled voices. What if Gadreel had gotten it wrong? Dread began to creep in at the thought that Adrastus might not be here at all.

"Watch your step." Gadreel's voice cutting through the silence made her practically leap out of her skin.

Gingerly, she tried to step over a large pile on the floor, but her toes caught on whatever it was. Something rattled as the pile clattered across the cellar. Kelera gasped, reaching down to stop it from making any more noise. Her hands met something smooth, and curiosity got the better of her as she picked it up to get a closer look. Her eyes adjusted to the darkness to reveal a skull with hollowed out eyes.

She jumped back, and it slipped from her hands. She held her breath, waiting for it to crash loudly onto the hard, dirt-packed ground, but Gadreel caught it. He held the skull in one hand and a finger to his lips with the other.

She couldn't contain her shock as she whispered, "Why are their bones in your family's basement?"

Gadreel placed the skull gently on the ground. "Likely some house brownies who disappointed my mother and met a quite unfortunate end."

It was no surprise that their mother, the Queen Consort, would have banished Lesser Fae to rot in the basement for doing something that she deemed displeasing. Kelera had seen Queen Beatrice's cruelty up close and personal, but it didn't make this scene any less heartbreaking. The Fae, both Lesser and High, deserved better.

The stairs leading to the first floor of the manor came into view, but before ascending them, she grabbed hold of Gadreel's sleeve. It was soft under her touch, made of the finest material Elfhame had to offer. A reminder of who and what he was.

In a hushed tone, she asked, "How is it that you and Adrastus turned out the way you did when the rest of your family delights in power and control, as they do?"

Gadreel's face was solemn as he answered, "Because we had each other."

The wooden floorboards creaked beneath Kelera's feet. Each step she took felt heavier than the last, like her legs were slowly filling with sand. The hall was dimly lit with golden candlesticks, making her and Gadreel's shadows appear ominously large.

There wasn't a servant in sight, which struck her odd. The royal family delighted in having mortals wait on them day and night. If this was, in fact, where Samael had taken Adrastus, then where was everyone?

She wanted to ask Gadreel, but was too nervous to speak. The silence was haunting, leaving only her beating heart ringing in her ears. They turned a corner, coming to a large room with open doors. The windows that lined the room were tall with beautiful lace curtains and the floor was made of polished marble. It must have been the ballroom.

Gadreel raised a hand, signaling for her to stay back. His voice was low and steady as he said, "You mentioned painted foliage on the walls, yes?"

Kelera nodded.

Gadreel glanced behind her to a set of closed double oak doors. "My father's study."

Her throat burned as she swallowed. She was in desperate need of food and water. She couldn't even remember the last time she had eaten. But there was no time for that now as Gadreel crossed the hall to the study. He slicked his frosty hair back and pressed his pointed ear to the doors.

Kelera shifted on her feet, unable to stay still. This was taking too long. If Adrastus wasn't here, then they were wasting precious time that they would need in order to track him down. "Gadreel."

He held up a finger to silence her. Then, turning to her with his brow wrinkled, said, "Listen to me, Kelera. I need you to control yourself in here. Do not—"

She pushed him aside and swung the doors open. It didn't take long to spot him. Sitting in the middle of the room, strapped to the chair with familiar chains around his wrists—chains she had seen in her vision—was Adrastus.

When she reached him, her knees buckled. His skin was a grayish-blue and his chest rose and fell slowly in shallow breaths. She knelt on the floor and tugged on the chains. They were so cold that they stung her fingers as she fumbled with them. Adrastus' head was hung forward, indicating that he was unconscious. He didn't look to be in much pain, but that only made her fear that the real battle was raging in his mind and in his heart rather than out here. Tears pooled in her eyes as she hissed at Gadreel, "Get over here and help me."

Tears were streaming down Gadreel's face as he joined her at his brother's side. "By the fates, what has he done to you?"

Kelera pressed her lips together to keep them from trembling. She'd never seen Adrastus in such a weakened state. The anguish at seeing him like this was suffocating. She shook her head as she said, "Samael gave me his word. He *swore* that he would not lay a hand on him!"

Gadreel pushed her aside gently and hovered his hands over the restraints. "Sure, but did he say anything about using magic?"

Kelera wanted to kick herself for not being more careful in her wording. She'd been so distracted with the horrifying visions Samael had conjured up that she had given him the loophole he'd needed.

Gadreel gave her an apologetic smile. "It's not your fault." His face twisted, and he chewed at his lip as he tried to use his magic to break through the chains. He panted as he said, "I have rarely used this sort of magic. That fight in Nevene was the first time in a long time. My talents are better used for pleasure, not destruction."

Kelera watched in horror as his magic only made things worse. Adrastus groaned as more frost spread across the chains. She pushed his dark hair from his face and rested her hand on his cheek.

Gadreel cursed out loud, "Damn these wretched things!"

Kelera put her other hand on Gadreel's shoulder to move him aside slightly. "Let me try."

She placed both hands just above the chains and closed her eyes. Embracing the warmth of her Seelie magic, she allowed it to flow from her and over the restraints. Steam rose from the metal as she melted the ice. Something clinked and when she opened her eyes, she found that the chains had snapped apart.

Gadreel was holding onto them with a strained look on his face as he set them down. He shook his hands out and grimaced as he hissed through his teeth, "Hot."

Kelera laughed through her tears, overcome with relief that her magic had done its job. Now there was the matter of getting him out of here before Samael slithered out of whatever shadowy corner of the manor he might be lurking in.

Gadreel put one of Adrastus' arms around him and lifted him from the chair. He grunted under the weight as he said, "Come on, brother. I know you're in there somewhere. You've gotta help us out."

Adrastus moaned in response, making Kelera's heart flutter. Somewhere deep down, he was still himself and he could hear them. She whispered to him as she leaned into take hold of his other arm. "You need to hold on, Dras. I didn't come all the way here just to lose you." She did her best to help hold some of his weight, but she was much shorter than the men.

The front door was within sight. Just a little further to go.

Gadreel looked around with suspicion. "I don't understand why Samael would leave him unattended."

"Perhaps he thinks he has already won and has no need for heightened security."

Gadreel scoffed. "That sounds like him."

Adrastus shuffled his feet slowly and methodically. It was as if every step took a great amount of effort. She encouraged him once again, "Dras, we need you. Please, fight whatever it is that's going on in there."

He gave no answer as they walked through the hall. Her adrenaline spiked as they came within reach of the door.

A velvety and confident woman's voice made the hairs on her arms stand on end. "Well, isn't this a treat?"

Kelera turned toward an open door to the left of them to see a grand dinner table. And at the head was Queen Beatrice in all her overzealous glory. Her fingers were lined with heavy jewels, and she wore a crown made of bone and pearls.

Kane sat beside her with his chair pressed against hers. He smiled arrogantly as he fed a grape to his mother. Kelera scrunched her nose at the unnatural display of intimacy that she had witnessed between them many times before in the Unseelie Palace.

Samael was standing only feet away from them with a sneer on his slim face. "Hello, Kelera. I hate to say I'm not terribly surprised to find you here. I'm rather disappointed those idiotic mortals didn't take your head, but not surprised. You do have quite the talent for survival." His eyes drifted to Gadreel. "But *you*, brother, now this truly is a shock."

Gadreel looked Samael in the eye as he said, "Come now, you didn't really think I liked you enough to go to war with you. You're smarter than that."

Samael's icy blue eyes narrowed. They were startling, even in the candlelight. "I am merely surprised that you had the balls to stand against me." He addressed Kelera as he continued to insult his brother. "You see, Gadreel was always the meekest of us. A little weakling, always standing on the sidelines whilst the rest of us learned how to become warriors."

Kelera snarled at him, "That is because he has a heart, while you... well I'm not sure what it is you have beating in that chest of yours." The frown that graced Samael's smug face was satisfying.

"It seems both of you have found your courage. No matter. You are already too late. Soon, dear Adrastus will be devoted entirely to me." He scratched at his chin. "I wonder which one of you I should have him slaughter first."

Kelera's magic burned in her veins, begging to teach Samael a lesson. She held it at bay as she warned him, "I am tired of your games, Samael. We may be outnumbered, but I still have access to Adrastus' magic. Or have you forgotten that we are bound?" She drew out the last words, relishing in the way Samael's jaw twitched. She knew it was a chip in his pride—knew that the fact that she had willingly bound herself to Adrastus must have been driving him mad with jealousy.

Though Adrastus' magic was fading from her, she couldn't let Samael know the effect the curse was having on the bond. He knew that having Adrastus' magic intertwined with her own made her a formidable opponent. Even with the power of the crown that he now held. It was why he had sent her back to Nevene to face a death sentence.

She and Adrastus might not be able to outmatch what was left of the royal family, but they could still put up one hell of a fight. And she needed Samael to continue to believe that. To keep him oblivious to the fact that the bond was weakening. And it was working. She could practically see the gears turning in his mind as he decided what to do next. She raised her chin, giving the impression that she had full confidence in her abilities.

Queen Beatrice, however, appeared out of the loop. She rose from her seat and slammed her hands on the table. "A detail you failed to share with your mother, Samael. What is the meaning of this? Why did you not tear this little twit's throat out the moment you found out?"

Samael ignored her as his eyes shifted between Kelera, Adrastus, and Gadreel. After an excruciating moment, he asked, "What do you think, Kelera? Should I kill you now? Or shall I let Adrastus do it?"

"He would never harm me." Kelera's heart was beating rapidly as she tried to keep her magic at bay. The urge to unleash her power was nearly blinding. But she couldn't do it. Not yet. First, she had to get Adrastus out of here.

Samael continued, "Are you so sure about that? You and I both know that you have already lost him. You may as well say your goodbyes. No matter how far you take him from me, he will still be a slave to my control. Face it. He is lost to you. And without him, the Seelie will not stand a chance against me."

Kelera was having difficulty swallowing as the dread set in. Samael wasn't afraid of her. And he was willing to let her walk out of here alive. It only proved how confident he was that his plan was going to work. She was speechless.

Gadreel shook his head. "You underestimate the Seelie Court, just as you underestimated us."

Queen Beatrice's face twisted in disgust. "You were always a weak little boy. I knew it from the moment I laid eyes upon you. I should have smothered you in your sleep."

Gadreel flinched, and it fueled Kelera's anger. So she did what she'd wanted to do since the moment she first met the horrible woman. With a blast of white light, she slammed the Queen into the wall. There was a sickening crunch of bones breaking and Kane rushed to his mother's side. When he looked back at Kelera, there was genuine fear in his eyes. She had not seen that in all the time she'd spent with him, and it was almost as satisfying as hurting the Queen. She met his gaze with a challenging one—daring him to come at her.

Queen Beatrice stirred. "The little bitch broke my arm." She shrieked at Samael, "You will not let them take one step from this manor!" She shoved Kane roughly. "Stop them!"

Samael held a hand up and Kane looked at his mother apologetically. Kane's voice was strained as he said, "I-I can't."

Queen Beatrice's eyes widened. "You bound yourself to him?" She rose slowly to face Samael while gripping her injured arm. "How *dare* you claim your brother's magic without consulting me first!"

Samael rolled his eyes. "You are not in charge here, mother. If you wanted a puppet, then perhaps you should have vied to place Kane on the throne." He looked Adrastus up and down and there wasn't a hint of love on his face as he did so. "Dear, sweet Adrastus here will soon complete his transformation. And when he does, he will do exactly as I bid. He will destroy the only woman he has ever loved, and I will enjoy every moment of it as I watch through his mind's eye. It's rather poetic, don't you think, Mother?"

Kelera's eyes burned as she stared defiantly at him. He ignored her, gesturing to Adrastus with a dismissive hand as he said, "Besides, the Queen will be dead soon, and without an heir, there will be no one to lead the Seelie Court."

Gadreel raised his chin. "An heir will rise."

Samael took a step forward and gestured to the door. Then he nodded toward Adrastus, who was still not fully conscious, and grinned. "Not anymore."

Chapter Twenty-One

G adreel was holding most of Adrastus' weight as they hurried toward the door. Kelera couldn't help being incredibly grateful that he was there with her. There was no way she ever would have been able to get Adrastus out of the manor on her own.

Once they were well away from the elegant house, she turned back to face it. Gadreel grunted under the burden of holding Adrastus by himself. "What are you doing?"

"He'll come after us. Maybe not at this very moment, but he *will* come." Her heartbeat wildly in her chest. "I can't allow that to happen."

Gadreel's voice wavered with uncertainty as he said, "Kelera?"

But her power was already in motion. She imagined the heat of the Beltane bonfire, remembering how its warmth kissed her face when she'd danced with

Adrastus. She'd been crowned the Goddess that night, but tonight she was something else. She was judge and executioner. Tonight they would burn.

Flames erupted around the manor, circling it and climbing up to the fearsome gargoyles. Panicked shouts were coming from inside the house, but she didn't care. Samael had threatened her world with a frost, but he'd underestimated her ability to melt it all away.

Gadreel stood speechless as his family's home became engulfed in flames. Kelera didn't have time to sympathize with his complicated feelings. She ducked under Adrastus' arm, taking up some of the weight. "Let's go."

As they left the manor and the roaring fire, inhuman screeches echoed through the trees. She shivered slightly, remembering the eyes of the gargoyles staring down at her. It only fueled her forward, wanting to leave them and the true monsters who were inside the house behind.

She and Gadreel tried to pick up their pace as they trudged through the Autumn forest, heading east. Her anxiety was at an all-time high, feeling the urgency of getting Adrastus to the lake. She blew a strand of hair from her face as she stumbled over fallen branches.

"What if Samael was right? What if we don't make it in time?" She hated herself for saying it out loud. Saying the words felt like giving up.

"I don't know, I really don't." Gadreel tripped, losing his hold on Adrastus.

The sudden weight pushed Kelera to the ground along with Adrastus' semi-conscious body. She gasped as the wind was knocked out of her. Scrambling to Adrastus, she took his face in her hands. "Dras, Dras, are you okay?"

He winced, but didn't speak. She ran her thumb across his stubbled jawline. Frustrated, worried tears streamed down her cheeks as all of her hopes and dreams began to slip away, with the man cradled in her arms. How would she survive a loss like this? To never get the chance to bicker with him, or best him in chess, or feel his lips on hers, or his hands on her body... it was too much to bear.

She leaned forward, resting her forehead on his. "You can't leave me. You promised me a life in Elfhame. I'm so sorry I left you with him. You have to wake up. You have to give me the chance to tell you how sorry I am."

Gadreel's hand was heavy on her back. Gently, he assured her, "He knows, Kelera. He knows."

She rose to face her friend and wiped the tears from her cheeks. "What did Samael mean when he said an heir wouldn't rise?"

Gadreel shook his head and gritted his teeth before answering, "He believes Adrastus is the lost heir."

Kelera wasn't surprised. She, too, had considered it numerous times. He was the strongest of all of them. He had Seelie blood... or had she been so desperate for an answer to their prayers—for a savior that would rise to lead Elfhame to victory—that she had allowed herself to believe? Judging by the frown on Gadreel's face, he didn't share the belief.

"You don't think it's him."

There was remorse in Gadreel's voice as he said, "I don't know what to think. All I know is that my brother has struggled with his demons for so long. He has done unspeakable things... In my heart of hearts, I suppose it is impossible for me to believe he is the ruler that the Elders prophesied."

Defensively, Kelera said, "He is not a bad man."

"No. He is not. But he is a haunted man. My father raised him as he believed a true Unseelie should be. There have been times where Dras has been as ruthless and violent as the rest of them. The difference is that he feels remorse for the things that he has done and tries to be a better man because of it. Ruling would be a struggle for him. He never desired the crown for himself, he only ever wanted to keep it out of Samael's hands."

Kelera looked back down at Adrastus, running her fingers through his raven hair. Her heart and her body ached, making it hard to imagine taking another step, but still, she said, "We need to keep going."

Gadreel stood, dusting himself off, and peered down the narrow path they needed to take. "It's going to take—"

The trees rustled behind them, causing her to snap her neck in its direction. Gadreel sank back down to the ground, crouching low beside her and Adrastus. A chill filled the air as his magic came to the surface.

A twig snapped with the sound of hooves clopping through the brush. Large eyes blinked at her in surprise. Eyes far too large and out of place on the small pony's face. Gadreel called on his magic, raising his hands out in front of him, but Kelera stopped him. "No!" She stood slowly, placing herself between him and the pony. "He's a friend... sort of."

The familiar midnight black pony bowed his head at her and took a step forward. Kelera inched closer to meet him. She reached her hand to pet his velvety snout, but Gadreel called out to her, "That's a pooka! It's not safe to..." He trailed off as the pooka nuzzled into her touch.

She spoke to Gadreel over her shoulder, "I was lost when I first crossed the border to Elfhame. He brought me to the Unseelie Palace." She gave the pooka a pointed look as she said, "He dumped me in a stream and thought himself to be very funny, but he still helped me none the less." She scratched at the pooka's chin. The woods must be his domain. He had found her once when she was in need, and it was as if fate had brought him to her again. Hope swelled in her chest and she asked, "I wonder if I might be able to ask for your help again?"

Gadreel sounded unsure as his voice wavered. "I don't know if that's such a good idea."

"He's strong enough to carry me and Adrastus into the Spring Court. Anything would be faster than the pace we're traveling at now." She took a step back, looking the pooka in his huge oval eyes. "No tricks this time?"

The pooka snorted and pawed at the ground before kneeling down on his front legs. Kelera wasn't sure if he was agreeing to no tricks or not, but it was worth the risk. She raced over to Adrastus' side and, with Gadreel's help, they lifted him up and onto the pooka's back. Kelera slid behind Adrastus, reaching over him to grab hold of the pooka's mane.

The pooka rose, sending Gadreel scattering a few feet back. Kelera made a mental note to ask him one day about what a pooka had done to him to make him so skittish. For now, she smiled down at him. "I am grateful to you, Gadreel. For everything."

"Anything for you two." He stared at Adrastus' face as if it might be the last time he would ever see his little brother. "Save him, Kelera. This world would be a much less exciting place without him in it," he tried to joke, but there was no smile to match the words.

The pooka pranced around, clearly ready to go. But Kelera took a moment to ask, "Where will you go now that Samael knows you do not stand with him?"

"To the Seelie Palace. I will join Oliver and the others." He smiled wistfully as he said Oliver's name, then sighed as he continued, "I believe Samael may also be tired of the games. I do not doubt that he will make his move on the Spring Court as soon as his forces are ready."

"Be careful."

"You as well." He wrapped an arm around his stomach and bowed to her. "May the stars guide you and the fates watch over you."

Kelera gave him a curt nod and kicked at the pooka's sides. With more speed than one would expect from such a stout creature, the pooka took off at a full gallop. As he raced through the forest, dodging branches and jumping over logs, she was reminded of the first time she had ridden him.

She had been frightened and alone in a world she didn't understand. It was remarkable how much could change in such a short amount of time. Here she was, once again, taking help from a strange Fae creature. Only this time, she wasn't alone. She was here, with the man she cared deeply for, flying through a realm she now appreciated and loved.

The night air whipped at her face as the pooka picked up speed. Bare autumn trees were soon replaced with massive evergreens. The path became more overgrown, and she feared that the pooka wouldn't be able to navigate through the thick brush. But he pushed on. He was a Lesser, solitary Fae and knew these woods well. Trusting in his ability to get her to the lake, she leaned into Adrastus—relishing in the familiarity and comfort his presence brought. He was slumped over and silent. Was that a good thing, or a bad thing? How much longer until his body began to change? Would his handsome, strong features be replaced with the shallow, bone-gray face of the Night Riders?

She tried to banish the thoughts from her mind, thinking instead of the way his dark, forest green eyes twinkled in the candlelight. And how his hardy laugh made her heart flutter. She thought of the night of the Beltane revel when he had taken her on the forest floor. Nothing else had mattered then. Not his sordid past as the Bastard Prince of Unseelie, and not her betrothal to the traitorous monster, Alexander. It had been as if she and Adrastus were the only two beings in the universe. It had been right.

Kelera's breath hitched in her throat as sudden agony shot through her chest. Something was wrong. Pain seared through her again and she clutched the pooka's mane tightly, trying to hold on. The pooka didn't seem to notice as he continued to gallop.

She gasped as the familiar chill of Adrastus' magic started to slip further away. She could feel it unwinding from her own, leaving her hot and feverish as her own power grew more unstable again. Like a thread being pulled from a shirt, his power was unraveling from her own.

She cried out to him, "Hold on a little longer, Dras! We're almost there. You need to fight!" Her mind raced as her fears began to come to fruition—their bond was breaking. That could only mean that the transformation was completing.

The trickling of water was music to her ears as the pooka brought her within view of a riverbank. He didn't slow his pace. He meant to jump it. Kelera pressed herself against Adrastus with all her weight. She closed her eyes as the pooka leapt into the air.

They hit the other side of the river with a jolt, and Kelera's mouth gaped in surprise. They did it. And with the river here, the lake must be close by. She held onto a small thread of hope as the Spring Court scenery blurred by them.

The pooka didn't slow until they came to a grove of elegant trees. The vast, white flowers hanging on the branches were in full bloom, filling the field with their fragrance. The pooka came to a full stop within reach of the crowded gray branches and knelt to the ground to let her dismount. He laid down gently, resting with Adrastus still on his back as Kelera approached the trees. She reached out her hand, but refrained from touching the thorny branches.

"These are hawthorn trees, right?' She spoke out loud without expecting an answer, but the pooka snorted in agreement behind her.

A strange sensation prickled at her body as if she was touching the thorns, though she hadn't dared to do so. They stared up at the noble trees that were said to represent life and healing. She reached for the locket hanging around her neck, as she had done so many times before, and ran her fingers along the engraving. She had always thought that the thorny branches etched into the golden locket was that of a blackthorn tree. A representation of the veil her mother had passed through in order to drop Kelera at her mortal father's doorstep.

The hawthorn tree drew her in like a bird to the sky. As she looked up at the enchanting flowers, a sense of familiarity and love filled her. This is what home truly felt like. This was what her mother had meant to leave her with.

Clutching the locket, she stepped forward, intent on leading the pooka and Adrastus through the trees. But as she placed her foot at the edge of the tree's stump, she was met with a solid wall of magic. It knocked her back a few steps, and she felt as if she'd slammed into a door.

"No," escaped her lips as she looked around in confusion. "Why isn't it letting us pass?" She spun to face the pooka, who was standing so close to her that she could feel his breath on her face.

He stared back at her helplessly. Kelera tried again and was met with the same invisible barrier. Had someone cast a spell to keep her out? Samael perhaps?

A beastly sound drew her attention to Adrastus. She ran to him and turned his face toward her. "Dras?"

A wicked, guttural growl came from his throat, and he opened his eyes to look at her for the first time. His beautiful eyes, which once sparkled like springtime in the forest, were now deep pools of darkness—much like the shadows Samael had burrowed into him. The darkness was jolting and gave her a feeling of emptiness as she looked into it.

Adrastus bared his teeth, and she felt more of his magic slip away from her. Her power surged, and she groaned as she struggled to hold on to it. Adrenaline shot through her and she gasped, trying to control her breathing. She had believed there was a war raging inside of him since Samael placed the curse on him, but now it was raging within her, too. It was as if she and Samael were battling for Adrastus' soul. And as of now, Samael was winning.

Chapter Twenty-Two

K elera grasped the sides of her head, trying to regain control. She couldn't allow the shock to deter her. She turned and flung herself at the hawthorn trees. "Let us through!" She pounded on the magic, sending sparks of white light flying through the air. "Let me save him!" She slammed her fist against the barrier. "I am born of the Seelie Court! Its power courses through my veins. I am sorry I ever tried to deny it. I am sorry that I never had the chance to know my mother and her people. But I am here now, ready to fight for them! I am here!"

Still, the magical wall held strong. She placed her hands on the barrier and sunk to the ground. A heartbreaking sob escaped her and her voice cracked as she begged, "Please, let me in. Give me a chance."

She gasped as the magic shimmered under her palms like ripples in water. She leaned away from it and watched as it sparked and lowered, revealing a path just big enough to let the pooka pass through.

Adrastus let out a manic chuckle, sending the hair on Kelera's arms straight up. His voice was ragged and strange as he said, "He says you're too late. He says I am to tear the limbs from your body and feed them to the wild dogs of these woods. The fenrir will devour you until there is nothing left."

It was as if a total stranger were speaking. This was not Adrastus. It was the curse talking. Kelera scrambled up and found her footing. She would not let Samael win. This was not how things were going to end. Ignoring Adrastus' menacing threats, she raced on foot toward the glittering lake surrounded by the hawthorn trees. The pooka's hoofbeats were close behind her and she glanced at him to make sure that Adrastus was still sitting securely on his back.

If Adrastus wasn't strong enough to dismount from the pooka, then that had to mean the transformation had not yet been completed. There was still time.

She didn't stop running until her boots splashed into the water's edge. She waved at the pooka. "Here. Set him here."

The pooka knelt down and Kelera grabbed hold of Adrastus' coat. It was torn and bloody, evidence of how his brother had treated him. How someone could treat their own flesh and blood with such brutality she would never understand.

Adrastus stared at her with black, emotionless eyes. If this failed, and he was turned, would he even recognize her anymore? Would he know what he was doing as he tore her apart?

The glamor that hid the scars Samael, Kane, and Ammon had given to him as a young boy of only eight years old dropped, revealing a marred face. She reached her hand up to run her fingers over them. She was sitting beside him in the lake now, but nothing was happening. The power of the water sent a tingling sensation through her where it met her skin. She was practically vibrating with its power. It stimulated her senses, like the drink she'd had at the tavern in the Summer Court.

Everything seemed clearer—colors more vibrant, the sounds of nature more distinct. So much so that she could feel the pain that Adrastus had endured by simply touching the puckered skin of his scars.

His hands reached up to caress her cheeks. She leaned into the familiar touch and hope bloomed in her chest. She whispered, "Adrastus."

His gentle touch turned to stone as he squeezed her face between his hands and pulled her closer to him. They drifted down to her throat and tightened until she could barely catch her breath. Frozen by shock, Kelera couldn't think of what to do. The pooka was whinnying wildly behind her and snapped her out of the heartache and terror she was trapped in. She gasped for air and struggled against Adrastus' hold.

She clawed at his hands, but he was too strong for her. With a fluid motion she'd seen used in the Unseelie fighting pits, she rolled on top of him and slammed her knee between his legs. It was the distraction she needed, because his hands loosened just enough for her to slip away from him.

She held her hands up defensively, prepared for another attack, but his body convulsed. It sent his limbs into violent jerking motions, and then he stilled. Slowly, she inched closer to him. Her feet kept slipping on the soft clay under the water, but she didn't stop. Pushing her hair from her face, she leaned down to listen for any sign that he was still breathing.

The gentle whoosh of his breath was coming slowly, but surely. With no time to waste, she splashed the water onto his chest, over his shoulders, and into his face in desperation. "Come on." Why wasn't it working? What if they'd been wrong about the lake? She choked back the tears threatening to fall and continued to beg, "Please, work. What do I have to do to get it to work?"

As if answering her plea, a soft melody filled the air. It drifted in the warm spring breeze with a hum. It was a familiar tune, one that predated any memory Kelera had of her childhood. Adrastus laughed wickedly, but as the humming grew closer, his eyes rolled to the back of his head.

A sweet feminine voice spoke from the middle of the lake. "There. That should hold it off for a bit."

Kelera spun her head to look out onto the lake where a strange woman had risen. She was draped in a thin veil of muslin, sheer enough to see her naked body beneath. Her face had a gray tint to it, and she appeared delicate and fragile. Her dull blonde hair was tangled with seaweed and pieces of what looked like barnacles were embedded in her skin. Yet there was still an unusual, beautiful quality to her. The sort of beauty that could be found in things that were not of this world.

Kelera turned back to Adrastus and tapped him on the cheek, trying to wake him up. "What did you do to him?"

"I gave him a bit of reprieve. His poor soul is quite tired." The woman drifted closer to them.

"Who are you?"

The woman put a hand to her heart. "Surely, if you came all this way seeking help, then you should know the answer to that."

"You are the Lady of the Lake?" Kelera asked. This woman looked nothing like the ethereal beauty in the painting she'd seen in the Unseelie ballroom.

"I am. And you have come here to save your beloved, have you not?"

"Can you do it? Can you stop the curse?" Kelera gazed down at Adrastus again. His chest was rising and falling steadily, and she gripped him tightly in her arms.

The woman gave her a pitying look. "I do not meddle in affairs of the heart."

Kelera's brow furrowed. She wasn't here to make someone fall in love with her. She was here to save Adrastus' life. "This is more than that," she said. "There is a war coming. We need him. *Elfhame* needs him."

The woman shook her head. "I cannot interfere with fate."

Kelera's magic surged with her frustration, sending waves through the water. "I do not care about fate!"

Water lapped up against the Lady of the Lake's ankles and her lips parted slightly. "If you are not careful, you will lose control."

Kelera growled in anger. "I did not come to ask for advice on my magic. I came to ask you to save him." She pointed to Adrastus and noticed his skin had become even more sickly. There was no way she'd come all this way just to lose him.

Before she could second guess herself, she reached for the water with her mind. With fierce determination, she imagined a rope and wove the water together tightly. Then, with every ounce of control she could muster, she swung it up from the lake and around the woman's wrists.

The Lady of the Lake's eyes widened in shock, and she tugged at the hold the water had on her, but it was too strong. Sweat beaded on Kelera's temples as she commanded the water to tighten even more.

The Lady of the Lake gave her a tentative smile. "You are as powerful as they said you would be."

For a brief second, Kelera wondered who *they* were, but she ignored her curiosity and asked through gritted teeth, "Can you do it? Can you save him?"

The woman's nose flared. Kelera had trapped an ancient being, but she didn't care about the ramifications. There was only one thing that mattered and she wouldn't leave until she'd done what she came there to do.

The Lady grimaced and said, "I can. But there will be a price." The grimace turned to a vicious smile, revealing rows of sharply pointed teeth.

Kelera didn't think twice as she said, "I don't care."

Surprise flashed in the Lady's eyes. "Is that so? Perhaps it is because you are not familiar with our ways, but most would hesitate at the prospect of owing a debt to the Elders."

"What do the Elders have to do with this?"

"They are the masters of this land's ancient magic. The very same magic that flows from the earth into this lake. Are you not frightened in the least bit?"

"The only thing I'm frightened of is losing him." It was the truth. She would not let anything stand in her way now. Her world would be a far darker place without him in it. That much had been made clear during their time apart. Adrastus had taught her how to find joy in the small moments. He had taught her to believe in herself. Most of all, he had showed her what love was.

The Lady tilted her head to the side as if to study Kelera. "That is very noble of you." She regarded her with a curious look, then began to hum the lullaby again.

"Does that mean you will do it?"

"I will."

Kelera released the hold she had on the Lady of the Lake's wrists. The water splashed back into the lake, and Kelera's heart beat rapidly as she waited to see if the woman would flee.

To her relief, the woman held her hands out over the water. It swirled around Kelera and Adrastus, sweeping him from her arms and further into the lake. She reached for him, afraid that if the Lady of the Lake pulled him too far, then he would drown. What if the Lady was working with Samael and planned to trick her?

The thought hadn't occurred to her before and for a moment, she was furious with herself.

Kelera played the Lady's words over and over in her mind, wondering if she missed something—some sort of twisted truth or loophole—but could think of none. So she resisted the urge to interfere and watched as the water began to rise, lifting Adrastus high enough that the Lady of the Lake could face him.

She placed her fingers on his chest and continued to hum the sweet melody. Magic shimmered like stardust as it glided from her hands and into his heart. Kelera held her breath in anticipation and heard the pooka dancing around in the grass behind her.

She had never seen magic look so lovely before as it twinkled in the twilight. It flowed effortlessly and Kelera envied the graceful way the Lady of the Lake wielded it. If only she could create such beauty with her own magic...

The color began to return to his face, replacing the rotting gray that had been seeping into his skin as the curse progressed. The Lady remained calm and concentrated, but her brow furrowed and Kelera caught a slight twitch in her jaw.

Kelera called out, "What's wrong?"

The Lady pursed her lips together then answered, "The curse has taken root far deeper than I had anticipated."

Adrastus stirred, showing signs that he was waking. In that foreign, ragged voice, he mumbled something intelligible. Kelera dug her nails into the palm of her hand, trying to steady herself.

"Then *dig deeper*," she commanded.

Surprise flickered across the Lady's face. "I am, little halfling. Even power as ancient as mine has its limits"

Something dark began to cloud around Adrastus. Shadows were seeping from his skin and spreading out along the surface of the lake. Each shadow left a layer of ice in its wake. Soon the water would be covered.

Kelera waded deeper into the lake. "Tell me how to help. Use my power. Take it."

The Lady regarded Kelera for a moment. She was waist deep in the water, looking up defiantly at the ancient Fae. They had come too far to fail now. She had already agreed to the terms to save him, but she would give more if she had to.

Finally, the Lady said, "You sense the immense power of Elfhame in the water, yes?"

Kelera nodded.

"Then grasp onto it. Like you did with the restraints."

Kelera did as the Lady of the Lake commanded, only this time, she envisioned the magic flowing to her in a soft current. It encircled her, just within reach. She closed her eyes, reveling in the brilliance of it. "Now what?"

"Now take what you need. Like picking at specs of sand, grab hold of the magic that nourishes life."

Kelera opened her eyes and glared at the Lady. How could she do that? How could she sift through all of this power and find one specific kind? The power of Elfhame was filled with different elements. She thought of Adrastus and the soothing power of his healing magic. The magic he had used when he'd healed her back after the lashes she had taken for the boy in the Winter Court and of the magic he'd used when he had tried to heal the scar on her face.

The power around her scattered with the memories, leaving behind only what she needed. Kelera held the palms of her hands up and embraced it as it flowed into them. She clutched onto it. She raised her hands over the water and extended them out to Adrastus, who was still suspended with the Lady of the Lake. For a moment, she rejoiced in the warmth of it—in the familiarity of it. Then she released it. With her eyes wide open, she watched as it swirled in a glimmering shine up to Adrastus and straight to his heart and head.

The Lady began to hum again and did not stop until every ounce of the power had left Kelera and reached Adrastus. The ice that his shadows had spread along the water melted away, leaving no trace that it had ever been there in the first place.

Kelera shivered as Adrastus' magic awakened, sending its icy shadows back into her. With a shuddering breath, she welcomed it back like an old friend returning from a long trip. The magic was working. He was coming back to her.

When they finished, the Lady lowered Adrastus' body back into the water and it flowed toward Kelera, bringing him into her arms. She pulled him back to shore and clung to his body as she waited for him to open his eyes. His eyes would surely tell her whether it had worked or not.

The Lady of the Lake lingered above the water and Kelera asked, "When will he wake?"

The Lady spoke confidently as she said, "When his soul is settled. It has been through quite a lot in such a short amount of time." Her voice had a hint of wonder to it as she added, "You did well."

Kelera ignored the compliment and gazed up at her as she asked, "And the price?"

"The Elders will call on the debt soon enough. A war is coming. It will be unlike anything the lands of Elfhame have ever seen. Brother will clash against brother. Neighbor against neighbor. And you, my dear, will not be able to escape it."

"I have already vowed to stand with the Fae to protect Elfhame."

"Yes. But you are not yet ready."

Kelera grimaced. "What is that supposed to mean?"

The Lady ignored her question as she said, "Goodbye, Kelera, daughter of realms." She started to hum the lullaby again and drifted down into the dark depths of the water.

Kelera shut her eyes, feeling for any trace of the magic that would bind her to the deal she had made. But there was nothing. No sign of an exchange or the debt magic she'd felt when King Cyrus had sentenced her to serve the royal family. It was as if nothing had happened.

Once the Lady of the Lake was gone, Kelera dragged Adrastus to the grassy shore. She grunted as she placed him gently on the ground. His skin was cold to the touch, though she didn't know if that was from the strain of the curse, or from the water.

Attempting to warm him, she shimmied out of her jacket and her linen blouse. Then she removed his jacket and shirt to reveal his bare chest. She tossed the wet clothes aside and curled into his body, sharing her heat with him. She called on her magic, summoning the warmth that it brought with it and nestled into the nook of his shoulder.

Hoofbeats clomped on the ground as the pooka approached. He bumped against Kelera's head as he laid down beside her. She shifted her body, pulling Adrastus with her so they were laying up against the pooka's fur covered pony shaped body. She was grateful for the pooka's glamor that allowed it to take on such a large form.

She sighed, happy to be in the pooka's presence. She owed him a great deal of thanks for aiding her not once, but twice. "I am lucky to have found you, you know. Or that you found me, I suppose."

The pooka snickered and Kelera laughed at the strange sound coming from what looked remarkably like the pony's she had grown up riding in the mortal realm. She patted him on the stomach and mused, "This is such a strange, *wonderful* land."

Her muscles began to relax and exhaustion threatened to send her into a deep slumber as all the adrenaline she'd been feeling started to wear off. Just as her eyes began to flutter, Adrastus jerked and coughed.

Kelera shot up like an arrow. "Dras!"

She held her breath as his eyes opened. The relief that came when she caught sight of the green rings around his pupils was like nothing she'd ever felt before. If she had pixie wings, she would have soared into the sky. Instead, she settled for leaping into him, wrapping her arms tightly around his neck.

She cried into his shoulder, breathing in the familiar scent of him. "I thought I'd lost you."

His voice was hoarse as he spoke. "What have you done, little thief?"

Chapter Twenty-Three

Kelera's heart skipped a beat, and she drew away from Adrastus. He sat up slowly, rubbing at his chest where Samael's shadows had been thrust into him. She moved back, giving him the space to get his bearings.

What have you done? She couldn't understand. She'd saved him. But why was he looking at her like that? His eyebrows were drawn together and his lips were pressed into a thin line.

Kelera sputtered, "W-what do you mean?"

His jaw twitched as his eyes scanned the lake. "What have you agreed to, little thief?" Hearing that nickname come from his lips again should have filled Kelera with pure joy, but instead it filled her with a sense of dread. Why was he in such a panic?

She tried to calm him, putting her hands on his, but he flinched away slightly. Just enough for her to notice.

She lowered her hands and shook her head. "It doesn't matter. You're safe now."

His eyes were hard as he said, "I may be safe, but you are not. What did you trade to save my soul?"

The forest surrounding them seemed to spin as his words sunk in. "It is a debt to the Elders. Surely it cannot be that bad."

"The Elders have not claimed a debt since the first Unseelie King was granted strength and the first Seelie Queen was granted beauty. Do you have any idea what those gifts cost them?" He grabbed hold of her arms and tugged her into him, wrapping her in his warm embrace.

He wasn't mad at her. No. He was frightened. He mumbled to himself as he caressed her hair. She hadn't seen him this distraught since Samael had forced her into the pits—when he had stepped in to claim her for himself.

All she wanted to do was lose herself in his arms. She didn't want to worry about some ancient presence that she knew nothing about. This moment was the only one that mattered. She tried to make him understand as she muttered, "There was no other way. We were out of time and I was so afraid of losing you. The things you were saying... I couldn't allow Samael to turn you into one of those crea*tures*."

He grasped her arms, looking her in the eye. Her eyes drifted to his mouth which lingered over hers, only inches away from her lips, and her desire rose. They'd been apart for only a couple of days, but the absence of him had been as painful as the guilt she'd felt for leaving him behind.

Adrastus' voice broke as he said, "You have to know that I never meant any of those horrible things I said. It was like Samael was inside my head. His commands were so loud and I could feel myself slipping away."

She swallowed hard. He never would have had to go through that if she hadn't run away from him and the others. Her voice trembled as she said, "I should never have left you."

Adrastus cupped her face gently as if he was worried he would frighten her. "You saw no other way. You had to do what you believed was right, and I knew that." He ran his hand through her hair, brushing it behind her ear. "You must know that I do not blame you."

His mouth inched closer to her lips and she waited in anticipation for him to kiss her. Unable to stand it any longer, she leaned in and pressed her mouth against his. His mouth opened in response, welcoming and warm. As their kiss deepened, so did her need for him. She climbed carefully into his lap, unsure if the curse had left any pain behind.

The pooka wandered away, finding a small patch of grass to nibble on down the lakeside. But Kelera was too lost in relief and joy to notice or care.

Adrastus' bare chest felt like polished marble against her own as she pressed her body against his. He stiffened between her legs, and feeling his desire only fueled her need for him. They were together again. She wanted to lose herself in him now. To rid herself of all the pain and guilt, if only for a little while. Her fingers fumbled with his pants as he caressed her back with calloused hands.

He buried his face in her hair and sighed her name. "Kelera." It was a divine sound coming from his lips and her burning hunger grew. She needed him now more than ever. They needed each other. It had been clear from the start, but she had been too stubborn and afraid to accept it.

That girl was gone now. The one who had feared both herself and the world around her. She had been replaced with someone strong and capable. With someone who was no longer afraid to admit what she wanted and to take it.

Adrastus pulled his pants down and Kelera stood to remove her own. There was something freeing about standing before him, naked, with the lake behind her. It was as if they were the only two people in the world. For now, this was their domain.

She climbed into his lap, sliding down onto him until they were one. She gasped, tilting her head back to the sky which sparkled with early sunlight. She and Adrastus moved in perfect harmony, anticipating the other's needs with expertise. Their magic breathed life into them, filling them with all the energy and strength they had lost while they'd been apart.

As they reached the height of ecstasy together, Adrastus drew her in with a kiss that said more than words ever could. With his hand wrapped in her hair and his mouth pressed firmly against hers, she knew deep in her heart that he was the flame to match her own. He was a soul that would forever be entwined with hers, no matter who or what tried to get in their way.

Their passion peaked, and it felt as if Kelera were floating back down to the earth. Back to Elfhame and its troubles. They would have to face it all now, but they would face it side by side. Before that happened, there was something she needed to say. She ran her fingers through his hair, where it curled slightly at the nape of his neck, ready to tell him what he meant to her.

Before she could find her voice, the beating of drums drew them out of their little world surrounded by the hawthorn trees. She lowered herself from his lap and looked in the direction of the sound. "Are those war drums?" She'd read about battles before but had never witnessed one firsthand. Suddenly, she was all too aware of how unprepared she was for the events to come.

Adrastus shook his head and tried to stand. Kelera was quick to lend him a hand, allowing him to lean on her for support. "No," he said.

The pooka came running to them and let out a strange whinny that sounded forced, like it was a noise he was making to match his glamor and not his natural one. His eyes were alert, indicating that he was sensing something she wasn't. Something that only the pooka and Adrastus were aware of.

"Then what is it?" The perfectionist in Kelera was reeling. She should have been learning everything she could about battle formations and signals... Everything she would need to know when it came time for Elfhame to face the impending war.

"It is a call for the Seelie council." He was panting as he continued, "Something has happened. Follow me." He handed Kelera her shirt, and she slipped it on quickly. It was still damp and clung to her body uncomfortably. Once he had his own shirt on, he took her hand and pulled her away from the lake. They jogged to the tree line and crossed through the magical barrier with ease. On the other side of the hawthorns, the tallest trees she had ever seen towered over them.

Beyond them was a small glimpse of a glistening, white-stone palace. The drumming was louder without the hawthorns surrounding them. Adrastus tensed, his muscles flexing in response to the reaction. Kelera tensed as well. Her instincts told her to run, but she wasn't sure what it was exactly that was making her feel that way.

Adrastus bent down and grabbed a handful of dirt and grass, allowing it to drop between his fingers. Then he turned to Kelera and gripped her arms tightly. "War is coming."

"We already knew that, Adrastus. What has changed?"

His hands trembled as he answered, "I can feel the shift in the very soil." It sounded as if he was musing more to himself than to her as he continued, "I can smell it like rot. Death walks amongst us." His jaw twitched as he said to her, "You need to go while you still can. It isn't safe here."

"Go? I just got back. I can't leave now." She couldn't understand why he was pushing her away. "I won't run away this time."

He ran his hand through his unruly hair. "It's just until this all passes. If you go back to Nevene, to your father—"

"They were going to try me for treason, Dras. They wanted me dead."

"Samael was right, then. He sent you back to face a death sentence." Adrastus' face turned red and his nose flared. "I had prayed he was wrong about that—had prayed that your people wouldn't betray you after all that you had risked for them."

"Alexander was working with Samael, but the council believed it was me." It pained her to say the words out loud.

A look that could only be described as pure hatred flickered across Adrastus' face. The old Kelera would have been ashamed to admit that the people she had tried so desperately to please had turned on her so easily. But the woman she had become was one that refused to dwell on it any longer.

His voice was venomous as he said, "I'll kill them both for this."

Kelera shrugged, "I'll help you. But I'm not leaving."

"You could go to the countryside, hide out and wait there until I send for you."

Her speech was rushed from frustration as she argued, "How can you ask me to abandon you and Elfhame when you both need me the most? I refuse to do that again." Adrastus opened his mouth to argue, but she held up a silencing hand. "How can I leave when I see every infinite possibility of happiness here, with you?" She grasped his face with both hands, running her thumb along his scar. "I *love* you, Dras. And I will stand by you until the end. I will remain by your side as you stand against your brother. And together, we will claim everything we deserve. We will take everything that the world has made us believe we were not worthy of." She let out a heavy sigh and waited for him to respond.

The drums filled the silence between them, beating to the rhythm of her heartbeat. Adrastus' hands trembled slightly as they rose to take hers. His face brightened and his lips parted as he leaned in to kiss her. It was like a weight lifting off her chest as she opened her mouth invitingly. Her pulse raced as the kiss deepened, saying everything that needed to be said between the two of them.

Adrastus pulled away, and gave her a curt nod as he said, "Then I suppose it is time for us to go."

The pooka knelt to the ground, offering a place for her on his back. She mounted the stout creature, and Adrastus took his place behind her. She gripped the pooka's mane as Adrastus placed his hands on her hips. He gave her a slight squeeze that brought heat between her thighs. It was so unlike the very first time they had found themselves on a horse together—when he had taken her back to the Unseelie Palace for sentencing.

He had explained that, however misguided his actions were then, that he had only been trying to protect her. But it was different now. Not just in the sense that she had come to know and love him, but that he was listening to her. Though she knew his instincts were to do anything he could to keep her safe, he was accepting the choice she was making for herself—her choice to stand by him through the turmoil that his brother was bringing to this magical land.

And that made her love him all the more.

Chapter Twenty-Four

T he pooka moved at a soft jog. The journey from the manor in the Autumn Court and all the excitement at the lake must have done a number on him. Even though he wasn't running at his usual frightening speed, he would still get them to the palace faster than if they were going on foot.

Kelera took the time to look around her. She had never seen trees so enormous before. They were the closest things to giants that she had ever encountered. It made her think of the stone giants they'd passed by with the Guardians and Bothwell. She wondered if they, too, had once stood this tall.

Adrastus pressed his body against hers and she leaned back, determined to appreciate every second of his presence. After coming so close to losing him forever, she would never take it for granted again.

The pooka's strangely elongated ears twitched, catching her attention. Horns blared from far off. Were they coming from the Seelie Palace? Perhaps it was just an accompaniment to the drums. But the pooka jumped around as if understanding something she didn't. Something else was wrong.

She patted him on the side of his neck. "What is it?" Prepared for another ambush, she allowed her magic to dance on her fingertips. It twinkled like miniature starlight, casting a soft glow around her hands. "Woah." She turned her hands over in fascination. She'd seen magic blossom with light before, but never so subtly. Never so beautiful and controlled.

She glanced back at Adrastus, whose mouth was hanging open in surprise. Unsteadily, he said, "Kelera…"

Pain shot through her chest, throwing her from the pooka's back and onto the ground. Had she been so distracted by her magic that she'd allowed them to be ambushed after all? Adrastus jumped from the pooka and cradled her as she moaned in agony. It felt like her body was scorching and rushing with water all at the same time. Her skin burned as if she were running through the blackthorns and allowing the thorns to tear into her flesh.

"Dras," was all she could manage to cry out.

His words came out with panic hitched in them as he said, "Hang on, little thief."

Another voice roared through the trees. The pain made it difficult to tell how close it was. "Prince Adrastus! Lady Kelera!" The excruciating torment blasting through her body blurred her vision so that all she could make out was a large man coming their way.

Once he was within a few steps from them, she saw Ragnor's familiar bearded face. The pain started to subside slowly, but the power of whatever it was that had been thrust into her still remained. It settled into her bones, filling up every crevice that her own magic did not take up.

Kelera could barely get the words out and they came as a whimper as she said, "Dras, do you feel that? The power?"

Adrastus shifted her in his arms. He gave her a puzzled look and blinked rapidly, as if realizing something that she hadn't yet. "It passed to you?"

She didn't have a chance to ask him what he meant as Ragnor's bearded face stared down at her in horror. "What's happened?"

Adrastus ignored the question and asked his own, "Are you here alone? Where are the others?"

Ragnor shook his head vehemently. "Scattered. There's been no sign of Samael or his men this close to the palace, but I've been sent to scout the area in case they decide to attack..." he drifted off as new bells began to toll at the palace.

"No," Adrastus growled.

Ragnor's eyes were glassy as tears started to pool in them.

Kelera's eyes darted between the men. "What is it? What do the bells mean?"

Ragnor wiped at the tears trickling down his face and he hung his head. Adrastus answered since Ragnor could not. His voice was low as he said, "The Queen is dead."

Kelera's stomach dropped. She felt a pang of sympathy for Ragnor, who had just lost his Queen. But more than that, she felt a surge of despair. With the Seelie Queen dead, Samael would not wait any longer. He would make his grab for power while the Seelie Court was in chaos and mourning.

Ragnor whispered, "I need to find the others."

Adrastus urged him, "Go. Kelera and I will go to the palace. Get the others and meet us there."

Before Ragnor could turn to leave, the ground shook violently, rocking him back. Adrastus held tight to Kelera, and they looked around wildly, trying to decipher what was happening. With each passing moment, it grew more intense until she realized they were thunderous footsteps and not a quake in the ground. She searched the area, seeing only trees standing with them in the forest.

The pooka must have spotted it first, because he rocked his head back and forth wildly and snorted in the direction of a few of the trees.

Alarmed, she tried to sit up and asked, "What? I don't see anything."

Adrastus pointed to the spot that had the pooka so alarmed and said, "There. Look closely." He lifted her up to stand and tried to hold on to her, but she shook her head. She was strong enough to stand on her own now.

She squinted her eyes and felt a buzz as they adjusted, giving her the clarity she needed in response to her magic. Whatever glamor the intruders were using dropped to reveal outrageously tall men emerging from the depths of the forest. Their stiff bodies were made up of a thin layer of bark and the harder she looked, the more clear they became. Their arms and legs were a tangle of tree limbs and their faces were bearded with heavy foliage.

The ground trembled violently as more of the creatures uprooted themselves from the ground. What had appeared to be trees in the forest were now monstrous creatures with the faces that only faintly resembled men. The one nearest to them stepped forward, forcing the pooka to dance a few paces back.

The tree-like man tilted his head, which was topped with lush green leaves. It gave what Kelera believed was a smile as the corners of its mouth twisted up with a creak. As it did, it revealed long, sharp teeth, made of stone that was the length of her arm. They reminded her of the arrowheads she used to dig out of the ground when she and Cierine were children exploring the countryside of Nevene.

Adrastus warned, "Steady." And she wasn't sure if he was talking to her or to the pooka, who was clearly in distress with his hooves digging into the ground and his head whipping around to each new tree that uprooted itself. Ragnor was wraith-white and frozen in place. They were all holding their breath.

Kelera whispered back to him. "Are they friend or foe?"

"I have absolutely no idea."

The tree that had stepped forward made an almost deafening creaking sound. Its brow furrowed, and it took a step back, as if trying to give them space. Was it attempting to ease their fear and show that it wasn't a threat to them?

Adrastus' magic quivered in her veins, as if he was trying to decide whether to draw it out or not. Kelera's breath caught in her throat as the tree leaned forward and squinted its strangely human-like eyes. Its eyes met hers with a steady gaze, and then it blinked. Something like recognition flickered in them.

A sound echoed from it like a tree crashing in the forest. Was it trying to speak? Kelera wasn't sure what it meant, but the other tree-like men around them seemed to understand as they repeated the sound, passing it through their ranks.

The sounds echoed through the trees, drowning out the beating drums and the chiming of the bells coming from the palace. Kelera clung to her magic, ready to defend her and Adrastus should these trees decide to act against them.

To her shock and awe, the trees began to kneel, one by one at first, until the rest followed suit. Now, every single one of the giant tree-like men were kneeling before them.

"Adrastus, are they kneeling to you?"

Fascination filled his voice as he said, "No, little thief, I believe they are kneeling to *you*."

Acknowledgments

Diving into Elfhame has been both fun and exhillerating. Celtic folklore has always fascinated me, and to have the opportunity to dive into classic lore, twisting it to make it my own has been incredibly fun.

First I have to thank you, my readers, who have shown me so much love and support. I know that reading is a passion we all share and for you to take the time to open my books means the world to me.

As always, I have to thank my family for their support. Without them, I would never have had the courage to take this leap. To my husband, Zach, who is my rock and always tries to bring a smile to my face (especially when the work becomes overwhelming). And to my babies... I can never express how much joy you bring me. You two are the greatest story of all.

Next, I would like to thank the brilliant writers in my writer's group: Danielle, Emily F., Emily H., Kate, Samantha, and Jess, who never hold back. You have shaped me into a better writer and have given me a thicker skin. You've taught me so much about how to build on my strengths and how to improve on my weaknesses. And more than that, you have given me encouragement, love, and support. I truly do not know what I would do without you all.

Lastly, to my beta team: Ardena, Catherine, Laura, and Christina. I am so grateful to have been able to entrust the roughest version of this book to each of you. Without your fresh eyes and guidance, this story wouldn't be what it is today.

One thing I have realized since starting on this journey is that it would be impossible without people around you who will love and support you. Through the ups and downs that have come with pouring my heart and soul into this story, every person mentioned here has kept me going.

My love to you all,
J.M. Wallace

ALSO BY J.M. WALLACE
A Legacy of Darkness
A Legacy of Nightmares
A Legacy of Destruction
Heir of Shadows and Ice
Heir of Embers and Ash

Novellas and More
The Princess of Sagon: A Smuggler's Tale (freebie in my newsletter!)

About the Author

J.M. Wallace is a proud military wife. She has spent much of her adult life moving from place to place with her husband and their two children, making stories of their own. As a young girl, J.M. was fascinated with stories that she read and that she dreamed up on her own. Even when she was horseback riding, she was never in her own yard; instead, she was in an enchanted forest or riding into battle alongside brave knights. Today, she puts those stories to paper, to share with the world. She does this in the little pockets of her day between giving her kids snacks, naps, baths, and putting them to bed. *A Legacy of Darkness* was her debut novel.

www.jmwallaceauthor.com

www.ingramcontent.com/pod-product-compliance
Lightning Source LLC
Chambersburg PA
CBHW051127190726
48290CB00006B/1721